UNDER THE CANYON SKY

Heart of Gold

Books by Dick Brown

Under the Canyon Sky Series
Book One: Canyon Crossroads
Book Two: Heart of Gold

Coming Soon!
Book Three: Guarding the Treasure

UNDER THE CANYON SKY

Heart of Gold

Dick Brown

SPEAKING VOLUMES, LLC
NAPLES, FLORIDA
2023

Heart of Gold

Copyright © 2023 by Dick Brown

All rights reserved. No part of this book may be reproduced or transmitted in any form or by any means without written permission.

As a work of fiction, the characters, places, and incidents are either products of the author's imagination or are used fictitiously. Many incidents are created for dramatic story-telling purposes; however, some events are loosely drawn from history. Any resemblance to actual persons, living or deceased, buildings, business establishments, organizations, events, or locales is entirely coincidental.

On the other hand, certain background incidents, historical events and characters are real. Teddy Roosevelt did indeed visit the Canyon on three occasions. Buffalo Bill stood in awe on the South Rim. Steam locomotives transported visitors to the very brink of the Canyon. Publishing magnate William Randolph Hearst raised wild speculation with his significant property purchases on and below the rim. And the Colorado River still glides quietly along in some places and roars loudly in others.

ISBN 979-8-89022-052-3

This historical novel is dedicated to the pioneering men and women who had a hand in the Grand Canyon's transition from unbridled backcountry to one of America's greatest national parks.

Acknowledgments

My very special thanks to my wife Donna who accompanied me on many of the Grand Canyon's grueling backcountry trails, exploring abandoned copper mines, trudging along on endless field trips, and patiently enduring my time away while I plunged into periods of historical research. And then at home, conducting critical reviews of manuscript drafts, cautioning me not to stray into a monotonous history report, offering her thoughts and perspectives, and giving me emotional encouragement and inspiration every single day, all the while keeping the home fires burning.

I also acknowledge my friend Gary Fogel, an author in his own right, for his constructive critiques and encouragement during the development of this trilogy.

I also thank my publisher and editor for believing in this project and making this story come alive on the printed page.

Preface

The wonder, intrigue and stunning beauty of the Grand Canyon are beyond measure. This historical novel brings to life the struggle of nineteenth and twentieth century pioneers against monopolistic corporations while enduring rapacious government control. It is a human-interest story where the Canyon itself takes on a life of its own. The story underscores the obsession of the Santa Fe Railway and its captive enterprises to drive the independent entrepreneurs—the men and women who opened the Canyon for all to experience—out of business and off the land. Despite constant badgering and accusations of being squatters and trespassers, the canyon pioneers still managed to leave their indelible mark on this grand stage. What we see today at the Grand Canyon is not only the work of nature but the work of brazen pioneers who chiseled trails out of stubborn rock, erected primitive tourist lodges on the rim, discovered rich copper deposits below the rim, and guided daring mule riders to the river. This is their story—a story of passion, dreams and challenges.

Chapter One

WINDSONG

On one hand, the sheriff is a pistol; on the other hand, a loose cannon.

Sabrina Jaffa, astride her chestnut mare Serendipity and trailing her mule Jenny, made her way along a primitive path across the Grand Canyon's Tonto Plateau. With worries about being followed, she constantly glanced behind, expecting to spot two harassing drifters, Morton and Sykes, trailing them. She knew those men could not continue west after a rockslide obliterated the trail. They would be closing in soon.

"Girls, we're about a day from intercepting the Jackson Trail, but we need a break." She guided Serendipity into a shallow draw and dismounted. "Let's hunker down here for a few minutes." She withdrew three apples from her pack, one each for her girls and one for herself. The two shady drifters had to be backtracking on the same route. She needed a diversion, a way to get them off her back.

About ten minutes into their break, Jenny brayed and Sabrina's heart sank. Then three burros crossed their route, not Morton and Sykes. Taking one bite of her apple, she mulled over some ideas on how to divert the trackers off her tail. Several more bites and a plan emerged. She needed a fork off her eastward leading trek.

Remounting and resuming her journey, and with just an apple core in her hand, she found a fork among the crisscrossing burro tracks. One branch, a well-trampled path, headed toward a deep ravine leading into Granite Gorge. The other branch headed in the direction of the Jackson Trail. Rather quickly, so that the girls had no chance of snatching it, Sabrina dropped her apple core about six feet along the Gorge branch.

After making about hundred hoof prints to fool her trackers, she cut a meandering path across the sagebrush and rejoined the main path, resuming her eastward trek. She chuckled with the thought that the two drifters may be well along in their descent into the deep ravine before realizing they had lost her trail.

***

During one of Kirby O'Brien's many runs to town for supplies, Sheriff Clint McCarty gave him a message for Monte Bridgestone.

"Hey boss, Clint has a party interested in purchasing the Shooting Star Mine!" blurted Kirby, in his usual excited but blunt manner.

"What? It's not for sale!" Monte, astonished about there being any thought of selling, with the mine producing rich ore, glared at Kirby. It irked him that no one had consulted him on the matter. Seeing the news upset his boss, Kirby hesitated in delivering the rest of Clint's message. After Monte calmed down, he repeated Clint's special request.

"Clint wants you to rush five or six tons of ore to complete a railcar load, as he is hard pressed for money," Kirby reported, "and he is rustling hard on the upcoming county election. He wants us to come to Flagstaff and campaign for him." Kirby added, "Oh, I forgot to mention that Clint wants you to take the ore from the good-looking vein we exposed on the second level."

Monte, still resenting Clint's requests, obliged, and the men hauled several more wagonloads to Flagstaff.

Clint won another two-year term as county sheriff. From his vantage point as an up-and-coming politician, he may have sensed the inevitable—creation of a national park which could spell the end of mining at the Canyon. With a growing interest in the tourist trade and an impending rail connection to the South Rim, he may have shifted his focus away from mining.

***

Monte and Kirby set out for Flagstaff with a final load of blue-green copper ore. They found the wagon road dry but dusty and made good time.

As they unloaded sacks at the Flagstaff railyard, Kirby asked, "Hey Monte, think there's any gold mixed in with this shipment?"

Monte paused, straightened his back, and said, "I doubt there's much at all. We're copper miners, Kirby, not gold miners. Why do you ask?"

Kirby put his hands on his hips and in a huff said, "Haven't ya heard? Everyone in town is talkin' about it! Someone made a huge gold discovery on the Klondike!"

"What's this Klondike yer rantin' about?"

Kirby almost fired a remark about Monte's schooling, but thought better. "It's a river in Canada's Yukon Territory," regaled Kirby, somewhat baffled about his out-of-touch boss. "I heard the Yukon is the most inaccessible, inhospitable country ever to host a gold stampede." Kirby continued. "Hundreds have perished while trudging over snow-clogged mountain passes to reach the goldfields."

"Well, it can't be any harder than what we're doin' here, hauling ore up several thousand feet to the South Rim by burro and then sixty-five miles cross-country by wagon." He motioned Kirby to get back to work.

Monte, so perturbed about McCarty's request for rush shipments, forgot to congratulate his partner on being re-elected sheriff. But that is not what angered him—the thought of selling the Shooting Star angered him.

Monte paid a visit at the Sheriff's office to unload on Clint. The office door creaked as he stepped inside, waking the deputy.

"Where's Sheriff McCarty?" he asked rather tersely.

"Oh, sorry, Mr. Bridgestone, you caught me snoozing. The sheriff is over at your old saloon, the Ponderosa."

It galled him that Clint found time to hang out in a bar while he hauled ore from the canyon and delivered on his partner's rush order. If he did not find Clint on official sheriff business, he would have a few strong words for him. Deep inside it bothered Monte that he did not still own the Ponderosa Tavern. He could use the extra income. As he reached the door, Clint came out with a young fellow in custody.

"Monte! I presume you are in town with another wagonload of ore for shipping. Good! Have you unloaded at the railyard yet? Give me a chance to throw this culprit in jail and we can visit over a beer." Clint sensed Monte had something on his mind.

"I don't have time for a drink. I have other business in town but we need to talk about your unilateral action in trying to sell the Shooting Star. Dang it, Clint! That's a decision for all the partners, not just you!"

Monte, angry and emphatic, clenched his fists, ready for a fight. Clint seemed to recognize no authority but his own. No one argued his authority as the sheriff, but as a mining partner, he alone had none. On one hand, the sheriff is a pistol; on the other hand, a loose cannon.

Monte, still flushed with anger, continued his tirade, "Besides, we are into the best ore we've seen since the mysterious explosion. Selling now is a bad idea," he charged.

"On the contrary, it's the best time to sell." Clint, always the devious businessman in their partnership, countered, "Prospective buyers want to see an active mine, a mine producing high-grade ore, better yet, native copper as we have been harvesting since the explosion. Besides, there is still the tourist potential. Kirby tells me you are still putting the finishing touches on the hotel near Summit Point. That may well be the way of the future. We need to look to the future; it's where we'll all be spending our remaining years."

"Clint, life is relationships and you and I go way back, but your politics is threatening our friendship and our business." Despite Clint's cockeyed optimism, Monte seemed to have regained his composure.

"But Monte, politics is compromise," said Clint, in a rather convincing tone and looking at his partner with a wary eye. Throughout this heated debate, Clint had one hand wrapped around the belt of the young culprit he planned to throw in jail.

"So, you are asking for compromise in our friendship!" Monte fired back.

"No, I'm asking the government to compromise. My sources tell me that sooner or later, the government will outlaw mining at the Grand Canyon."

Monte, still agitated, fumed, "That may well be. Clint, let me put it plain and simple. We are not selling the mine!" With that he turned and walked away, clearly in a foul mood. Clint and Monte disagreed on the goals of their enterprise many times before, but this time it seemed much more serious.

Monte and Kirby returned to the Canyon with a wagonload of boards from the Kennedy lumber mill for a major construction project—the Grand Canyon Hotel. He admired the strength and fine-grain of the pine and understood why the transcontinental railroads favored ties cut from ponderosa logs. He constructed his hotel of ponderosa—mud-chinked logs for foot-thick walls, gabled roof, and plank floors—a special combination of romance and roughness to instill in his guests a sense of the pioneering spirit.

***

As miners worked their claims and transported ore to the rim, other forward-thinking entrepreneurs descended upon the Canyon—men with both the canyon's mining potential and tourist potential on their minds.

The Federal government, which had taken its first step in preserving the Canyon in its natural state by establishing a forest reserve, wrestled with how to begin implementing administrative measures. It favored the Santa Fe Railway and its subsidiaries over the hard-working pioneers. Obsessed with ridding the Canyon of independent entrepreneurs, the men and women who opened the Canyon for all to experience, the Santa Fe tried to drive them out of business and off the land. Constantly badgering the pioneers, the government went so far as calling them trespassers and squatters!

Aware of increasing interest by entrepreneurs and influential corporations in the canyon's rich copper ore deposits, Monte and his partners formed the Canyon Copper Company. Loosely organized, it served as an informal bond—a miner's partnership.

Several tons of ore stockpiled on Windsong Mesa needed sorting and sacking and lifting onto jacks as one-hundred-pound loads. A pack train master then needed to drive the burros up the trail. With the establishment of the Canyon Copper Company, Monte began to keep records of ore hauled to the rim.

He made the work assignments. "Jeremy, where is that young feller, Jeremy Livingston?" He found Jeremy sitting on a rock in the shade of a scrub cedar.

"Yes, boss?"

"Jeremy, I want you to wrangle jacks. Mark, Mark Warren, I want you to work with Kirby who took Ben Saxton's place on our team, and pack supplies down and ore back up. Remember, one hundred pounds per jack, no more." Monte worried that Mark and Kirby might overload the pack train.

Slim Broadway volunteered to haul water from a tank the men had constructed in a ravine near the hotel site. "That's good Slim, we need water; however, the last I saw the tank, it was getting a mite low, so we need to conserve as much as possible."

"Monte, I meant to mention something to you. Talking about water reminded me that some time back I watched two fellows paddle across the river to where it passes Skeleton Creek. They called themselves Morton and Sykes, no first names, and both were rather closed-mouth, as if they did not want me to know anything more about them. I think they may be on a wanted poster somewhere."

"Never heard of those two, but thanks, Slim, for letting me know two unsavory characters may be snooping around our part of the canyon." Monte went back to organizing his work party.

Kirby and Jeremy rounded up eight jacks from Cottonwood Creek. They loaded five to seven jacks per train. The more tedious work fell to Monte. He did most of the sorting while the other men sacked and packed ore. Return trips always carried food supplies, water barrels, empty ore sacks, or timbers for the mine.

Water is vital for survival but more so at the Grand Canyon than other wilderness areas. Only after an arduous journey, even for pack animals, could one reach the Colorado River, inaccessible in most places. Summit Tank on the rim, entirely dependent on rainfall and snowmelt, proved to be an unreliable source. The men considered it a stock tank, more suitable for animals than humans.

The men fortunately discovered a spring at the head of a gulch below the east wall of Windsong Mesa. The miners scooped out a bowl-shaped depression in the soft shale at the base of the Redwall. Water, ice-cold and sugar-sweet, trickled from fern-covered clefts in the wall and filled the basin. Monte named this watering hole Arrowhead Spring because he found a small arrowhead nearby; the spring became one of the most reliable sources below the rim. Each day, Kirby or Slim descended the Redwall with a string of burros, each burro with two barrels strapped to its back, to haul precious water from the spring.

Mining copper from the mesa proved to be back-breaking work; picks dulled on the rock, and the clatter of ore chunks being dropped into iron buckets echoed in the tunnels. Passageways needed constant shoring. Glowing light from kerosene lanterns diffused in tunnels full of limestone dust, a miserable place to earn a living. Without high-grade pay-dirt, no man would accept such grueling work.

Christmas would have been a routine workday if Mark Warren had not brought his traditional wagonload of Yuletide provisions. Like the year before, for the North Rim asbestos miners, the men sung carols around a roaring campfire. On this trip, Mark also brought the latest edition of the *Frontier Times*. He would return to Flagstaff with two thousand pounds of ore.

Sitting at a small table in the mine's rock house, Monte spent the evening hours perusing the local paper. It carried news about plans for another railroad from Flagstaff to McCarty's Landing at the head of Pioneer Trail. The railroaders completed a survey of a sixty-eight-mile route, with construction scheduled to start in the coming year.

The railroad expected to enhance the tourist and freight business at the Canyon. Shipping copper ore from the mines south of McCarty's Landing formed the most important part of the freight business. Monte knew he had the best ore; however, the proposed railhead would be of little use to his operation. He doubted the venture would ever proceed beyond paper. "Yep," he said, "seems the rugged stage road would remain the only viable means of transporting ore."

Even with his mind dwelling on railroad plans and shipping ore to smelters, another story caught Monte's attention. "Hm-m, what's this about town fathers deeding five acres to a fella named Percy Lowell for Flagstaff's first permanent scientific facility—an astronomical observatory!"

When townsfolk learned that Lowell would study planet Mars from Observatory Mesa, they began calling the site Mars Hill. Lowell funded construction of the observatory himself, including a large telescope with a mechanical clock drive.

As Monte folded the *Frontier Times*, he said, "So now folks will see shooting stars through a big telescope. I'll stick to my own Shooting Star—the best copper mine in the West!"

***

With growing investor speculation in mining and tourist industries, and with sporadic talk of a Grand Canyon Railway and a Grand Canyon National Park, mining properties began to change ownership. The first pioneer to settle on the South Rim sold out first. Clancy Jennings transferred ownership and rights to his trails and ramshackle hotel to Jeff Fox and Jay Watts, owners of the Grand Canyon Stage Line, for fifteen hundred dollars. A year later, Fox established the Starlight Camp at McCarty's Landing.

Jeff Fox warned Jennings, "Clancy, you can keep your claim to the land under the homestead laws, but you cannot engage in the canyon guide business or attach your name to any trail within thirty-five miles of your old hotel." That agreement soon faded from Clancy's memory. He continued the life he loved—guiding tourists and spinning yarns.

Sitting at the rough-hewn table in the rock house in mid-January, Kirby and Monte read about Clancy selling out in the latest edition of the *Frontier Times*. Another story drew their attention: "Clint McCarty has brought in six tons of copper ore and expects more wagon teams Saturday or Sunday. The ore is destined for the smelter in El Paso."

"Monte, the mine is looking splendid. It is improving every day as we sink deeper on the mineral. Sure feels good to be taking out rich copper ore." Kirby seemed to be reassuring Monte all was well.

"I agree, Kirby. Now, it's getting late; time for you to rest. You have the next shift. Before I turn in for the night, I need to write to my son in New Mexico Territory and then go see how the men on night shift are getting along."

By this time, a team of ten men worked at the Shooting Star Mine. Two men labored underground on each shift and a third man installed timbers. With the system for mining being a manual operation of digging, sorting, screening, sacking and packing, they could not recover great quantities of copper mineral, but they overcame this shortfall with quality.

A month later, the *Frontier Times* carried another encouraging report on the mine. "This week Clint McCarty received assay returns on ore he sent to Denver from the Shooting Star Mine in Grand Canyon. The assays ranged in value from ninety to one hundred and ninety dollars per ton. The returns showed a fair percentage in silver and gold, but the greatest value is in copper, ranging from fifty to eighty-five percent. As work on the mine has developed a large body of rich ore, it may someday prove to be the best copper property in Arizona." Even Colorado mining men marveled at the high grade of the copper ore.

Monte returned from the mine. "Kirby, you're still here."

"Yeah, I couldn't sleep. I keep thinking about the mine. How's the shift work going?"

Monte pulled up a chair and summarized their operation. "Well, bucket-loads of ore are reaching the surface, the timbering of drifts and stopes is continuing, and two men are beginning a new crosscut to connect the two drifts on the eastern face of the Redwall. With that one hundred and thirty-foot shaft we sunk to these drifts, we can extend more stopes from the crosscuts."

Kirby listened to Monte, noting a touch of pride in his descriptions. "Kirby, I'm especially pleased with how our mule-driven hoist is raising ore from drifts near the bottom of the shaft—where the mineral occurs in its richest concentration. Also, I like the track layout with ore carts riding rails to the dump at the lower drift. Tomorrow, I'd like you to check on our dump. I don't want waste rock blocking the opening to the side canyon."

With ore stockpiled on the mesa and on the rim, and with roads clear for wagons making the three-day haul, ore accumulated in Flagstaff. There, men loaded it into railcars for shipping to the smelter that made the best offer to the Canyon Copper Company. The stockpiles had another five hundred tons ready for shipment. Clint continued to play the market to find the best returns.

***

An added dash of excitement at the Canyon helped draw tourists below the rim. The camp cook, Simon O'Reilly, during a break from his chores, discovered two caves on the west wall of Windsong Mesa. He squeezed his rotund body through an opening in the Redwall and knew he had made an important find. O'Reilly rushed back to camp to report his discovery.

"Kirby, where's Monte? He needs to see this." Kirby pointed to the rock house. He watched O'Reilly stumble over a copper kettle as he entered the building.

When Monte received O'Reilly's report, he suspended mining activities for the day and diverted the men's energies to cutting a down-sloping trail along the craggy cliff and enlarging the entryway. They found the first cave to be an intricate network of tunnels and rooms extending two thousand feet into the mesa. Translucent stalactites hung from the ceiling. Reflected orange lantern light darted from one pendant to the next. Beneath each stone pendant stood a coral pink stalagmite, frozen in its perennial quest to unite with its partner.

The second cave had higher ceilings and more grotesque limestone formations. Pieces of stalactite lay shattered on the floor, strewn like rubble in a petrified forest. Monte wondered if the mine explosion may have jarred these formations. Crystal-studded curtains clung overhead. Compartment after compartment boasted of diverse stone formations, each teasing the imagination as to what it might represent. In a few places, the splat of water drops, relieved of their tortuous percolation path through the limestone, broke the hollow, crypt-like silence.

Monte addressed his miners, "Men, we're locating a new claim along the western edge of Windsong Mesa to encompass the caves. I'm calling it the Copper Kettle Mining Claim. This way we can control and protect the caves which have the potential of becoming a major tourist attraction here at the Canyon."

The Flagstaff paper, in a special edition describing the mines and caves, congratulated the owners of the Canyon Copper Company: "All will rejoice with us that success has crowned the well-directed effort of these our fellow citizens."

The men located the Copper Kettle Mine in the names of Monte Bridgestone, Clint McCarty, Slim Broadway and Kirby O'Brien, and recorded it with Coconino County. O'Reilly railed against Monte about not listing him as a locator. Slim placed the claim notice, folded and sealed in a tin can, inside a rock pyramid. Later O'Reilly, still angry he did not at least garner an honorable mention, added his name to the notice in the can.

An assay report showed the Copper Kettle rich in silver and lead with more than enough gold to pay working expenses. That summer, discovery of the Windsong caves boosted tourism at Summit Point. Flagstaff's Grand Canyon news correspondent, Ryan Perkins, reported a surge in the number of tourists traveling the Summit Trail. He added the trailhead had water for stock and campers, but also a word of caution. Summit Point offers an adventure in vertigo, as if standing upon nothing—being instead suspended in mid-air—a fatal five-hundred-foot sheer drop at the tip of the boot. Back in prehistoric times, fifty-foot-deep cracks must have split the rock surface of this craggy formation, giving one the intense and disturbing impression that stepping across a crevice could send the whole affair tumbling into the canyon.

During an interview with Monte, Perkins asked, "How did Windsong Mesa get its name?"

Monte set his coffee cup down on the rock house table. "Well, that's an interesting question. When we were exploring along the west wall of this mesa, we sometimes heard a whistling sound. At first, we thought it was a songbird or maybe just the wind playing tricks on us. When our cook discovered the caves, we realized it was the wind singing through the limestone catacombs. So, it turns out the name Windsong was a good choice."

"So, you didn't know the reason for the whistling sound until after you discovered the caves. Got it. Thanks Monte." Perkins tucked away his notebook and started back up the Summit Trail.

***

After discovery of the caves, Monte and his men resumed work on a small addition to their log house at Summit Point. After that, the men spent the fall months harvesting ponderosa logs for a much larger project—the Grand Canyon Hotel. Monte envisioned a two-story log building twenty-four feet wide and sixty feet long.

The men did not have to go far to fell trees of necessary height and diameter. A majestic stand of tall, straight ponderosas thrived a few hundred feet back from the rim. Monte's construction crew comprised the Livingston brothers Jeremy and Dexter with his Navajo girlfriend Moonflower Yazzie, Kirby, Slim, Mark and himself. Mooney kept the crew supplied with fresh drinking water and oven-baked flatbread served with a sweet spread she made from prickly pear cactus.

"Okay men, here's the plan. We'll build the walls using straight logs with precision, hand-cut dovetail notches and inverted V-notches at the corners to lock the logs in place for structural integrity and stability. And we'll use light-colored lime chinking to seal the cracks. Jeremy and Mark, I need you to cut log rafters for structural support of the walls and roof. Slim, for solid flooring, I need you and Dexter to unload those wood planks Kirby and I hauled from the Kennedy sawmill." Monte pointed to the wagon.

"Kirby, you are our best mason. We need to build chimneys of stone from our quarry and mortar them in the same way we did at the Windsong rock house." Monte went on to describe how they will cover the pitched roof with cedar shingles, and how the hotel will feature eye-catching dormers and gables, many windows and several doors. Kirby convinced Monte to use the roof to collect rainwater and snowmelt, a system of gutters and drain pipes to channel water to cisterns crafted with oaken barrel staves.

The main building included ground-level, wood-frame extensions to serve as kitchen and storerooms. Adjacent outbuildings served as woodsheds, toolsheds, and livery stables.

The men spared the ponderosas near the hotel but trimmed their lower branches so as not to obstruct canyon views. They cut down scrub oak and cedars and cleared away brush so that visitors could appreciate the immensity of the Grand Canyon.

After many months, the men completed construction of the rustic log hotel. Just ahead of its grand opening for the coming tourist season, Clint McCarty visited. "So, working on this hotel construction explains our drop in ore production."

Monte let the comment pass and explained how the Grand Canyon Hotel is destined to become the new terminus for the Grand Canyon Stage Line. He hoped the new hotel would become the hub for a new community named Summit.

"I imagine ol' Clancy Jennings will object to the change, but I understand he no longer owns his tent complex," said Clint.

Monte continued the tour. "As you can see, we offer the first modern accommodations here at the South Rim, including comfortable rooms, a spacious lounge, and a dining room, soon to include a continental chef. We're using Navajo rugs from Mooney Yazzie's clan to cover the floors and walls. These rocking chairs facing the fireplace were hand-crafted by our friend Francois LaRue. And I've hung deer antlers and wolf skins above the mantle, giving the lounge the look of a hunting lodge. Look at our spacious dining room with oak tables and chairs, also crafted by LaRue. And here's my private museum."

"Monte, I see you plan to fascinate visitors with a rare glimpse of frontier life at the Canyon. I suppose those white crystalline stalactites come from our caves and those bright blue mineral specimens from our mines." Clint made a mental note that the hotel will be an excellent place to entertain prospective buyers.

"So, you see Clint, this is why I have no doubt the Grand Canyon Hotel offers the best accommodations on the South Rim. All we need now is rail service."

"Yes, a railroad to this point would serve tourism and our mining operations. Monte, I urge you to get back to mining." With that, Clint offered his congratulations on the hotel construction and went on his way.

***

If Clint saw troubled times ahead for mining, Buckey O'Neill did not share this view. He found mining to be an exciting enterprise, considering the risks involved in buying mineral-producing properties in a fluctuating market. He also saw it as the key to building a railroad from Williams to the South Rim. Pursuant to this, he located a series of mining claims for Black Diamond Development Company at Prospector Flats. The best claim in the area produced ore valued at only twenty dollars per ton—much lower than that produced by the Shooting Star Mine. Clint shrugged this off as risky speculation.

Instead of sinking shafts into the limestone caprock at Prospector Flats, the miners used an open cut method, exposing a vein from the surface and scooping ore into wagons. O'Neill felt that the low expense of making open cuts went a long way in mitigating the meager value of Prospector Flats ore.

Ever since the World's Fair in Chicago, the irrepressible Buckey O'Neill tried to convince eastern capitalists to invest in copper mines at the Canyon. Intrigued by copper claims along Shaski Wash and near Tusayan Well, he believed the high-grade ore mined at Windsong Mesa alone would clinch the deal if the rails also extended east to Summit Point.

Known to be an adventurous and reckless man, Buckey found mining at the Canyon an exciting enterprise, but more as a promoter than a hard-rock miner. His earliest efforts to promote such enterprises led to establishing the Black Diamond Development Company following the World's Fair. Building a railroad from Williams stimulated the company's interest in developing mines at the South Rim.

With the help and influence of Buckey's Chicago and Washington connections, the company pursued a right-of-way for their railroad through the forest reserve. Had he lived, he would have witnessed the construction of the Grand Canyon Railway and the advent of large corporate holdings at the Canyon.

In late December, Buckey, operating as an agent for Black Diamond and the owners of the Shooting Star Mine, executed a purchase agreement for the sale of their canyon properties for forty thousand dollars. With the deed and agreement placed in escrow in Jesse Parks' bank, any further action waited until Spring.

***

Clint reminded Monte that Buckey O'Neill and his business associates continued to express their interest in buying their properties on Windsong Mesa. In fact, he learned from Buckey that the company wanted to see the mine and planned to arrive at Summit Point any time. He advised Monte by mail: "If the men want the mine, sell it to them. If they don't want to buy, don't bend. Cash up front and no grumbling, or there can be no sale."

On the same trip, the Black Diamond party expected to visit the mining properties around Prospector Flats where thirty men worked on copper claims.

All indications pointed to the potential for continued production of high-grade ore at the Grand Canyon. But O'Neill may have misrepresented his own feelings about the Prospector Flats venture to Clint McCarty while the two tried to hammer out a deal to purchase the Shooting Star Mine.

The wily sheriff, not easily bluffed, shared his thoughts about Prospector Flats with Monte. "Ya know, O'Neill claims the mines have no depth to them. Can't always tell what he is saying. They are locating new claims out there all the time but what they are taking out are rather sorry-looking pieces of rock. Don't see why they should want to locate any more claims if they think they are no good."

Monte had an explanation. "Clint, you know as well as I, it is just human nature to rave about an unproven lode, and to promote it as a surefire bonanza. If it were a true bonanza, the discoverer or developer would hold it in secrecy for himself."

The men knew Buckey planned a ruse. But copper showings just south of the rim, in paying quantities, may be all that is needed to bring rails to the brink of the Canyon.

***

When Buckey let the time for execution expire, perhaps intentionally, a new purchase agreement needed drafting and signing to keep the deal alive. About this time, a series of eight mining camps extended from Prospector Flats to Promontory Point on the South Rim, along the future route of the Grand Canyon Railway.

Black Diamond owned and operated four camps, including Prospector Flats—now a robust camp in a sheltered draw with a log dining hall; tents serving as the assay office, foreman quarters, and miner's dormitories; and a frame building for visiting officers of the company. A cabin that Buckey and Kirby built, three miles from the rim, served as headquarters for the company superintendent. Tusayan Well supplied water to all the camps. Black Diamond finally procured Cole Campbell and Slim Broadway's claims eight miles from the rim.

All the mining claims in the so-called copper belt featured shallow locations—denuded veins in a blanket of broken limestone, thought to be part of a massive ledge extending north fifteen miles across the Coconino Plateau from Prospector Flats to the rim.

In a conversation between Clint and Monte during another ore wagon delivery, Monte raised the question, "Clint, do you think the Prospector Flats outcroppings could be part of canyon ore bodies or just isolated surface deposits?"

Clint responded, "Now that is an intriguing question. If the ore is not deep at Prospector Flats, investment would be risky, perhaps disastrous. And you know Buckey thrives on taking risks. Because of him, speculation is already wild."

"And he talks like one could make a fortune if one invested wisely," said Monte, "and so far, development is signaling bright prospects. Apparently, he is expecting a rise in the importance of land near Starlight Camp because he staked a series of tangent quartz placer claims along the rim between Panorama and Sunset points."

Clint added, thinking Buckey may use a delay tactic, "Maybe that's why he had to draft up a new purchase agreement."

Copper prices fluctuated and untimely declines signaled potential ruin to marginal ventures. The financial panic and the creation of the Grand Canyon Forest Reserve had already stifled canyon prospecting, and economic depression retarded mining development. Republicans blamed Democrats for the Great Panic and scored a landslide victory in the mid-term elections.

The next presidential election fought economic issues, ending with a decisive victory by pro-gold William McKinley over pro-silver William Jennings Bryan. President McKinley named the independent firebrand Theodore Roosevelt, who loved the West and westerners but also loved politics and publicity, as assistant secretary of the Navy.

With the McKinley administration came signs of restoring confidence in the national economy. Perhaps as a good omen, two ships laden with Klondike gold arrived in Seattle and San Francisco, confirming rumors of a great gold strike in the Yukon. The news spread nationwide, although newspaper magnate William Randolph Hearst's *San Francisco Examiner* missed the boat, giving the story only a few lines of print. The celebrated Klondike Gold Rush offered a chance to restock the nation's gold reserves and brought a modest jump in copper prices.

Meanwhile, at Captain Clancy Jennings' place, the old-timer entertained a group of new arrivals gathered on the veranda of his homestead cabin. His stories thrived on the crowd's naivety and lack of canyon knowledge. This time he had several folks full of questions, albeit some designed to invoke a nonsensical story.

A young whippersnapper sassed Cap about rocks. "Mr. Jennings, do rocks in the Canyon sleep at night?"

Jennings nodded, "No one's ever asked me that before but I reckon that's true. I sometimes camp overnight under a rocky overhang in Redrock Canyon. That dang rock has kept me awake many nights with its relentless snoring!"

"How's the hunting around here?" queried an elderly gentleman.

"Recently shot a big buck next to that big ol' ponderosa over yonder," boasted Clancy, "got 'em good too, my bullet went clean through him, dropped like a rock, had venison stew for weeks." Feeling he needed to add credibility to his answer, he added, "Need proof I killed that deer? Look over here." Clancy walked over to the ponderosa and pointing with his walking stick, he said "There's the bullet hole, right there."

The crowd moaned, unsatisfied with the explanation.

"Does the wind always blow like this, Mr. Jennings?" asked a tall gentleman in the back, one hand on his derby hat.

Clancy had a quick answer, "No, only half the year."

"Oh, thank goodness," praised the lady next to the gentleman.

Clancy added, "The other half of the year it blows in the opposite direction."

"What?" Another gentleman exclaimed, "Let's be on our way, Claudia. That old-timer has spent too much time below the rim."

"I heard that," said Clancy, and speakin' of being below the rim, if you get lost, get out your pencil and paper and draw up an escape plan. Then take that route to safety. Don't always work but try it."

"Mr. Jennings, it feels like it's getting late, do you know what time it is?" asked a young woman.

"Who knows, the Canyon is timeless—no one here carries a timepiece. There's no telling time here," said Clancy, seeming annoyed. "Time goes right along by and I go right along with it. I do not allow clocks or any such ticking mechanisms to regulate my life."

"Well Mr. Jennings, I wish I had a timepiece. I lost two hours this morning and have been looking for them all afternoon." The crowd gave a cheer to the young lady for her timely retort.

"Now folks, speakin' of losing time, I can squeeze in just one more question." Looking around, no one seemed to want to ask about anything else. Tiring of the unbelievable answers from this peculiar old-timer, some additional folks left. "Well then, I'll close with a story about a gunfight I had with one of my mules in this side canyon." Clancy turned and pointed to Red Rock Canyon. When he turned back, he saw his remaining listeners walking away.

Chapter Two

A STAR FOR OUR FLAG

Grand Canyon, remote and beyond compare.

Ryan Perkins, the veteran newsman, arrived at Summit Point, seeking an update on the Shooting Star Mine and the new Grand Canyon Hotel.

"Ryan, good to see you. Please join us for dinner." As they walked over to the hotel, Ryan leading his horse to a hitching post, Monte continued. "You are the exception to visiting newspapermen. I recall several reporters associated with one newspaper or another—sometimes a country editor and his entire family, sometimes tramps representing themselves as special correspondents for eastern papers—expecting reduced rates. I managed to keep them all out of the dining room."

"Mr. Bridgestone, consider me a paying customer and a friend who wants to tell newspaper-reading Americans about the great success you are having. I'm planning two articles, first about your copper mines. Then on my next visit, I'd like to feature this magnificent new hotel. The *Frontier Times* has always been generous with favorable reports about your enterprises. We don't waste print on such nonsensical stories as Clancy Jennings spews." With that, Monte told his mining story while Ryan ate lunch, making notes while he chewed.

Monte liked Ryan, a newspaperman with money to pay for his grub, but more importantly an honest reporter delivering the best publicity yet for the Shooting Star Mine: "McCarty and Bridgestone own a rich mine in the Grand Canyon. The ore has copper concentrations as high as seventy-five percent, and silver averaging twenty ounces per ton.

The men have already shipped considerable copper ore to smelters in Denver and El Paso."

Another article in the same edition signaled changing times. Flagstaff had grown to a town of fifteen hundred year-round residents, the Bank Hotel had installed new-fangled electric lights, residents lined up to peer through Percy Lowell's telescope, and a railroad to the Grand Canyon had turned from idle talk to construction planning.

Both Flagstaff and Williams wanted the railroad spur line. Flagstaff promoted a seventy-five-mile line for the potential tourist industry, but the townspeople offered few investors. Williams promoted the advantages of a shorter sixty-five-mile line to the mining industry, with tourism and the needs of stockmen as secondary, and clinched their offer with more financial support than Flagstaff.

Buckey O'Neill had finally attracted Black Diamond Development Company's interest in both the proposed railroad venture and the mining potential of the Grand Canyon region. Expecting good ore production from the Prospector Flats mines, and spurred on by the largesse of Williams' investors and the Territorial Legislature which revived the railroad-building tax incentive, the company incorporated the Grand Canyon Railway, with Buckey named as one of its directors. The company planned to build a railroad and telegraph line from Williams to Starlight Camp on the rim.

Like President Harrison, President William McKinley used the Creative Act to establish national forest reserves, including the San Francisco Mountain Forest Reserve. Through an act of Congress, the Grand Canyon Railway received permission to enter and traverse Harrison's Grand Canyon Forest Reserve. The charter read, "from the town of Williams to the town of Black Diamond on the rim of the Grand Canyon." Construction did not start until March when most of the winter snows had melted.

***

While mining and railroad transactions took place at the Canyon, Congress considered new legislation focusing on mining activities in forest reserves. It passed the Organic Act, which attempted to rectify the conflicts that arose between the Mining Act and the Creative Act. It reinforced the intended dominance of the Mining Laws, even to the point of placing mineral value higher than forest value.

There had been no intention to close the national forest reserves to prospecting, locating, developing and patenting mining claims. The Organic Act recognized and reconfirmed prospectors and miners have a statutory right, not just a privilege, to enter upon national forest reserves for purposes of prospecting and mining. It cautioned against impairing their rights or making them burdensome. Unfortunately for canyon miners, the reserve boundaries encompassed the Grand Canyon Mining District, and although the Organic Act had provisions for returning forest land better suited for mining to the public domain, such reversion did not take place at the Canyon. The issue would become more complicated as Grand Canyon evolved into a national park.

Sheriff McCarty, by now famous for his shrewd ability to manipulate the law to his personal advantage, heard about President McKinley approving the new legislation, which threw the Grand Canyon Forest Reserve open to mining.

Kirby wrestled with how some mine developers claimed parts of the Canyon to control traffic, springs, viewpoints, and tourist lodging—anything but what the mining laws intended. While resting with Monte at the saddle on the Summit Trail, Kirby launched into a serious discussion.

"Monte, I'm concerned about fraudulent claims here at the Canyon. Sooner or later the government is going to crack down on claims held for reasons other than mining." He recalled Monte and Clint staking mining claims at the north end of the stage road. He knew the current system did not put a time limit on holding a claim nor did it require proof of valuable minerals, thus allowing large areas to be claimed on speculation that it is worth mining, when it is possible the intent of a claim may have nothing to do with mining.

"Kirby, if you are worried about our caves, the entrance is on a legitimate mining claim and the caverns cross into our Shooting Star claim."

"Here's my idea on how to prevent abuse of the mining laws." Kirby took a deep breath and launched into his spiel. "I think the locator should first present a statement of intent to file to the County Recorder who in turn posts a public notice for a hundred-day period. During that time the locator, if he is serious, must sink a thirty-foot exploratory shaft on his lode claim. Then he collects and submits an assay sample from the vein. If the assay report proves mineral is present in paying quantities, he proceeds to file his valid claim and marks the claim boundaries on the surface."

Monte sighed. "That's a long, drawn-out process. It could take four or five months before the locator can start mining."

"But at least he knows what he has, and the public knows he has a valid claim. And another thing, why allow the locator to claim up to twenty acres when a smaller plat may suffice? I say make the claim area variable and smaller to suit physical conditions."

"I understand your concern but what you are suggesting does not seem practical," said Monte. He tried to say more when Kirby interrupted.

"And another thing, I believe the annual assessment work, the one hundred dollars' worth of manual labor required by the Mining Laws to hold a claim, was intended to be spent on shaft and tunnel development, not trail maintenance, living quarters or tourist facilities."

"Kirby, if you feel this strongly, you should run for Congress and work toward closing the loopholes in the Mining Law."

"No, Monte, not me. Maybe Clint McCarty: he seems to thrive on holding public office."

"For reasons I care not to get into, I do not think Clint would be a good choice. Let's resume our climb to the rim."

***

Buckey O'Neill continued to mastermind the purchase of canyon mining properties for Black Diamond Development Company. Already the company had gained the Prospector Flats and Campbell-Broadway operations and now set its sights on the Shooting Star Mine.

Newspapers made it no secret: "The Black Diamond Development Company may soon control all the mines in the Grand Canyon Mining District. The next bond or purchase will be that of the McCarty-Bridgestone property, with its Shooting Star Mine being the best in the district."

The aging agreement between Buckey O'Neill and the owners of the Shooting Star Mine provided for the forty-thousand-dollar sale of that mine and three others, the caves, the Shooting Star mill-site with its resident Grand Canyon Hotel, and the Summit Toll Road.

But Clint and Monte added a provision to the agreement; one that stipulated that O'Neill, within ten days, hire and put to work at least six experienced miners on the Shooting Star Mine. Until the receipt of the last of four equal payments, the owners maintain possession and free use of all buildings, toll roads and water rights.

In early August, a *Frontier Times* article publicized the agreement: "The Black Diamond Development Company now holds all the copper properties at the Grand Canyon. The latest acquisition is the McCarty-Bridgestone mine."

O'Neill honored the new agreement by resuming ore production at the mine. He himself spent considerable time on Windsong Mesa—supervising the sinking of a second shaft. For a while, he kept six miners working six days per week.

During the third week of November, special agent Bradley Miller of the Interior Department's General Land Office in Washington City visited Clint McCarty in Flagstaff and Monte Bridgestone at Summit. This Washington bureaucrat had a two-fold mission: to investigate the properties of the Canyon Copper Company and to determine the advisability of upgrading the Forest Reserve to a National Park.

Miller had the look of a bureaucrat—a short man in a derby hat, a freckle-faced perfectionist with slanted eyebrows imparting a perpetual expression of surprise.

At Summit Point, Miller, narrowing his piercing eyes, opened the conversation. "Mr. Bridgestone, you need to understand that my boss in Washington City is a forest-saving crusader. He supports the withdrawal of forest lands from the public domain and designating such lands as forest reserves, outlawing timber cutting, livestock grazing, roadway construction and, yes, mining."

"So, what's your point, Mr. Miller?"

"My boss is more interested in managing forest resources than losing them to national park designations."

"Special Agent Miller, I may as well set your mind at ease right up front," Monte announced, taking deft aim at the high-strung agent. "I assure you we cut all timber on our five-acre Shooting Star mill-site, the Summit Toll Road is for access to the mine and, although we do not solicit tourists, we charge tolls to offset maintenance costs, and we located all mining claims before any presidential proclamations."

Miller maintained a stern countenance and an air of defiance as Monte continued.

"Sir, we are not mining here on the rim. Look down there; you can see our Shooting Star Mine and there's not a tree in sight," argued Monte.

"Ah, perhaps you cut them down for firewood or tunnel supports," countered Miller. Monte resented this agent's prickly disposition and blustery stubbornness.

Miller peered down his long, pointed nose as he made notes. With an abrupt change of attitude, tone and temper, he put on an air of leniency. "I apologize for getting riled up so. I'm under a lot of pressure and I find the Mining Laws to be rather ambiguous and therefore abused. With your assurances on your operations here, I'm no longer concerned, and my report will be positive."

Miller seemed well satisfied but as he folded his notebook, it appeared he had something else on his mind.

"Mr. Bridgestone, this has nothing to do with my investigation. Have you run into a female prospector in the Canyon? Rumors circulating in town say she appears occasionally, then disappears."

"Interesting you should ask. She's quite a mystery lady. We've crossed paths two or three times, the most recent being about two months ago. She seems quite the loner, almost out of place gallivanting around below the rim." Monte hesitated to say much more until he had a better inkling about what Miller had on his mind.

"What's her name?" asked Miller.

"She goes by Sabrina Jaffa. I assume that's her real name. Why the interest?" Monte wondered about Miller's off-handed questions about Sabrina.

"Oh, just curious," volunteered Miller, adding, "Is she having any luck?"

"Well, I question her prospecting skills. I've seen her snooping around in the black rocks of the gorge, then another time looking at brown sedimentary sandstone. Anything we find that's any good is always in the limestone." Monte felt he had said enough, but added, "She avoids contact with us miners."

Miller felt he had pried enough. He bid farewell and left the Canyon. When he returned to Washington City, he filed his report recommending protection to prevent vandalism, destructive fires, overgrazing by sheep, and hunting wild animals. He supported making the Grand Canyon Forest Reserve a national park although he believed park status should not interfere with the fullest possible development of the Canyon's mineral resources.

The General Land Office, the Secretary of the Interior, and the local forest supervisor all recommended establishing Grand Canyon National Park. But only Congress can create a national park. The canyon pioneers breathed a sigh of relief as the government shelved the idea for a few more years.

That winter, the railroad completed its survey under the skillful charge of a young surveyor named Travis Holmes, a brother of railroad advocate Brayton Holmes. He also worked as a miner and trail guide and later became an early forest ranger at the Grand Canyon.

***

When Cuba revolted against Spanish rule, America dispatched the armor-plated cruiser, USS Maine, to Havana to protect American interests. The sheer size of cruisers and battleships, armed with big guns capable of hurling ten-inch shells toward an enemy, inspired the names of several South Rim rock formations.

One fateful night, while anchored in Havana Harbor, the Maine exploded and sank with the loss of two hundred and sixty-eight men. Many speculated someone had detonated an explosive device under the ship's gunpowder magazines, obliterating the forward third of the ship. Others believed spontaneous combustion of coal dust in the fuel bunker next to the magazines led to the mysterious explosion. It did not matter—the sinking enraged Americans.

Articles in Hearst's *New York Journal* blamed Spain for the disaster, but the paper distorted facts, and even fabricated news when none fit its story. Tensions escalated, Spain rejected an ultimatum to withdraw from Cuba, and by April, Spain and the United States had declared war on each other. Congress passed the Volunteer Army Act calling for a volunteer cavalry and President McKinley ordered a naval blockade of Cuban harbors. "Remember the Maine, to Hell with Spain!" became the battle cry for America's first overseas war.

***

It would be another year before the tracks approached the rim. Those not associated with the railroad already felt the pressure, a sign of coming trouble for the Summit complex. The railroad and its attendant hotels at Grand Canyon Village drew strength from each other. This powerful synergistic monopoly perched itself near the head of the Pioneer Trail. With financial assurance from eastern capitalists, and with well-placed connections in national government, the railroad's South Rim foothold endured, much to the dismay and disadvantage of many of the canyon pioneers.

The winter months were some of the worst canyon miners had ever experienced, with several three-foot snowfalls hampering travel between the South Rim and Flagstaff. Clancy Jennings, returning from the Canyon with Stuart Casey, made a decision. "Casey, this journey across the Coconino is so strenuous on our horses and us old-timers, I have a mind to spend the winter months right here in Flagstaff."

"I feel the same way, but what will you do? I have a family to go to. Where will you hunker down?" Casey had an idea but he waited for Clancy's response first.

"You don't have an extra room, do ya?"

"No, my house is too small, and you know I have a large family. But Cole Campbell's old residence on South San Francisco Street is for sale."

Clancy purchased Cole's place and set about remodeling the house. This was quite a change for a man used to surviving in the canyon wilderness. In ordering lumber for the remodel, he asked the salesman at the Kennedy yard if a set of plans came with his purchase. He had spent little time in town over the past fifteen years, limiting his forays to re-supplying his outfit. His extended stay in Flagstaff presented an opportunity to spin yarns to townsfolk. One of his favorite stories featured a big mountain lion that entered his cabin and would not leave.

Townsmen, lumbermen and prospectors gathered around a rowdy faro game at the Ponderosa Tavern. They all knew Clancy Jennings. "Before you fellas take another gulp, tell me whether you've heard about the mountain lion that invaded my home on the South Rim," started Clancy.

"Several times, but tell us again," answered one player. Clancy, eager to hold their attention, started again.

"One day when I went out to get firewood from my pile behind my cabin, a big cat strolled through my door. Mind you, I planned to be gone only a minute or two. Well, he would not let me back in. I waited until the feline marauder fell asleep and then stepped across my squeaky porch with the plan to reach inside and grab my rifle. He heard me sneaking around and launched into a round of loud growling." Clancy looked around; he had only a few patrons' attention, unlike entertaining wide-eyed gullible tourists on the rim. He raised his voice and continued. "After the growling spell, the critter went back to sleep, this time right in the doorway. I needed my gun but the cat would not let me pass. If I could just reach it, I would have a good supply of meat for the winter."

Several men got up to leave. Brushing by Clancy, one whispered to the other, "I've heard this story several times before, but last time it was a bear in his cabin."

Undeterred, Clancy resumed his long-winded spiel. "I waited for the cat to drift into a deep sleep and then made my move. I remembered my six-gun hanging behind the door. I reached around and removed it from its hook. The door creaked, the marauder woke up, and I skedaddled. About fifty feet out I turned around and aimed. I said to myself: 'When my gun fires, it will be fresh meat in the pot—and it's already half-cooked.' I pulled the trigger, I pulled it again, and one more time. No bullets."

With this, Clancy again checked on his few remaining listeners. "Now here's the good part," he continued. "I stood stone-still, petrified, knowing this was the end. That big cat ran right past me, chasing a deer that had just happened along. Would you believe it—that deer saved my life! And I got my cabin back!" The barkeep and a few men at the faro table roared with laughter as Clancy added, "I believed if there had been no deer running interference for me, I'd be the big cat's dinner!"

"Clancy, every time you deliver that story, it's different," criticized one man at the bar. He noted, "Last time it was a bighorn sheep, before that an antelope. Next time, I dunno, maybe a bear."

With such a tough winter, townspeople listening to Clancy's mountain lion story could have used the extra meat in the pot, whatever kind of animal he bagged. Although the deep snow made traveling impossible, northern Arizonans took comfort in knowing there would be plenty of snowmelt for stock and spring water for the upcoming tourist season at the Canyon.

Even before the snow melted, the Flagstaff *Frontier Times* promoted the wonderful caves of the Grand Canyon. Visitors could make their way to the entrance where Monte Bridgestone and his men had cleared a platform on the west wall of Windsong Mesa. From there, adventurous souls could enter one of two large limestone cavities and then decide on several passageways, each leading to an intricate series of tunnels and compartments. Since their discovery, the caves attracted as much attention as the Canyon itself.

Ownership of the caves, mines, trails and hotel became questionable as Buckey O'Neill missed his first payment. Then in March, the paper reported that he had transferred his interest in the Grand Canyon copper claim to Black Diamond Development Company for stock in the South Rim Improvement Company. Buckey had formed that mining investment branch of Black Diamond to show confidence in the production potential of mines from Prospector Flats north to the Canyon.

Shortly after this transaction, the thirty-eight-year-old answered the call to arms by volunteering for Army service in the Spanish-American War. A wave of patriotism swept the nation following the sinking of the Maine. Many brave men left their ranch, family and mining life behind for service to their country.

O'Neill helped form a regiment of western men under volunteer Army Colonel Theodore Roosevelt. Buckey took command of Troop A, 1st U.S. Volunteer Cavalry, a contingent of hard-fighting cowboys, miners, and frontiersmen of Arizona Territory. Five hundred men from New Mexico Territory, nearly two hundred from Oklahoma Territory and many more from eastern states joined the Arizona volunteers, all of whom went down in history as the famous Rough Riders.

As Captain O'Neill and his Rough Riders, including the reclusive miner Sam Thornton, boarded the train in Prescott, he tried to console his misty-eyed wife. "My dear, the war will not last long, and I will return in ninety days."

The Army didn't ship enough horses to Cuba in time, so the gallant troops fought on foot. While awaiting orders for the Battle of San Juan Hill, O'Neill stood erect among his men crouched on the ground. Bullets zipped above their heads. A sergeant urged his captain to take cover, but, perhaps intent upon inspiring his men by his own example, he declared, "The Spanish bullet that would try to kill me has not yet been molded." At dawn, a sniper's bullet struck O'Neill in the mouth. He died just hours before Teddy Roosevelt's daring charge up San Juan Hill. The recklessness, the compulsion to "buck the tiger," always a part of his life, finally proved fatal to Buckey O'Neill.

Roosevelt's gallant charge up San Juan Hill encouraged his troops. As the first to reach the enemy trenches, he killed one defender with his pistol, allowing his men to continue the assault. His leadership and valor turned the tide in the battle. Newsmen attached to his regiment reported his actions back to their editors in the United States. Teddy's superiors recommended the Colonel for the Medal of Honor.

American troops had attacked Spanish forces in mid-June and by July third the U.S. Navy had defeated the Spanish fleet in Santiago harbor. While right about the war not lasting long, but wrong about the circumstances of his return, O'Neill broke the promise he made to his wife.

News of O'Neill's tragic death flashing over the wires in Arizona caused widespread sorrow in the hearts of its citizens. This dashing adventurer had the invincible courage, patriotism and intrepidity that distinguished the derring-do western frontiersmen.

After ten weeks of fierce fighting, hostilities ended that August. Spain suffered a humiliating defeat and the collapse of her empire. The United States gained several island possessions—Guam and the Philippines in the Pacific, Puerto Rico and Cuba in the Caribbean. The victory marked America's entry into world affairs and a period of growth and prosperity that would last decades.

When Roosevelt returned to New York City, hordes of cheering citizens called for the 40-year-old Spanish-American War hero to run for Governor. He consented, but first toured the country with other Rough Riders and took part in several reunions. Sixteen of his Rough Riders re-enacted the San Juan Hill battle in Buffalo Bill's Wild West shows.

Meanwhile, back in Prescott, Buckey's wife mourned the loss of her beloved husband. In an emotional speech at a memorial service for Rough Riders who lost their lives, she said: "To you who celebrate our nation's success in battle, when your spirits are raised in triumph and your songs are the loudest, remember that we—grieving wives and mothers—sitting and weeping in our darkened homes, have given our best gifts to our country and our flag."

Tears streamed down her face as she tried to regain her composure. Several minutes passed before she could conclude her speech with a question. "I ask, how many hearts have been broken in the cause of patriotism?" The local paper, where Buckey once served as the editor, repeated her mournful message.

In November's national election, Roosevelt cruised to victory and became Governor of the Empire State.

An honor guard of Rough Riders laid Buckey O'Neill to rest at Arlington National Cemetery, on the gentle rolling lawn of Lee Mansion, where, as a boy at play he had led many an imaginary charge. His headstone carried the inscription "Who Would Not Die for a New Star on the Flag?"

The Arizona Rough Riders' gallantry in the battle for Cuban independence not only impressed the nation, it boosted the territory's gamble for statehood—indeed another star on the flag for Arizona. In addition, New Mexico and Oklahoma would gain statehood. The three new states contributed eighty-five percent of the Rough Riders in the Spanish-American War.

O'Neill's untimely death robbed him of the rewards of his crusade—the building of the Grand Canyon Railway he championed, the prosperity of the copper mines he promoted, the acceptance of Arizona as the forty-eighth state, and ultimately the preservation of Grand Canyon, remote and beyond compare, as a national park.

***

Construction of the Grand Canyon Railway, slow and sporadic for more than a year, turned around in the summer months. With rails and fastenings and rolling stock on their way, the railroad pushed north, despite added financial woes compounded by an inoperable Williams smelter because of the Santa Fe's refusal to supply water.

With the turn of the century, the railroad started transporting copper ore from Prospector Flats to Williams. Canyon tourists could ride the train to Prospector Flats and complete their trip to the rim by stagecoach.

But the railroad achieved only a partial success; it carried ore and passengers, as intended, but it needed to complete its tracks to the rim. Without the Williams smelter, ore still had to be shipped to more distant smelters. Transportation costs soared while ore quantities dwindled. The combination thrust the railroad into a serious financial crisis. In September, the company went into receivership.

The Santa Fe offered to buy the bankrupt line. Black Diamond Development Company, eager to rid itself of a losing proposition, accepted the Santa Fe's offer. With completion of the final sale and transfer, the Santa Fe instilled new hope that a railroad would finally reach the South Rim of the Grand Canyon.

***

All indications pointed to Grand Canyon Village becoming the center of tourism. But the Zebulon Branigan party of Boston felt differently, visiting the great hotel at Summit and Windsong Mesa instead of the Village. As an author, lecturer and photographer, New York publishing houses sought Zeb's travelogues, including Grand Canyon excursions. At the time of this canyon venture, Monte had closed the mines. On an earlier trip, Zeb had stayed at Clancy's tent camp where he endured some of the pioneer's wild tales but this time, he looked forward to his first visit to Summit Point and its Grand Canyon Hotel.

"Mr. Bridgestone," commented Branigan, "as our host, I cannot express enough in praise of you and the fine comforts offered by your new hotel. There is a warm, cheery atmosphere about its interior, a sense of the pioneer spirit in the stout log construction." Branigan continued, "And to my great surprise, you have a white-aproned, white-capped European chef presiding over your cuisine."

Zeb contrasted Monte's down-to-earth character with the nonsensical but entertaining Clancy Jennings, "Sir, unlike ol' Jennings, you are a man of few words, but those few words are always to the point. I see nothing of romance in your soul."

Monte never had anyone talk to him in such fine language. "Thank you, Mr. Branigan," replied the proud hotel proprietor, "it has not been easy."

Branigan, somewhat facetiously, continued, "Well, I know that when a mountain lion occupies your cabin, it is not the lion that gets to stay, and when you see a beaver, you admire his industrious nature, and as for hanging from the brink of the mighty Canyon by a dangling tree root, you have not wasted your time in such perilous adventures, but instead have sawn wood and hewn rock and built the mighty Summit Trail."

Monte, still reeling from the accolades, led the Branigan party down the trail on an overnight horseback excursion. The riders found the descent to be a series of steep zigzags that commanded their full attention. The trail ran along slopes so vertical that the builders could not lay long winding curves but instead zigzags that required sharp changes in direction, corkscrewing in and out of crags and crevices. None of the visitors had ever experienced a trail that dropped at forty-five-degree angles and bridged gaps between narrow ledges, where one could look down hundreds of feet. By noon the canyon caravan had reached the rock house on Windsong Mesa.

Monte felt obliged to explain the lack of activity. "As you can see, the mine has not fulfilled its promise, I'm sorry to say."

"Why is that, Monte?" asked Zeb, by now both being on a first name basis.

"Well, the cost of transporting ore has been a major factor. I have not given up, but for now the trail remains our best asset. In time, I believe it will become a source of profit, when tourists, like you fine folks, discover the new world that awaits them below the rim."

The party paused at the mining camp where the cook offered his special miner's soup and canned meats in battered tin cans. They sat in straight-backed chairs at a rough-cut pine table beneath an open building, draped with flapping awnings to provide shade from the noon-day sun. That afternoon, Monte guided his party through the caves. He unlocked a wooden door at the entrance. The adventurers squeezed through a low portal, filed along crystalline corridors, and at one point crawled on their hands and knees between the half-closed jaws of rock into a mammoth chamber. At the end of another corridor, they used dangling ropes to scale a wall, with lighted lanterns swaying from a belt, and lowered themselves into a dank and dark cathedral of stalactites and stalagmites. The party ventured over one thousand feet into the catacombs beneath the mesa before Monte directed them back to the world of daylight.

Early that evening, the party retired to one of the one-room, weather-wracked shanties on the mesa. The wood-frame buildings featured primitive construction, with a pitched roof, shuttered windows, and walls of warped pine boards. Fading shafts of sunlight squinted through cracks and knotholes and pierced the dark interior. Sunlight also filtered down between warped slats of a swayback roof, raising questions about what happened when it rained. Zeb asked his host, "Pardon me for my bluntness, but do you expect us to sleep under thin layers of shoddy workmanship like this?" The cabin in which the party settled contained six cots, each with its bedsprings mounted three feet above the plank floor. Zeb could not help commenting on the sleeping arrangements.

"These sleeping-machines," he noted, "are not as comfortable as the bare ground on which we slept while at the foot of Clancy's trail."

"Sleeping-machines? I've never heard them called that before," said Monte, "but having killed a rattlesnake yesterday, not forty-five feet away from here, you'll find the extra elevation of our cots reassuring." Monte wondered if folks back East called beds sleeping machines.

A cast-iron wood-burner occupied the center of the room, and several sections of stovepipe extended through the roof. The miners had placed a massive pine cabinet in a dark corner. On its saddle-brown surface rested a kerosene lantern, a spare six-shooter—no doubt for prowling snakes—and a row of brass cartridges. The only door faced South.

At sunrise, Monte organized the group for a trip to the river. They met behind the rock house where the Summit Trail dropped into Cottonwood Canyon and passed through the old miner's camp at the fork. Monte and his party dismounted in the shade of trees a short distance below Cottonwood Camp. Only on foot could they manage the remaining distance to the river. To their great surprise, they found a saddled chestnut horse tethered to a spindly cottonwood.

Monte called out, but no one answered. A brief search did not locate the mysterious rider, so the party continued their trek to the river. Single file, they skirted the east branch of Cottonwood Creek and finally dropped below the Tonto on the northwest side of Windsong Mesa.

Then they saw her—a woman wearing clothes more becoming of a prospector: Striped cotton shirt, baggy trousers, floppy broad-brimmed hat, a long braid down her left shoulder, and a small pick in her right hand.

"Sabrina? Sabrina Jaffa, is that you?" shouted Monte. "Folks, I ran into this woman down here a couple years ago. Claimed she was prospectin'. First time I've seen her since then!"

Directing his attention back to the woman, Monte asked, "Sabrina, you still pokin' around down here lookin' for a good dig?" No response. "And how come we haven't crossed paths until now?" Monte added. Zeb Branigan, unable to take his eyes off this ravishing woman, seemed as curious as his trail guide.

"Well, if you quit askin' questions, I'll tell ya. I remember you. You and your partners were just as surprised to see me back then as you are today. I've been comin' down here for years, just keepin' to myself, knockin' about these side canyons, lookin' for a good place to stake a claim," confessed Sabrina. She wondered if they would buy her story.

"Well, I'll be," stuttered Monte, again aghast at the sight of an attractive female prospector. She had not aged at all. She still sported flashing green eyes, a bewitching smile and a friendly, though standoffish, disposition.

"So, how's it going? Having any luck? You ain't gonna find anything good in those black granite walls. That metallic-looking glitter fooled us years ago," volunteered Monte. By now Zeb and his party appeared antsy, wanting to continue their adventure.

"I figured that, but just had to take another look. I know you think it's strange that you haven't run into me," Sabrina explained, "but I've avoided encounters with other prospectors and tour guides. When I see a fellow human, I skirt him widely or just hunker down and wait for him to leave the area. I'm about to head back but it's nice to see you again." Then turning to Zeb, she whispered, "Be careful going down that gulch to the river, lots of loose rocks." And with that, Monte's party headed north, looking back a couple times to see Sabrina negotiating her way back to the stand of cottonwoods and her waiting horse.

Red buttes shrank against the skyline, serving as depth gauges, as the party climbed down into the gorge. At last, the drainage channel they had been following opened to the Colorado River. Far from the haunts of men, the visitors gazed at the brown flood sliding past large boulders deposited at the foot of the trail.

"Monte, who was that woman back there?" queried Zeb.

"I don't rightly know; none of us miners do," confided Monte still perplexed himself. "And that was only the fourth or fifth time I have seen her. Stuart Casey told me he ran into her around Six-Gun Creek a few years back—she's quite the mystery lady."

The Branigan party spent the rest of the day climbing back to the South Rim and to the comforts of the Grand Canyon Hotel. At the supper table, several of the visitors wished they could have another look, not at the Inner Gorge, but at the mystery lady, before departing on their long trip back to Boston.

Chapter Three

A GRINDING HALT

Prospecting around canyon rockslides is strictly with the unconditional consent of geology, subject to change without notice.

The McCarty-Bridgestone mines included the Shooting Star Mine and four others below Summit Point. Some stakeholders wondered if the Shooting Star had underground connections to the Broadway diggings which looked like a field of potholes. Slim Broadway, Francois LaRue, and the Bergner brothers owned these operations south of Tusayan Well. Men mined ores below the rim and quarried ores on the rim.

For several months, Clint McCarty expressed his frustration with the McCarty-Bridgestone mining operations. The owners despaired of ever reaping financial gain from their canyon properties. Meanwhile, the Black Diamond Development Company had more mining operations than it could handle. The company defaulted on all its purchase agreements. The various mining properties reverted to the original owners. Then McCarty hatched a scheme for the owners to pool their resources. He wrangled power-of-attorney agreements and proposed to sell all fifteen mines to a wealthy New York heiress named Amelia Granger.

With the owners of the Shooting Star Mine experiencing hard times—no money to pay miners—and with the possibility of selling the mines to Granger, Clint again called for increased ore production. He knew higher yields would hold Granger's interest and fetch a higher price. He also lobbied for a new railroad, despite the line making its way to Starlight Camp. Clint continued to maintain that the mining and tourist industry at the Canyon would benefit more from a rail connection at Flagstaff.

Because Clint's political life kept him busy in town, he depended on Monte to manage their canyon properties. Kirby showed signs of tiring of the manual labor in the mines. Slim, involved in both mining groups, wanted the Shooting Star Mine to operate at a profit, and it bothered him that they could not find more men willing to do the physical labor. As for Monte, he became discouraged by the fluctuating copper market. Proud of his Summit enterprise, he tended more and more toward mining the pockets of tourists than the pockets of copper hidden in Windsong Mesa.

Mining men bided their time in hopes of an upswing in the price of copper that would clinch their deal with Granger. Completion of either railroad would bring more tourists to the Canyon, and then the partners could capitalize on their investment in the mines and in their hotel and outfitting businesses.

Continuing his push for a separate line from Flagstaff to the South Rim, Clint advocated using the right-of-way already on record. He extolled the fact that eight thousand tons of ore sat on the dumps of the Broadway mines and one thousand tons sat ready for transport from the McCarty-Bridgestone mines. He estimated another eighteen thousand tons lay exposed on the various properties. Clint once commented to Monte, "If only Flagstaff had a smelter; we'd all be making money."

At a public meeting of Flagstaff officials, Clint burst through swinging doors and interrupted a discussion about business opportunities. He spoke as a mine promoter, not a town sheriff, "Our town needs to approve one hundred thousand dollars to construct a smelter with a capacity of two hundred and fifty tons per day! Gentlemen, I'm telling you such a copper smelter will provide employment and pay for itself by eliminating the cost of shipping to faraway smelters!"

One of the town officials, annoyed by the outburst, responded, "Are you suggesting we enter the smelter business?"

"No, of course not; that's something for the mining industry to address, but we can encourage and support such an enterprise. And remember, with a rail line to bring the ore to the smelter, there is an added benefit to my proposition—tourism. Last year, eight thousand visitors traveled from Flagstaff to the Canyon by stagecoach, each paying a round-trip fare of twenty dollars. A railroad could bring fifty thousand visitors per year at a reduced fare."

"I don't like it, McCarty," said another official, leaning forward in his chair, "you are suggesting passengers share the ride with ore cars and from what I've heard about the El Paso smelters, they stink and fill the air with black smoke!"

"So do trains!" countered Clint, with a hint of frustration in his voice as he stormed out of the meeting.

Flagstaff townsfolk believed two competing spur lines to the Canyon would hurt business for both lines. After McCarty left, the mayor announced, "Gentlemen, the Grand Canyon Railway just reached Prospector Flats so it's a foregone conclusion that Williams, not Flagstaff, will service the Canyon."

Anticipating more tourists, whether they travel by stage or train, Slim and two other men labored on the Pioneer Trail, making improvements between Canyon Gardens and the river. They also moved the trailhead and claimed a new mining site four miles west of the Pioneer Trail, naming it the "Buckey O'Neill" in honor of their lost friend.

***

As the proprietor, Monte advertised the Grand Canyon Hotel as being situated a mile above the Colorado River, with fine trails and the best guides. He boasted his place commanded a grand view of twenty-five miles up the Canyon and one hundred and forty miles beyond. The renowned photographer and travel lecturer, Matthew Wilson of Hartford, made Monte's Grand Canyon Hotel his base station for two months one summer. He chose Summit Point because of its easy access to the inner canyon, points of interest along the rim, and ancient cliff dwellings just under the rim. Under Monte's guidance, Wilson captured the Grand Canyon in all its glory on photographic plates. His classic prints of heavily corseted, skirted ladies astride mules on the Summit Trail helped promote visitation at the Canyon.

That winter saw an increase in prospecting activity. Casey and Jennings located many claims between Grindstone and Bridgestone canyons. Operating alone about a mile west of Grindstone Creek, Casey located several more claims, including one special copper deposit he called the Whirlwind. He and other prospectors staked more claims on the north side of the river, in what old-timers called Dancing Ghost Canyon, that drained the sprawling Haunted Mesa into Skeleton Creek. And still others located new claims along Six-Gun Creek. Sabrina Jaffa, still avoiding contact with mining men, continued poking around side canyons but had yet to record her first claim. And Monte, convinced of the tourist potential at Summit, staked his claim to additional properties on the rim. He located five claims around the hotel and one, the Navajo Lode, to encompass Summit Point and its access road. Later it became embroiled in controversy when forest rangers challenged its validity. Monte located the Yucca, Lizard, Bobcat and Rockfall mining claims on the rim near the hotel. To capture additional water rights, he and Clint located claims at Summit and Red Horse tanks. Their Red Horse claim included the well-built, now abandoned, log cabin at the old stage stop on the road to Flagstaff.

Despite the remoteness and lack of development in Northern Arizona in the early nineteen hundreds, tourism on the South Rim increased at an astounding pace. Among the many summer visitors came a plump thirty-eight-year-old spinster. She stayed on as the shy housekeeper at the Grand Canyon Hotel. Anna Bigelow had a broad smile and a snub nose that wrinkled the freckles on her round face. She became a close companion of Monte, but with guests on hand she often stayed in the background.

By this time, Fox's stages no longer drove from Flagstaff, but instead from the railhead at Prospector Flats to Starlight Camp. At this new stage terminus, Fox erected cabins and wood-floored tents. This new tourist camp—a "tent city" of flapping white canvas—marked the beginning of the Starlight Hotel and included O'Neill's old cabin on the rim. Built with railroad loan money, the Grand Canyon Railway maintained the hotel.

Late that year, the railway passenger agent advised Monte that tickets issued by their Williams office reading "over stage line to Grand Canyon" would only be valid for Fox's line. Monte expressed great dismay with this unexpected announcement. "Now I need to establish my own line to shuttle my patrons fourteen miles to Summit."

In the meantime, the country elected William McKinley to a second term, handing William Jennings Bryan a second defeat. Teddy Roosevelt, who had campaigned for McKinley during his first run for president, had signed on as McKinley's running mate, bringing with him his war hero fame and his passion for conservation. Arizonans felt uncertain about how McKinley and Roosevelt viewed the transcontinental railroads thrusting spur lines into the Nation's pristine wilderness. At least Vice President Roosevelt's sensitivity to public discontent with big corporations and political machines tempered some worries about the McKinley administration.

Tracks would reach the South Rim long before Teddy's first visit, risking the Canyon to being overrun with development and private industry. The railroad and its attendant hotels represented a monopoly with well-placed connections in national government. Canyon pioneers felt powerless as the Santa Fe continued north, determined to stake its position at the head of their Pioneer Trail.

Only Captain Clancy Jennings seemed to be unconcerned with the impending commercial development. He wasted no time finagling room and board at Starlight Camp. Quite the kidder, he would tell stories to unsuspecting tourists milling around the village. He liked to prey upon parties of eastern women. They listened with absorbed attention to Cap's high-pitched voice as he described how he and his partner dug the Grand Canyon. He would never crack a smile, just in case one of them suspected that he may not be telling the truth.

On one occasion, a petite New England school teacher, who had kept silent during his graphic account of how hard they had worked, looked up with a triumphant air and said, "That story may be true, Captain Jennings, but what I want to know is what did you do with the dirt and rocks you took out to make the Canyon?"

With a hearty laugh, ol' Cap responded, "Easy 'nough to answer that. Why, with the diggins I built the San Francisco Mountains!"

When the tourists went home for the season, Clancy retired to his cabins below the rim and whiled away the winter days prospecting. In the Spring, he would return to the rim with more whoppers.

Monte began operation of his own stage line from Prospector Flats to Summit Point. Arrival of the first train at Grand Canyon would bring an abrupt end to Fox's stage line; but Monte's daily stage continued between Starlight Camp and Summit Point for many years, carrying both passengers and supplies. Guests of the hotel rode without charge.

Monte seemed more interested in running his hotel and stage line than operating the mines, but the other partners expressed renewed interest in reopening the Shooting Star Mine since shorter hauls to the new railhead would replace the long wagon hauls to Flagstaff. Slim wanted to lease their mine and put it back in operation while the partners waited for heiress Amelia Granger to accept their proposition. Slim explained: "I don't think there is a fortune in it anymore but as I am doing nothing, and I believe the property would sell much quicker by being operated than by resting idle, I'll take a lease on it and try developing it." No one seemed willing to take him up on his offer, perhaps believing Slim could not muster a work force, so the mine continued to lay dormant.

Clint and Monte had been contemplating construction of a smelter on the rim and then putting the mine back in operation. They would need a permit from the Secretary of the Interior for firewood to make charcoal. A gasoline engine could drive the blower. They would also need a good man to operate the furnace—one willing to take the heat and accept payment in copper rather than dollars. Clint regretted that they had not built a smelter on the rim years earlier, saying, "We would all have plenty of money now."

That winter, Slim reminded them again they needed to be thinking about the Shooting Star Mine and hotel properties. He still wanted a lease but with Monte snowbound at Summit and Kirby working at Prospector Flats, the partners never responded to his offer.

***

While a storm raged on the Coconino, Stuart Casey worked alone on his Whirlwind mining claim a mile downriver from his base camp at Grindstone Canyon. Casey, inured to strenuous work and the dangers of prospecting alone, thought about Sarah. "If she could see him now, she'd raise a ruckus," mused the wiry old-timer, "she'd call this pure foolery." Sarah, a good-hearted but overbearing woman, worried about his asinine mining escapades and never hesitated to scold her husband or express, in no uncertain terms how she felt—abandoned, unappreciated and dejected. It mattered little now as their marriage ended in court with a divorce.

Casey triggered a rockslide while cutting a new prospect hole in the black diamond rock formation. He had traipsed all over the site—an unstable gulley full of loose rock and rubble. He and other prospectors called it the Whirlwind Slide and for good reason—no solid footing, no trees or bushes to grasp, and nothing to stop one from sliding with the whole shebang into the gorge. As soon as Casey stepped onto a tilted slab of black granite, it moved. He knew prospecting among canyon rockslides is strictly with the unconditional consent of geology, subject to change without notice—and he knew he made a formidable error—the last he would ever make. Smaller slabs on either side also moved. In an instant the entire gulley slid as one, with unbridled fury, like jumbled logs riding ahead of a flashflood. Casey lost his balance, fell backwards and found himself at the mercy of the moving mass of rock.

He never saw it coming, but a monstrous raft of black rock rolled over his right leg. Feeling his bones crush and punch through muscle and skin, he screamed in excruciating pain. As if on cue, the entire caboodle of sliding, grinding rock slowed to a stop at the edge of a cliff. Casey found himself trapped with his mangled leg pinned under a massive rock slab. To make matters worse, no one would think to look for him for another week or two.

The Grand Canyon, with its perpetual interplay of eternal forces and the human spirit, is a noble adversary that tests the mettle of all who challenge her. The last thing a man wants to do is the thing he does last. Casey's desperate cries for help ricocheted off canyon walls with hollow mockery. He would succumb but only after days of writhing in pain and agony.

Casey could squirm just enough to free his arms and withdraw his pencil and daybook from his shirt pocket. He recorded his dying thoughts while pinned to the Canyon he so dearly loved. Held captive by the giant bone-crunching rock slab, he spent his final days developing a dramatic record.

Clancy Jennings, hunkered down at his camp on Whiskey Creek, became alarmed at Casey's long absence. When Clancy reported his old partner missing, Slim organized a search party. He and Clancy found Casey's body within ten feet of a fifteen hundred-foot drop to the river. From notations in his leather-bound diary, the men determined that he died twenty-five days earlier. Casey had suffered a lingering death, evident by his clenched jaw, twisted body, outstretched arms, and chips of rocks around his fingertips. His mining friends used a block and tackle to lift the slab, drag the body out from under, roll it in a tarpaulin and cover it with stones. "The poor fellow," Slim mumbled, "he left nothing but crushed bones and his daybook."

Casey's oldest son, close to his father during their cattle ranching days but less since he abandoned his family, remembered sobbing in the dark that night at his father's campsite. Clancy, who recovered Casey's daybook, reported his findings to the coroner's jury as it conducted a hearing in camp.

Clancy shared Casey's demise with fellow pioneers. "Day 1—cannot feel my right leg—should have heeded Sarah's warnings. Day 2—thirsty, scorching sun, pain in hip comes in unbearable piercing jabs. Day 3—heely monster took one look at me, wagged his black tongue, and moved on. Day 4—crying for help useless, reckon I'm a goner for sure. Day 5—so dry, shaking, can't—."

"That's it," Clancy reported, "ol' Casey stopped writing—and stopped living."

Clancy tried to change the somber atmosphere by telling a humorous story, but no one laughed.

Years passed before Slim and Kirby retrieved Casey's remains. Although Clancy wryly commented that he thought the old fogy too dead to bury, the men laid Stuart Casey to rest near the head of the Pioneer Trail.

A late February memorial service in Flagstaff honored the fallen canyon pioneer. Townsfolk remembered him as an honest, upstanding citizen and one of the earliest of the pioneers in the area. Cole Campbell, who had known Casey the longest, told the small gathering, "I will always remember my old partner as a strong-willed visionary. He saw it all, endured it all, and savored it all. We both grappled to read the rocky pages of that ancient book known as the Grand Canyon."

Clancy Jennings added, "No one should die this way. Unlike me, ol' Casey was sparing with his words. I'll never forget smoking our pipes in the hour of canyon twilight; he always wanted me to conjure up another wild tale."

Monte Bridgestone expressed his feelings as best he could, "Casey inspired respect and confidence. Despite the Canyon's adversity, he was ever the optimist. I believe this good-natured pioneer is now very much at peace with himself."

Stuart Casey, survived by his estranged wife and eight living children, left a hole in canyon mining exploits and a hole in the hearts of his many friends. His long-time partners, Cole and Clancy, let most of his mining claims go by default, although Clancy negotiated the sale of some remaining asbestos mines. In earlier times, the owners valued the mines at twenty-five thousand dollars, but the Great Panic reduced their value to a quarter of that. As a result, no one developed the mining properties any further.

***

Progress on the railroad remained very slow, and production at the Prospector Flats mines stopped when the price of copper tumbled again. With no ore to ship, the primary need for the railroad vanished. In June, Black Diamond Development Company foreclosed. The Grand Canyon Railway sold out to the Santa Fe for the bargain price of one hundred and fifty thousand dollars. The new owners pledged to complete the remaining twelve miles of track to the Canyon and predicted that trains would run to the South Rim by the end of September.

At this juncture, Jeff Fox sold his interests in the Grand Canyon Stage Line and the lodge at Starlight Camp to Jack Keystone, a thirty-four-year-old pioneer railroad engineer who came to Arizona with the Atlantic & Pacific Railroad. He once served as deputy sheriff under Clint McCarty. This industrious entrepreneur would later purchase the Jennings place, where he planned to operate a small cattle ranch and build a sixteen-room, wood-frame hotel.

The Santa Fe's newly acquired Grand Canyon Railway faced the formidable task of laying the remaining track from Prospector Flats to Grand Canyon Village in three months. Despite seeing rails and ties stockpiled at the Flats, visitors and workers scoffed at the company's prediction of passenger service to the Canyon by the end of September.

"How many rails did we set yesterday, Joe?" asked Hank DeWitt, knowing no one had been counting.

"I have no idea, but for each pair of rails I know we put down twelve ponderosa ties," answered Joe Stewart.

Hank and Joe came west with the railroad in the eighties. Back then their supervisor, Jack Keystone, now the new Starlight Hotel proprietor, threatened to fire them if they did not work harder.

"I wonder if ol' Jack will come down to see how we're doing," added Joe. "He has wangled his way out of this back-breaking railroad business—managing the Starlight now—much easier on the backbone."

As the line progressed northward up Shaski Wash, a Shay engine nudged a line of loaded flatcars ever closer to the brink of the Canyon. Hank and Joe worked as part of a fourteen-man crew. Four men had the job of offloading ties from flatcars, setting them in place along a line of survey stakes and dumping crushed rock ballast between them. Then ten men carried five-hundred-pound steel rails, setting them on the next section of ties, and driving two dozen spikes to pin each rail to the ties.

"Yesterday we were on the tie gang, today the rail gang," observed Joe. "I'm not sure which is easier," responded Hank, adding, "it takes me four hard blows per spike."

Joe added, "For me too, unless I hit a knot."

After completing a couple more sets of rails and ties, the hissing engine moved up the line, its crushing weight testing the workmanship beneath heavy wheels. With no side line, the workers had no way to clear away empty cars so the distance for manhandling materials became longer with each completed section.

"Hank, I just hope our foreman is paying close attention to the survey lines," commented Joe, not noticing the foreman standing behind him. "I would hate to rework a section because we strayed off the line." Hank nodded his head in silent agreement.

"You two just pay attention to laying track," barked the foreman, "there are thousands of steel rails to set on thousands of wood ties, and we've ten miles to go."

***

The Grand Canyon Hotel at Summit Point, being the only first-class hotel at the Canyon, hoped for a profitable fall season. Its stage left Starlight Camp at eight-thirty every morning. The hotel charged two dollars per day, saddle animals one dollar and fifty cents, trail guide two dollars and fifty cents, and carriage rides, not exceeding six miles, round trip, one dollar per person. Trail guides included Clancy Jennings, Slim Broadway and Francois LaRue.

Convinced that the railroad would extend the tracks to the Pioneer trailhead, Clint launched his own tourist enterprise. He acquired full ownership of the Pioneer Toll Road by purchasing his partners' shares, gaining control of one of the main accesses into the Canyon. He purchased the Red Horse Station building and hired men to move it to a site next to the Starlight complex. Log by log, the men dismantled, transported, and reassembled the old station on a site near the tracks, then added a second story and a wrap-around porch. This building, with its squared logs and frontier character, became the McCarty Hotel while Starlight Camp became the Starlight Lodge. With Clint's foothold firmly established on the South Rim, he assured himself a place in the Canyon's development. In the coming years he would face formidable competition—the Santa Fe-Trails West coalition.

Meanwhile at Summit, Monte and Slim discussed a new disturbing development.

"Slim, I was notified earlier today that the forest supervisor has ordered the district ranger to take full possession of our Summit Tank."

"What's that mean, Monte? It's not theirs to take," argued Slim.

"Well, according to Ranger Travis Holmes, they are taking it and holding it for exclusive use by forest rangers."

"That means the Summit complex will depend solely on cisterns and spring water hauled up here by burros," concluded Slim.

"Yeah, and, in times of drought, we may be forced to purchase water from the railroad," grumbled Monte, shaking his head in disgust. "This hostile action is just another sign of troubling times. It's especially hard on canyon settlers and residents who are finding it more difficult to live and thrive in the Forest Reserve. First timber and grazing permits, now the confiscation of a water supply we worked so hard to establish. It's downright criminal."

Just as Monte finished his rant against forest rangers, Stephen Zimmer, accompanied by his sixteen-year-old daughter, arrived at Summit with two hundred pounds of cameras, plates and flash lamps, ready for the trail. Monte had invited the well-known commercial photographer to visit Summit for the purpose of creating promotional views. He escorted them to all the important viewpoints, including the Whiskey, Redrock Canyon, Summit and Pioneer trailheads. At each trailhead, Zimmer and his daughter ventured part way down for a different perspective while Monte waited on the rim.

"Look Pa, I see a rider on the trail down there!" Zimmer's daughter pointed to a sharp switchback several hundred feet below them.

The photographer trained his camera to the spot just as the rider disappeared around a rock abutment. A few minutes later he caught sight of the rider again.

"It's a woman on horseback trailing a pack animal. Looks like she's headed down, perhaps planning an extended stay in the Canyon."

When she reappeared, Zimmer pressed the button on his camera.

"Got her, but she's a long distance from us. She may not even show up on the plate."

A month later, Monte received twenty-eight prints for review. The batch did not include a picture of the mystery rider.

***

That summer, McCarty, Bridgestone and Broadway leased the Shooting Star Mine and associated properties to a compendium of eastern capitalists and Arizona investors. A Harvard graduate led the investment group. Bradley Cooper, a mining engineer, served as the Coconino County representative in the Arizona Legislative Assembly, where he became familiar with mining and land development at the Canyon.

The lease included a purchase option. It specified the same properties that the late Buckey O'Neill tried to buy—Shooting Star, Downhill, Copper Kettle and Polaris lodes, the Summit Toll Road, and the Shooting Star mill-site with the hotel. Cooper masterminded the agreement and then proceeded to formally organize the Canyon Copper Company and file registration papers with the County. He felt strongly about developing the Shooting Star Mine into a high producer. With the railroad about to start regular train service to the South Rim, any property on the rim would be a good investment.

Within days of completing the lease agreement, Cooper staked six new lode claims on Windsong Mesa. He also located the Cooper mining claim in the gulch below the east wall of the mesa, securing the water rights to Arrowhead Spring. On Summit Point, in early September, he located the Summit mill-site and the Summit stone quarry, not realizing that Monte Bridgestone had already claimed the site as the Navajo mining claim. In years to come, considerable controversy would surround these overlapping claims.

As the new proprietor of the Canyon Copper Company, Cooper set about designing improvements for transporting ore to the rim. Anything would be better than slow-moving burro pack trains. He heard about aerial tram systems to haul Klondike miners and supplies over

Chilkoot Pass that separated Alaska from the Yukon. He also heard about such systems being used to haul ore from high-mountain silver mines near Park City, Utah.

Bradley sketched designs for a tram to transport ore from the Shooting Star Mine to the rim. He envisioned a series of wood-frame towers to support pulleys and cables, ore buckets, and a mule-driven wheel on the rim to power the conveyance system. His design called for a loading station on Windsong Mesa, ten support towers, three miles of steel cable, two or three teams of six mules to turn the wheel, and large wooden bins to catch ore as it dumped from moving buckets.

Bradley estimated the cost to build would be less than fifteen thousand dollars and time to construct about six months. He thought to himself, "All I need now is a group of enthusiastic investors to finance the construction."

As he rolled up his plans, he noticed Monte, Slim and Kirby conversing on Summit Point.

"Hey fellas, wanna see my idea for a tram?"

The men walked over to Bradley. "You have an idea for a train?" frowned Kirby.

"Not a train, a tram," replied Bradley, eager to explain the machinery that could make a miner's life easier.

"What's a tram?" returned Kirby as the engineer spread out his design drawings.

"It's a system of cables, two in fact, one stationary to support a string of suspended ore buckets and the other a traction cable to move the buckets along the line," explained Bradley.

Monte interjected, "You've gotta be kiddin', cables all the way from Windsong Mesa to here where we're standin'?"

Slim interrupted. "Sounds like a fascinating plan—it would get the mine back in operation and the production up to where it would be worthwhile."

"That's my plan; here, look at this," and Bradley revealed details as the men hovered over his drawings.

"There would be a terminal on the mesa for loading ore buckets as they arrive on the cable. I figure each bucket will carry about three or four hundred pounds of ore; that's four times what a single burro can carry."

"Wait a minute," Monte interrupted, "you expect these buckets to be loaded while they're still moving?"

"Well, I haven't worked out the details on that part yet," confessed Bradley. "Now spacing of supporting towers will depend on the lay of the land, which as you know, is steep in most places. Some spans could be a thousand feet!"

Monte had to ask, "What keeps the buckets from slipping backwards on steep sections?"

Bradley had no answer. "How should I know? I'm still working out the details."

Monte quipped, "Well, yer the engineer!"

Bradley changed the subject, "We must select the most direct route to the terminal on the rim which will be on the Summit mill-site."

Monte objected, "Ya know, that filing is right on top of my Navajo claim."

"Yeah, well we'll clear that up later," mumbled Bradley, half to himself but knowing the others heard, adding, "That terminal will have wheels and rollers just like the lower terminal, and there will be dangling ropes to tilt buckets and get them emptied as they swing by for the return trip."

In Bradley's mind, the tram would operate in the reverse of Park City, instead of extending from a lofty mountain position to a valley, it would convey ore from a "valley" to a lofty point, albeit the highest point on the South Rim.

"Hey, fellas," volunteered Kirby, "I wonder if we could substitute a chair for an ore bucket so that workers could ride up and down on the tram!"

"Ya know, when I was mining in Colorado, I heard of a mining town called Telluride. They say the name is a contraction for 'To Hell You Ride.' That's what I think of yer crazy cable car idea," jabbed Monte as he sauntered off to his Summit homestead.

Deep down, Monte wished he had thought of some alternative means of conveying ore to the rim. He resented having lost control of the Shooting Star mining operation.

Slim had been silent while others spoke their minds, but now he inserted himself into the discussion. "I understand Monte's skepticism. The cost per-ton to convey ore from the Shooting Star to Summit Point will be the deciding factor on whether this is a viable scheme. It all depends on how many tons of ore the tram can haul each day, how many workers we need at the loading and dumping stations, how many pounds each ore bucket can carry, and last, but not least, whether government agents will approve such an operation."

Bradley shrugged. He had no response.

"Another thing," added Slim, "I have my doubts that six mules trodding in a perpetual circle can hoist a string of loaded ore buckets. You may need a giant steam engine and that requires large quantities of wood for fuel and water."

Bradley shrugged again and scratched a note on his drawings as he returned to his quarters in the Grand Canyon Hotel. He expected stronger interest by Bridgestone. In his room, Bradley asked himself,

"Is my plan too grandiose, too expensive, and too obtrusive for this magnificent landmark of the American West? We need to work out many technical details and project financing and resolve several controversial issues." One thing for sure, Bradley needed to harvest all the copper he could before the government set aside the Canyon as a national park.

***

In a series of transactions, McCarty and his partners leased, and then sold, all their properties. In time, Bradley Cooper became President and Stephen Herrington became General Manager.

Other stockholders of the Canyon Copper Company included Ernst and Otto Bergner; merchant Casey Horton; notary public Amanda Mitchell; former Vermont Governor Carroll Page; Maud Rogers, a wealthy Vermont widow; and Dr. Roberto Torrez, a pioneer pathologist and a student of southwestern archaeology interested in the cliff dwellings in the San Juan and Colorado watersheds.

As a matter of public record, the Flagstaff paper announced the sale of the Shooting Star and Summit properties, and the county recorded the transactions.

And Monte, in the doldrums, felt downtrodden—a complete failure in all his enterprises—no longer owner of the bustling Ponderosa Tavern or the Canyon's copper jewel, the Shooting Star Mine, or the stately Grand Canyon Hotel, once the envy of all canyon accommodations. Monte needed an angel to brighten his days.

Chapter Four

RIBBONS OF STEEL

Where the rim meets the sky, the rails meet the rim.

One evening Cole Campbell and Slim Broadway walked from Canyon Gardens toward the point on the Tonto Plateau which offered mind-wrenching vistas of the deep gorge. There, the Colorado River snakes between vertical bands of pink and black granite. The day's blazing sun toasted everything it touched on the Tonto, even searing hardy blades of gramma grass.

"Step lightly, Slim," warned Cole, "there may be rattlers hereabouts."

"I'm well aware, Cole. Rattlers are much maligned—they have no way of knowing there is no malice in our hearts," Slim explained, all the while looking where he placed his feet. "Some folks hunt them relentlessly, often without reason."

The men plodded along the hot dusty burro path. Each step brought them closer to the northern edge of the plateau and a dizzying view of the river far below.

"We are intruders in the rattler's domain. It's best to keep a sharp eye on his movement, and a sharp ear for his tail-shaking," said Slim, adding, "a rattler always sounds a warning before striking, even when it could attack more effectively in silence."

Cole countered, "I'd say the warning, as you call it, and the strike, occur about the same time. Anyway, watch where you place your feet; there could be a lashing tongue ahead, searching for some hint of our intentions."

The men came to a torturous row of fractured boulders about waist high. They scanned the lower crevices for dens and resting places, while steadying their clamber over rubble with one hand on the boulders. Suddenly Cole stepped back to avoid a rattlesnake's menacing hiss and rattle on top of the rocks!

The snake, coiled and spring-loaded, sunk his crescent-shaped fangs with their deadly venom deep into Slim's right hand.

"Eee-ow!" cried Slim, "I've been bit!"

Cole drew his revolver and fired a bullet into the five-foot long body, then ripped the strip of rawhide from his field glasses and wrapped it around Slim's forearm.

"Let's start back, Slim, we need to get help right away."

Cole fired two more shots in the air, hoping to get someone's attention before the poison took effect. The two had not gone but a few hundred feet when Slim slumped to the ground. They both knew, with dreadful predictability, time had run out for the gentle, good-natured prospector. He had escaped death by an explosion while blasting rock for the Pioneer Trail, but this time rattlesnake venom would take his life. "Cole, I can't see, I can't breathe, I can't ___" Slim Broadway died within minutes of the fatal bite.

Cole reported the accidental death to the County Sheriff and organized a work party to retrieve Slim's body. Friends held a simple funeral service in Flagstaff and buried him in the local cemetery as its sixteenth entry. They remembered Slim Broadway when he mined on both sides of the river, when he helped haul the prize rock, and when he volunteered to help Monte build the first cabin at Summit.

***

In mid-September, LaRue guided an eccentric sixty-three-year-old widow and her younger sister on a trans-canyon trek. The intrepid lady,

Maud Rogers of Bellows Falls, Vermont, was a close friend of Governor Page who suggested the ladies visit the Grand Canyon. Maud, well-educated and blessed with considerable wealth, seemed fearless yet cautious, eloquent yet playful, and dignified yet rough-and-ready.

Three years earlier, Maud joined a party of tourists guided by LaRue on the Whiskey Trail. After spending the night at Jennings' river camp, she left the group and started back alone on the trail. She encountered Captain Jennings, headed down, driving fresh saddle horses for the party. Stopping Maud on the trail, he asked, "Ma'am, what are you doing out here by yourself?"

"Going home."

"See that shady overhang, Ma'am? Sit there and wait for the others. I'll tell Francois where you are." Maud seemed disoriented, lost in a vast sea of rocks.

The returning party helped Maud back up the trail. She rode the stage to Flagstaff and boarded an eastbound Overland Express.

Maud returned with her sister Sadie as clients of LaRue, now guiding his own trail parties. With three pack animals loaded with provisions, they set out for the North Rim. The adventurers descended the Pioneer Trail and arrived at the river crossing near Skeleton Creek. LaRue, in his distinctive French accent announced, "We will now part with our animals, and prepare for our crossing."

Maud, undaunted by her previous experience, remarked, "The sight and sound of this river rouses me to a considerable pitch of enthusiasm, pounding and pulverizing, smashing and crashing."

LaRue responded, "You are hearing a ferocious rapid upstream."

Maud added, "My word, the Colorado looks dirty. And look! There goes a big log! In the East we would call that a navigation hazard."

Sadie chimed in, "And there's another log! What if a log hits our boat?"

Blake Jensen, who worked for LaRue, waited by their wooden scow, a boxlike craft with high sideboards, a blunt bow, three crossboards for seats, the center one serving as a rowing station. As a hired hand, he served as a trail guide, river master and prospecting partner.

"Blake, I present Maud and Sadie Rogers, paying customers from Vermont," announced LaRue as he motioned to the two sisters, both wearing inappropriate black dresses and straw hats with blue tie-down ribbons fluttering in the breeze.

"Howdy ladies; I'm your trusty river guide. Ever done anything like this?"

"No," responded Maud, "but we sure hope you have."

"You have nothing to worry about. The river's running well today; nothing like this time last year," replied Blake, seeing an opportunity to put a little scare into these novice women.

"Whatever do you mean, Mr. Jensen? It looks treacherous enough to me," Maud stated rather matter-of-factly, as the guide stowed gear in the boat.

With no sign that anyone wanted him to go on, Blake, feeling cocky, tried to launch into his standard river-running story. As he started, he caught LaRue shaking his head, not wanting him to describe their harrowing experience.

With considerable trepidation, Maud and Sadie stepped into the boat. Blake threw a few more sacks in and took the oars as LaRue pushed off. The boat soon struck the sandy landing on the other side, a considerable distance below the point where their river voyage had started. Then Blake, with care and courtesy, helped his passengers ashore.

With the two women and sacks of provisions left on the north side, Blake and LaRue shuttled back and forth across the river several times that afternoon. By the time they had ferried all their provisions to the sandbar, darkness had set in. They built a fire of driftwood and set about preparing supper by firelight.

"We're having canned beef and beans," announced Blake, the self-proclaimed bean master. Then, turning to Maud, he commented, "Down here, we call beans canyon whistles." Maud had to ask why as Blake turned away to hide an inward giggle.

"Well, if you must know, for their gas effect, and an invasive aroma the next morning." LaRue glared at Blake in protest to his use of inappropriate conversation in the presence of two refined ladies. Then he also turned away, half grinning, half snickering. Maud and Sadie, not amused, ate their meal in silence.

The intrepid travelers spread their bedrolls on the soft sand. Throughout the night they heard the flapping noises as the river swirled past their camp.

The next morning, as shafts of sunlight brightened the opposing side of the gorge, smells of outdoor cooking filled the river camp and puffs of smoke curled from the flickering flames, like fog swirling around a tall butte.

Blake made the call, "Come and get it, flapjacks, sizzling bacon and cowboy coffee." The bleary-eyed women staggered over to eat their breakfast, spiced with a side order of Blake's tall tales—whoppers for sure. The men guzzled their coffee, but Maud and Sadie just sipped, trying to strain the floating grounds swirling in their cups.

LaRue announced, "Time to start toward the North Rim." Maud, surprised as she and Sadie had swallowed little coffee, prepared to lodge a protest but Blake had already scrambled up the rocky trail along Skeleton Creek where they would mount burros for the ride to Firelight Camp. Maud mounted a burro named Tyler while Sadie mounted Jasper.

"What a clear mountain stream this is. It is not unlike our creeks, right Sadie? Swishing willows and tall grass line its rocky sides, and it comes splashing and dashing down pure and sweet," declared Maud. Sadie did not respond. It seemed no one listened to Maud's endless trail comments.

They passed a side canyon that LaRue called Dancing Ghost Canyon. Maud asked about its name but the only information the men divulged included something about a trickle that drained through it from Haunted Mesa. Maud rambled on. It seemed her burro enjoyed the chatter as his ears seemed to twitch at the start of each commentary.

The burros skirted narrow ledges and trudged up rocky steps. Many sycamores, cottonwoods and alders shaded the flowers and ferns along the creek, in a verdant symphony of bright and muted colors. Maud pointed out one drawback of the lush gulley. "Francois, these mosquitoes are out for blood!"

The trail turned into a tremendous climb. Maud met the challenge by clinging to the coattails of her guide with one hand and sometimes with both hands, he holding tight to the burro's tail. Tyler accepted this and did his best to haul them up the streambed. Sadie, being younger and lighter, rode Jasper with considerable ease.

At Firelight, they set up camp for the night below a roaring spring that contributed most of the water in the creek. Sadie felt compelled to comment on their overnight accommodations. "This is how you camp here in the Canyon? We are all in a heap together—rolls of bedding, campfire, burros, knapsacks and saddles—all in a very cramped space!" cried Sadie.

"Yes, sometimes we look disorganized," said LaRue, who then changed the subject. "I find the north side of the Canyon more beautiful and diversified than the south side. I contend that no one can know the

Canyon unless he, or she, crosses the river and climbs to the rim on this side."

Maud agreed, "The landscape is spectacular, and I understand why many folks want to make Grand Canyon a national park. But it is so rugged and remote, who would want to travel like this. We're just getting started and I'm already having second thoughts." Sadie added, "It borders on inaccessible. I'm for turning back in the morning."

After spending a cold, miserable night confined in a small camp, Maud's courage almost failed. Like her sister, she contemplated giving up, but then vowed to continue. They started again and ascended a steep, loose trail in the manner of the previous day. They came across springs of excellent water trickling out from under the cross-bedded sandstone.

His timing not the best, Blake felt compelled to point out large footprints near the springs. "Them's mountain lion tracks. We all need to stay alert. Those big cats stalk deer, not humans, but just the same, you don't want to get crossways with ol' Diego."

Alarmed beyond description, Maude gasped, "Diego?"

"Yeah, we named him on a trip last year," interjected Blake, attempting to calm Maud's nervous disposition. "Diego snarls and paws the ground when we meet each other, but so far he has left us alone, right Francois?"

"So far, so good; ladies, don't worry, Diego is probably miles away and has already dined on fresh venison."

The party reached Gunsight Saddle and then followed a long trail to the North Rim. Winding through scrub oak and sagebrush, past browsing mule deer and skittering tassel-eared squirrels, the travelers felt the end of their journey near.

The men ordered Maud and Sadie to dismount and finish the climb on foot with the aid of their burros' tails. After such slow plodding, the burros suddenly seemed to be in a hurry and sometimes very unceremonious with the women. Maud looked up at the north wall of the Canyon, looming in all its grand cliff-and-terrace symmetry.

The party finally reached the rim and stood spellbound by the magnificent views. A great salient promontory stood before them, and beyond lay an irregular horizon of chiseled tablelands. They watched the sun squinting on the western horizon. Before them lay a majestic wilderness of changing shapes and gliding shadows, golden shafts of sunlight sprayed desert towers and ramparts—the real American West. "Wait," cried Maud, "I want to Kodak this view." After several clicks, Maud tucked away her two-dollar Brownie box camera. However, the absent-minded photographer packed only one roll of film which had only six exposures.

"C'est magnifique!" said LaRue. "This is why Grand Canyon needs to be a national park. Blake here thinks Grand Canyon is too big, too inaccessible and impossible to manage as a national park."

"I agree with you, Francois. We need to preserve this great chasm in its present state. There must be a way to do that and still allow future generations the opportunity to see what we are seeing. I hope ol' Diego will share his domain with caring humans."

The party spent a cold blustery night on the plateau, listening to the mournful howl of a lone wolf. It snarled at the stinging cold wind rushing through the dark forest. The wind carried a message, and the wolf caught it in its bared teeth. The scent of humans raced through the Arizona night. What a long, spine-tingling wail he made. A restless night awaited the travelers.

After a breakfast of beef jerky and canned tomatoes, washed down with black coffee, grounds and all, they started back down. It occurred to Maud that the rocks ahead, or any blind corner on the trail, might be a perfect place for an encounter with a grumpy mountain lion. She shuddered to think of the snarling and clawing.

Returning to Firelight Camp, Maud and Sadie collapsed on their bedrolls and fell asleep in minutes.

After another restless night and a campfire breakfast, Blake spoiled the mood. "Time to go, Mrs. Rogers."

Francois countered, "Hold up Blake. Let's take a few more minutes to watch the sun light up the Canyon in all its reds, oranges and yellows. Nothing like this in Vermont, eh, Mrs. Rogers?"

"Do you know Vermont, Mr. LaRue?

"Yes, Ma'am, I'm originally from Quebec, just across the line from Vermont."

"Oh yes, I think you mentioned that once before," remembered Maud.

They retraced their footsteps and navigated the streambed. At the river, LaRue ferried them across to the south side where they mounted burros and started back up the Pioneer Trail to the South Rim. Maud and Sadie Rogers returned to their home in the East with cherished memories, and six photographs of an unprecedented rim-to-rim experience at the Grand Canyon.

Francois LaRue, attracted by a shocking headline, picked up an edition of the *Frontier Times*. "Hey Blake, someone shot President William McKinley point blank. When he died eight days later, Vice President Theodore Roosevelt became our twenty-sixth and youngest president."

Blake looked up, "Who's this Roosevelt feller?"

***

Three days after McKinley's passing, the whistling and clanking of a steam locomotive signaled the beginning of regular train service to the South Rim. That train comprised an engine, a tender, three water tankers and one passenger car.

The new tracks extended to the brink of the Canyon, with the first train from Williams arriving only two days later. The terminal included a maze of tracks and switches allowing a train to pull into the makeshift station to disembark passengers and unload water and freight, then back up on a wye, realign itself with the main track, and back into the depot for embarking passengers.

Monte Bridgestone, among the canyon pioneers witnessing the first train's arrival, had just ended his regular run to the Village. He took in the sight—a smoke-belching steam locomotive sitting on bright steel tracks—what Santa Fe officials so eloquently called ribbons of steel. But in the Santa Fe's passion and fervor to create tourist access to the Grand Canyon, it added clamor and disruption to the once quiet life on the South Rim. Its shrill whistles became harsh reminders of the train's ability to shatter the reverent silence of the Canyon.

The Santa Fe vowed to make the Grand Canyon a popular tourist resort during the next year by erecting a more permanent station, a large modern hotel, and improving the Pioneer Trail, although it did not belong to them, and building miles of road along the rim.

The railway established daily passenger service, with round-trip fare at four dollars, from Williams to the Canyon. It pulled out of the Williams depot mid-morning, rolled along for a distance of sixty-five miles, and arrived at the temporary Starlight Hotel and depot early that afternoon. The following day, it left at nine in the morning and returned to Williams by early afternoon.

The black, grimy locomotive, with its clanging bells and grinding wheels, seemed most unnatural at the Canyon. Its intrusive tooting spilled over the rim and echoed from one butte to the next. President Roosevelt, a strong proponent of both preserving the quiet reverie of America's backcountry and expanding the nation's network of railroads, would have mixed feelings on future train rides to the Canyon.

By reaching the South Rim, where the rim meets the sky and the rails meet the rim, the railroad had marked the beginning of a new era. Although its roots lay in the mining industry, its lifeblood lay in the multitude of canyon visitors. As the dominant conveyance for years to come, the railroad became a lifeline for local residents in Grand Canyon Village and became highly influential in developing the Grand Canyon as a tourist attraction. A telegraph line, routed along the railroad right-of-way and operated under contract by Western Union, gave electric life to the Village.

With its first train to the South Rim, the Santa Fe Railway, operating its spur line as the Grand Canyon Railway, surveyed a location for a more permanent depot near the Starlight Hotel. Under the act which granted railroads the right-of-way through public lands, the government allocated twenty acres for yard track, sidings and station. The Santa Fe made plans for construction of the Grand Canyon Station and tourist accommodations, including enlarging the Starlight Hotel to two stories and erecting more tent cabins at Starlight Camp. As the proprietor, Jack Keystone made sure that Buckey O'Neill's historic log cabin became an integral part of the hotel complex.

Long after inaugural riders left the train, a dark figure lurking in the passenger car stepped off and disappeared among the ponderosas. The Santa Fe accused Clint McCarty of placing recruiters on the train. Their mission—to persuade passengers to book rooms at McCarty's hotel rather than the Starlight. While no one could prove such hijacking operations, some suspected two drifters of passing out advertisements before the train's arrival. Keystone floated two names, Morton and Sykes, as possible informants for hire.

The strategic location of the McCarty Hotel near the tracks and the Pioneer trailhead irked the Grand Canyon Railway. One of the local officials commented to his colleague, "We need to do something about that McCarty fellow. He's trying to siphon off passengers and divert them to his tiny rustic hotel."

McCarty resented what he called government-sponsored business barging in where he had done the groundwork. His outright defiance of the Santa Fe resulted in the railway moving its new depot further east, leaving the McCarty Hotel less accessible to arriving passengers. Rumors spread like wildfire that the railway planned a second, grander hotel east of the Starlight. Construction of the Canyon Queen Hotel would not begin for another two years but the Santa Fe intended to assign management of the two hotels to the Trails West Company.

Clancy Jennings became well-pleased with regular rail service to the Canyon. With train passengers at the Village, Clancy had a steady supply of greenhorns to listen to his tall tales.

Although Grand Canyon Village seemed destined to be the center of visitor activity on the South Rim, Monte Bridgestone's Summit enterprise refused to die. His original log cabin and hotel building became headquarters for the Canyon Copper Company. As Bradley Cooper drew plans for an annex to the hotel, Monte homesteaded a new location south of Summit Point.

While Monte continued to manage the Grand Canyon Hotel, he built a modest four-room bungalow for Anna and himself, and a line of wood-framed, pitch-roofed buildings which he operated as the Summit Hotel. His small stage line transported train travelers from the Grand Canyon Station to both hotels. In time, despite two independent operators—McCarty and Bridgestone—trying to snag customers from the

Santa Fe-Trails West monopoly, it would be the only big corporate operators left standing on the South Rim.

Monte determined that the Canyon exhibited its greatest depth and commanded its best views at Summit. Although his Summit Hotel sat back from the rim, obscured by the forest, it occupied the highest point on the South Rim. In many respects, Summit Point became the showplace for unrivaled canyon scenery.

From Summit, not the Village, a visitor could carry away one of the most vivid mental pictures of this wondrous land—utterly mesmerizing. At Summit Point, one could stand at the apex of the great arc the river carved in stone, where it pivoted west, past terraced temples and palatial colonnades. Monte often thought to himself, "If only the rail terminus had ended at Summit, it would have become Grand Canyon Village."

As manager of the Summit Hotel and Stage Line, Monte outfitted parties from his well-stocked hotel stables. He provided seasoned trail guides, camping equipment and sure-footed saddle animals at reasonable rates. East and west of the complex, visitors could ride on horseback or by carriage for miles along the rim.

"Folks," Monte said, addressing a small party who just arrived from the Village, "we have just improved the Summit Trail with a direct connection to where you are now standing. Here you have the easiest descent into the Canyon, and access to lateral routes on the Tonto Plateau." Monte pointed to the flat terrain of the Tonto.

"With an early start, you can descend to the esplanade, skirt around Whiskey Canyon and reach the river at Whiskey Rapids. After a rest in the sand dunes watching the roaring torrent, you can then return to the rim on the Redrock Canyon Trail, all in a single day."

As Monte explained his offer of two-day trips westward across the Tonto to the Pioneer Trail, an elderly man in the party interrupted him.

"Is that storyteller, I think his name is Clancy, hereabouts?"

Monte ignored the question. "Now, upon returning to the rim, you can either catch the train to Williams or the coach to Summit—a delightful fourteen-mile ride along the forested rim, I might add."

The man more interested in meeting Clancy Jennings seemed to lose his patience, but then Monte finally obliged.

"No, we do not see Clancy around here anymore. If you came here for magnificent views and real canyon adventure, you came to the right place. If you came for outlandish stories, you should have stayed in the Village." He regretted his last remark, but it hurt no one's feelings.

***

When not minding his own enterprises, Francois LaRue worked for Bradley Cooper guiding trail parties on the Summit, conducting three-day trips to the Little Colorado, and piloting longer trips to Havasupai country in Cataract Canyon.

Cooper and his associates had been leasing the Summit mining properties, but, in mid-November, they exercised their option to buy three of the claims and the famous Summit Toll Road for ten thousand dollars. Proceeds from the sale went to the originators. Monte and Clint invested their shares in their respective hotel ventures.

Ore production under the new owners went well, with large bodies of high-grade copper ore being extracted. Monte had long believed a greater copper bonanza lay waiting discovery under Windsong Mesa. The company used sixty pack animals to carry ore from the mines to Summit Point and needed more because it planned weekly shipments to the El Paso smelter. Monte still had his hotel operation but, in some ways, regretted selling out. Being so close to the Canyon Copper

Company and the mines he had once developed, owned and operated, made matters worse.

One afternoon, Monte ran into Bradley Cooper coming up from the mine.

"Hey, Bradley, do you have a few minutes? I have something I'd like to discuss with you."

"Sure Monte, what's on your mind?" Bradley, his beard and shirt flecked with cigar ash, dismounted and hitched his mule to a juniper. The men sat down on two shaded rocks, with a commanding view of Windsong Mesa.

Monte started the conversation. "First, some time back you were working on a scheme for a tramway between the mine and the rim. I apologize for my skepticism."

Bradley interrupted, "No apology necessary. I've put that crazy idea out of my mind."

"I haven't. I've been kicking it around for some time and I thought I'd run it by you. Now, hear me out." Monte pointed to the mine.

"We all know Windsong Mesa is chock-full of high-grade copper ore. I suggest you revisit your drawings, update the design and build that tram."

Bradley, startled by Monte's change of heart, let him continue.

"Start a campaign to set aside this area as a small but special mining district. You'll need some political help in Washington City to get that approved. The district should include all of Windsong Mesa and the spring below the east wall plus the mill-site we are sitting on. It would finally serve its intended purpose. Your tram idea would work but not if it is mule powered. You need a steam engine to run the pulley system. Use the tram also to haul spring water for the steam engine and a smelter."

Bradley had to interrupt. "A smelter? You mean to refine the ore here on the rim?"

"Yes, set the smelter back from the rim so it does not spoil the view. There's plenty of timber up here to fuel a smelter. Send any byproduct material back down to the mine and combine it with mine tailings as backfill. You want no visible dumps on the mesa to spoil the view. Follow me so far?" Monte noticed Bradley scribbling notes as fast as Monte laid out his ideas.

"Now, Clint has been kicking around ideas for an East Rim Scenic Railway. With train service at the Village, all you need is a spur line between there and Summit, with a siding at the smelter. The rail spur's primary purpose is to serve as a scenic railway, but its secondary purpose would allow occasional freight cars for shipping refined copper to market. To get such a plan approved, you would need to pledge to remove tram cables, towers, terminals, steam plant and the smelter when mining operations cease. What do you think, Engineer Cooper?"

"Monte, that's a wild plan, and many things—government approvals, financial investment, natural resource protection—need to come together to make it work. I can see you have given this a lot of thought. I know you care about protecting this awesome canyon so I'm rather surprised you would place an industrial complex in the middle of what may someday become a national park."

As he said this, Bradley wondered about the plan's technical feasibility. "I'll run your idea by the owners and see what kind of response I get."

The men parted company. Monte felt like he had handed a viable concept to the Canyon Copper Company, but deep down, he too had reservations about an industrial complex in this magnificent place on the planet.

Chapter Five

DANCING GHOST

Close to copper bonanzas, far from prosperity.

The early years of the twentieth century represented a time of transition and mixed feelings at the Grand Canyon. Investors bought and sold properties; partners organized and reorganized companies. Canyon prospectors, miners and settlers—though they longed to profit from their hard labors—grew apprehensive about interloping corporations. Some pioneers resented the greed and influence of these companies.

While the miners had discovered minerals worth recovering, and while most of them advocated tourist developments, they feared the takeover nature of large commercial enterprises. The quiet solitude of the Grand Canyon gave way to steam locomotives, hordes of tourists, and boomtown hotels, and the possibility of screeching cable systems threading their way into the canyon depths. On one record-setting day at Starlight Camp, nearly four hundred visitors stood in awe on the South Rim, a new, exciting, yet disturbing pattern for the future.

***

On a cold blustery Sunday afternoon in early January in Flagstaff, a skeptical crowd gathered around two coughing, sputtering machines with hard rubber wheels. Arizonans viewed steam-powered locomotives to the Canyon as a novelty, but Martin Griggs, a wealthy entrepreneur from Los Angeles City, planned to demonstrate an alternative mode of transportation using the old stage road. He hoped to exploit the use of newfangled carriages to shuttle passengers between Flagstaff and Grand Canyon, making the round trip in a single day.

For this highly publicized event, Griggs challenged another entrepreneur, Travis Hawthorne of Denver City, to a race to the South Rim. He selected the Grand Canyon Hotel at Summit as the finish-line. Ten days behind schedule, he sent a telegram to Monte Bridgestone: "Leaving Flagstaff Friday or Saturday with two steam-powered automobiles for your place, with four men aboard each. Request you have three barrels of water for my auto and the same for my Denver competitor." Telegraph service extended only as far as Grand Canyon Village, but Teresa Cordova volunteered to run the message out to Monte.

As mid-morning approached, the men boarded their hissing automobiles—Toledo Eights—ready to steam out of town and become the first auto to reach the brink of the Canyon. Griggs' party included himself as the driver; Winfield Oppenheimer, a Los Angeles newspaper reporter; Jesse Parks, the highly respected Flagstaff banker; and Seth Westbrook, the local guide. Westbrook had been living in Flagstaff for thirty years. At age twenty-one, he had the honor of witnessing the gold-plated spike being driven at Promontory Point, Utah, marking the completion of the first transcontinental railway. For that historic event, passengers from the West brought San Francisco Bay water while from the East came Atlantic water—for blending at Promontory, close to another sprawling body of salt water—symbolic of the union. Griggs viewed this canyon automobile race as a similar historic event. Travis Hawthorne made his fortune in gold mining around Cripple Creek, Colorado. His passengers included the well-known reporter, Jake Peterson, of the *Rocky Mountain News*, and two local cattlemen who claimed familiarity with the stage road.

Newsman Ryan Perkins predicted the historic auto race would take six days or six years. Griggs thought six hours would be sufficient, since, in a speed test between Toledo City and Detroit City, his machine had reached forty-two miles per hour under one-hundred and seventy pounds of steam pressure. Reports of dry stage road conditions and little snow at the South Rim bolstered Griggs' confidence. With a gross weight of twenty-two hundred pounds, he felt that neither mud nor snow nor ice could impede the overland progress of this eight-horsepower horseless carriage.

While the turn-of-the-century automobile fulfilled the practical concept of a horseless carriage, townsfolk remained skeptical about its touted substitution for the horse. They viewed the auto as a novelty, not a mode of travel that would replace the horse, although automobile builders measured traction in "horse" power and believed their commodity held great promise for the future. No one could have dreamed it would become the backbone of a great industrial nation.

"Griggs, before we depart on this futuristic contraption, explain some of these gadgets," insisted Oppenheimer, ready with his notebook and pencil.

"Gentlemen, here's the information our reporter friend here wants," said Griggs. "The steam engine of this Toledo-built automobile includes a flash boiler, water coil, and sixty-gallon water reservoir. The right driving wheel is fitted with a cyclometer to register distance traveled in miles. I'll tell you more along the way." Giving a side-long glance to Hawthorne briefing his crew, he shouted, "Mayor John Atkins, let's get this race started!"

Mayor Atkins, now serving his third term in office, waddled over to the two coughing, smoking Toledo Steamers. "Dang it, I forgot my starting gun. Does anyone have a gun I can borrow?" A scruffy cowboy handed him his Winchester.

"Mr. Griggs, is your machine ready?"

"Yes, Mr. Mayor, let's get on with it."

"Mr. Hawthorne, is your machine ready?"

"Yes, ready—we think."

The mayor seemed unfamiliar with the carbine. After waving it around in front of the crowd, he found the trigger. "Very well, here goes!" He fired the shot and the race started.

Both automobiles operated well for the first ten miles through the San Francisco Mountain Forest Reserve and did not suffer any breakdowns until well out of sight of townsfolk. When Griggs' luggage trailer bore down too hard on his rear axle, he abandoned it. This problem remedied; their journey continued.

Unknown to Griggs, Hawthorne's automobile lost its steering. When he crawled out from beneath the undercarriage, he grimaced. "Gentlemen, I have bad news, the steering rod has snapped. The race is over for us."

The Griggs team stopped for the night at the sheep ranch of Hans Litzinger. They had made no provisions for camping, expecting to arrive at Summit Point that evening. Litzinger invited the men to bunk with his three ranch hands in their mountain cabin. The cowboy hospitality included a supper of beefsteak, biscuits with honey, and, of course, strong cowboy coffee.

"Mr. Griggs, what do ya use to heat the water to make steam?" one cowboy asked.

"They call it gasoline, a combustible fuel derived from crude oil."

"Is that like kerosene we use in our lanterns?" The cowboy seemed very inquisitive.

"Yes, kerosene and gasoline are both products distilled from crude oil."

Another cowboy piped up, "Distilled? you mean like whiskey? Dang, I wonder if your auto would run on whiskey."

Griggs felt the conversation had gone far enough. He preferred to concentrate on how he could make up time on the road. There was no sign of Hawthorne after leaving him behind on the forest road. He wondered if Hawthorne would overtake him during the night. He thought about lightening his automobile load and regretted carrying four men. At least he had discarded their bulky luggage and trailer. The last thing he heard before falling asleep was the howling of a lone coyote.

The next morning, Griggs found his automobile frozen solid. He lost considerable time and precious gasoline thawing the engine. With the riders set to go, the cowboys lined up to see them off. Their broncos snorted and reeled every time the cylinders belched steam.

Griggs shouted, "See you on the return run," then turning to Westbrook, "Are you sure this is the most direct route to the Canyon? We are making many wide curves through this pine forest."

"Don't worry, this is the way, the only way. The road will straighten out once we get out of the trees." Suddenly there was a loud pop. "What was that?"

"Darn if I know," said Griggs. The machine became enveloped in a cloud of steam when the water pressure gauge burst, and the valves came to a halt. The auto coasted into a rocky draw. There, the harried and frustrated crew plugged the gauge line, rendering the gauge itself useless but allowing them to restore steam pressure. Unknown to the men, this mechanical failure signaled the beginning of their troubles that day.

After another two miles, Griggs announced, "Gentlemen, we have now used all the Los Angeles gasoline contained in the two feed tanks under that seat." He pointed to where Oppenheimer was sitting. "Fortunately, we have a reserve. We can refill the tanks with cans of Flagstaff fuel, alleged to be gasoline."

When they started again, it became clear that this inferior fuel could not produce the amount of heat required to keep up sufficient steam. But it could produce dense black smoke pouring out of the ventilators, enveloping the men, making them all look like coal miners.

The Griggs automobile crawled along for several hours, making about three miles an hour. Somehow, they had wandered off the stage road. Deciding to further lighten their load, the party abandoned its remaining baggage, and perhaps unwisely, its precious water and most of the Flagstaff gasoline. They also left other non-essential equipment on the ground, including field glasses and all but one camera. The four men piled onto the machine, hoping to reach the Canyon during the night. After another mile, however, they heard a sharp metallic clank—followed by a harsh rasping sound.

Westbrook broke the bad news, "Griggs, your sprocket chain has parted."

After three hours of repairs, the expedition continued its traverse of the Coconino, albeit not by the stage road. Griggs had lost all confidence in Westbrook's guiding skills. By midnight, it had turned bitterly cold—and the wind made conditions worse. They had exhausted most of the kerosene oil in the side lamps which now cast a pale light only a few feet. Two men had to walk ahead to direct the way. Hours later, they stopped in a stand of cedars and bedded down around a large blazing campfire. Jesse Parks, the Flagstaff banker, who had been quiet most of the trip, just had to say something.

"Fellas, I'll bet you miss the comfort of the rooms you enjoyed at Flagstaff's Commercial Hotel."

Oppenheimer followed, "Yeah, camping in the wilderness in the middle of January is hardly my brand of adventure."

Dawn came early. No one dared mention hunger or thirst. For breakfast they each had a piece of beef jerky as they frowned at the cursed automobile. They had only a little gasoline left in the tanks and a little water in the boiler. Westbrook estimated they needed to travel another eighteen miles to reach Monte Bridgestone's place. He and Parks started a fire under the boiler while Oppenheimer scribbled several lines in his notebook. After building up a head of steam, the machine chugged along with only Griggs onboard. The others walked alongside. Westbrook, having lost his bearings, offered no direction except to go north. Two miles later, the machine, with a final gasp of escaping steam, died. With no road or trail to follow, the men abandoned the auto and plodded on foot, hoping to reach the rim in the vicinity of Summit Point.

At noon Westbrook sighted Craddock's old cabin in the forest, with a weathered sign declaring the Grand Canyon to be only five and three-quarter miles away. Oppenheimer and Parks remained at the cabin while Griggs and Westbrook agreed to summon help. They had covered half a mile when Westbrook collapsed of exhaustion.

"Griggs, I must rest; I'm stopping here."

"Westbrook, go back to Craddock's cabin, I'll continue alone." He wondered how a hearty frontiersman and guide could have been so overcome with exhaustion and concluded it must be his advancing age.

Griggs trudged north through the forest all afternoon, perplexed and exasperated by the sign at Craddock's. He mumbled to himself, *"Why not post the distance in round numbers?"* Around five o'clock, after covering about eighteen miles of that five and three quarters distance, he vowed to find the man who put up the sign and kill him without mercy. Griggs then noticed movement at the bottom of a swale.

At first, he thought it might be the man who put up the sign, and his heart leaped for joy. Delirious, he made out the object to be a wild turkey. Griggs clamored down the swale, several more turkeys scattered ahead of him, and he skidded to a stop beside a shallow pond. He scooped up handfuls of ice-cold water and guzzled as much as he could. It did not matter turkeys and other critters had waded through the pond. He shivered as he swallowed more of the dirty brown water.

An hour later, tired and footsore, Griggs emerged from the trees at the brink of the Canyon. Twenty minutes after that, he staggered into the Grand Canyon Hotel to arrange a rescue of the other three adventurers.

When Monte asked what he needed, Griggs replied, "All I want is water and food and the whereabouts of the man who put up the sign at Craddock's cabin."

Monte served him water, a can of tomatoes and some stale crackers.

"Oh, one more thing; any news of Travis Hawthorne and his team?"

Monte had no reports of Hawthorne's progress and assumed the other team was still on its way.

About eight o'clock that evening, Monte returned to the hotel with his four-horse team—and chauffeur Griggs, banker Parks, reporter Oppenheimer, and guide Westbrook. With business very slow in winter months, the survivors became welcome guests. Before the intrepid foursome retired for the evening, they each signed the hotel register.

***

The next day, Monte and Oppenheimer drove to the Starlight Hotel and telegraphed for gasoline. While Monte checked on supplies at the depot, Oppenheimer sought Clancy Jennings in hopes of soliciting one of the captain's famous stories. In Flagstaff he had heard rumors about Dancing Ghost Canyon that branched off the prominent fault line that formed Skeleton Canyon on the north side of the river. He wondered about the origin of the name; a dancing ghost had a tinge of mystique about it.

Most of the old-timers credited Clint McCarty with the name because he had an unobstructed view of Dancing Ghost Canyon from the second floor of his hotel. Luckily Oppenheimer found Clancy huddled in a cabin at Starlight Camp. He posed the question, hoping to spur him into telling the story.

"Yes, McCarty, and well, me too, gave it that name," Clancy said, as he opened the door of his woodstove and stirred the hot coals with a poker stick. Clancy hesitated for a time. Conditions were not right—he preferred large audiences—but then realized Oppenheimer, as a Los Angeles newspaper reporter, had a wide readership. He closed the stove door and said, "I'll tell ya how it was."

"We never know'd where she came from, but she appeared on the rim one day, looking out of place in these outlandish surroundings, spellbound by the solitude and tranquility. This place does that to yer mind, ya know."

Cap peered at the reporter and assured himself that he started taking notes. Oppenheimer, taken aback by Clancy's language, as he sometimes spoke like an old bumpkin too long in this country yet other times, like a gentleman educated in literature, had a question.

"So, you are saying the ghost was a woman?"

"Hang on to yer britches, reporter man. You wanna hear this story or not?" shot Clancy. "Yes, a free-spirited young woman. We called her Darby. She seemed shy. Sometimes, when we tried to get close, she got spooked an' would jest melt into the vastness of this mystical place, like some kinda supernatural being."

By now, Oppenheimer realized he had latched onto a wild tale.

"Then other times Darby seemed real, even mischievous and wild at heart, but also intriguing and alluring. She captivated the hearts of all us boys whenever she would come into view. When close, you could see her cryptic smile and blue eyes. Her capricious moods and confusing gestures tantalized us old curmudgeons and sent young hearts fluttering." Oppenheimer, surprised at Clancy's sophisticated language, scribbled more notes.

"Take young Joe Stewart, McCarty's hired trail hand," offered Clancy. "Once this tinhorn confessed that he had a weird dream about Darby; says he was working on a washout down on the trail and looked up and saw Darby standin' on an overhanging rock. Joe tells me he envisioned her yielding easily, collapsing into his arms. He felt the animal in him rising—eager and forceful—but a squawking raven wrenched the whimsical image from his mind and the feeling from his body."

"What happened?" prodded Oppenheimer.

"Wal, jest like that, she was gone. I told Joe he must be workin' out in the sun too long. She was never there. Out of nothing Joe had conjured up a sensual encounter, an apparition. Another raucous squawk from the droning raven directed him back to the task at hand."

Clancy leaned back in his chair and fumbled for his pipe.

"Oh sure, we old-timers could also conjure up thoughts of tenderness, beauty and happiness—and we have great memories of our heart-pounding younger days—but time has passed us by and—I'm straying off the subject, aren't I mister? As I was saying, the boys and I all fell in love with Darby."

Oppenheimer continued scribbling in his notebook but, so far, he had no answers on the origin of the name for Dancing Ghost Canyon.

"Late one afternoon," Clancy resumed, "Darby walked right over to McCarty and I, snatched two pink ribbons from her hair, and said 'Take these, fellas, and think of me.' We almost fell off our sittin' rocks. It was the first, and I might add, the only time she ever spoke to us. Teardrops welled up in her celestial blue eyes. She spun around with a swish of her flowing blond tresses, some catching on her tear-streaked cheeks as she started down the Pioneer Trail." Clancy waited for Oppenheimer to catch up.

"We stared at her fer hours, with field glasses mind you, watchin' her mosey down the trail, gazing at the wonderful, magical sights. I found her as mesmerizing as the dancin' flames of a campfire. We watched her comely form shimmer along the trail but felt she may not return."

Oppenheimer, hooked, appeared flustered, desperate to know where Clancy planned to take this strange tale. "What happened next? Did you see her again?" he panted.

"Wal, if you'd quit interruptin', I'd tell ya," Clancy snapped.

Oppenheimer dropped his pencil and bent down to pick it up. "I hope yer getting' all this," Clancy moaned, "because I ain't gonna tell it to ya a second time."

He waited for the reporter to retrieve his writing instrument from under the woodstove, then continued.

"There was a ghostlike haze hangin' in the canyon that afternoon, an' long about sundown the yellowing rays colored up that haze like gold. I grabbed my field glasses from Clint and that's when I thought I seen a tiny ghost dancing among the towers and ramparts on the far side of the canyon. The gold faded to bronze, then to brown and then darkness, and, just like that, the deep canyon shadows swallowed our dancing ghost girl." He paused for a moment. Then his story seemed to take on a mournful tone.

"It doesn't happen often, but when we find the canyon napping under late afternoon clouds, we sometimes see a figure hovering a little west of Skeleton Canyon—and we jest know it must be Darby. An' that's how that side canyon came to be known as Dancing Ghost Canyon."

Oppenheimer closed his pocket notebook. He had an exclusive story, first-hand from the legendary Captain Jennings. As he turned to leave, the captain added, "An' there's a mesa above Dancing Ghost Canyon we old-timers call Haunted Mesa, but that's another story."

Oppenheimer hesitated. Did he have time for a follow-on story, perhaps one of spooks, the sigh of the night wind, even the groans of lost spirits? No, he thought, not a ghost of a chance that anyone would believe such a tale. He grinned at Clancy and then turned away, pleased he had captured a wild tale from the venerable Clancy Jennings, but the more he thought about it, the more he wondered, could Darby have been real; could Joe Stewart's dream have been Clancy's dream? He had no time to collaborate with Joe or any of the other canyon pioneers.

***

The gasoline arrived by train the next day and Monte hauled it to the abandoned automobile. He and Griggs nursed the machine up to the rim by way of the old stage road, arriving, albeit without its discarded luggage, five days after leaving Flagstaff. The men drove the Toledo Eight out to Summit Point where Griggs brought it within six inches of the rim while Oppenheimer took a picture with his Kodak box camera.

Early the following morning, they drove to the depot where Westbrook, Parks and Oppenheimer boarded the train. Just before Oppenheimer stepped aboard, he asked Monte about Clancy's story of Darby, the Dancing Ghost.

"He spun that tale for you?" queried Monte, wondering how a reporter could be so duped. "It's just something Clancy conjured up one day for the telling. He's always dreaming up new tales; but this one's been around a while and gets wilder every time someone new like you comes along."

Oppenheimer seemed deflated as he said goodbye to Monte and thanked him for his hospitality and services. While gazing out the train window, he wondered if he had a story worth printing.

Several days later, Martin Griggs, with Monte Bridgestone as his honored guide, made the sixty-seven-mile trip from the Grand Canyon Hotel at Summit to the Commercial Hotel in Flagstaff in seven hours, ending the first automobile expedition to the Grand Canyon. On that return run along the old stage road, the men diverted twice to retrieve abandoned luggage and the trailer, all the while keeping a lookout for Hawthorne and his team. Griggs, realizing they had not strayed very far off the road, said "Monte, I wish I had you as our guide instead of that Westbrook feller."

As a crowd gathered around the automobile, still belching steam from its return trip, an elderly fellow, sporting a fifty-caliber Sharps carbine on his shoulder and a ten-inch Bowie knife on his belt, stepped forward and introduced himself to Monte.

"Mr. Bridgestone, I believe?" inquired the old feller, "I'm Levi Jackson; I believe we have crossed paths a few times in the eastern part of the Canyon."

"Levi! It's been years since we rescued each other from that ol' river; how has life been treating you?" Monte, clearly surprised to see the old-timer, extended a handshake.

"Yes, about twenty, maybe. Say, what is this hissing contraption that's causing all the fuss in town?" asked Levi.

"Well, Griggs here calls it an automobile. Other folks are calling it a horseless carriage."

While the newfangled automobile had not yet run riot, Monte shared Griggs' vision on how it would someday command an unlimited market. Pony Express mail service already ousted the horse and transcontinental trains replaced wagon trains.

"Griggs is already predicting we will need new roads, even special roads dedicated to automobile traffic, and accompanying rules for speed and safety. I think he's right. He is so infatuated with what you call a hissing contraption he's almost certain it will not only challenge rail transportation to our beloved Grand Canyon but maybe even eclipse it in our lifetime."

Monte, still excited about encountering Levi, wanted to shift the conversation to the old pioneer.

"Monte, I don't share your enthusiasm, but the times are changing," Levi reckoned, as he turned to leave.

"Wait, Levi, what have you been doing all these years?" Levi drifted back to where Griggs and Monte stood.

"Well, Molly and I gave up ranching long ago and, until recently, we were living in Tuba City. Our four married children and their families were living nearby. But then the government uprooted us Mormons to expand the Navajo reservation," winced Levi. "Our family received a few thousand dollars for improvements we made to the land, then we scattered. Molly and I settled in Joseph City out on the flatlands, then we moved further south to Taylor, which is where I'm headed now."

"Well, safe travels to you, friend," returned Monte, "it's been a pleasure seeing you again." Griggs seemed to enjoy hearing the two pioneers of the area talk about how times are changing.

Monte learned that Travis Hawthorne's auto broke down very early in the race. They walked back to Flagstaff to summon help. So, neither Griggs nor Hawthorne won the auto race; in fact, it was not a race at all. Despite the problems plaguing that historic auto trip to the Grand Canyon, it showed innovation in motive power and speed. If the automobile dominates roadways, footmen and horsemen will have to look to their safety. Monte believed the auto would dazzle folks and impress them with the vast prospects of this new transportation enterprise.

***

With the railroad having established a foothold on the South Rim, and the rush of tourists inevitable, several canyon pioneers scrambled to claim more of the Canyon for themselves. Francois LaRue filed a location notice for his six-mile Powderkeg Trail, a right-of-way from his camp at Cliffhouse Springs on the west side of Sunset Basin. The trail skirted around several points, stayed high above the Redwall before descending into what he called Lakota Canyon, and extended beyond his rock house to where Lakota Creek reached the Colorado River.

About the same time, Clint McCarty located the Sunset Basin Toll Road which extended northwest from Tusayan Well to the rim above Sunset Basin, then down into the basin and along Sunset Creek to the river. This eight-mile trail intersected the River View Toll Road where it crossed the creek. The River View Trail, also known as the Tonto Trail, meandered sixty miles, beginning at river level at the mouth of Redrock Canyon and then headed west in and out of side canyons along the top of the granite to Lakota Canyon.

McCarty also located the Garden City and Moonshadow mining claims at Canyon Gardens to straddle the Pioneer Toll Road and reinforce his stake at this popular resting place. Then he made one of his boldest moves in trying to control development on the South Rim. He located the Battleship Rock and Cliffrose, two mining claims situated end-to-end on the rim, encompassing his hotel site, the head of the Pioneer Trail and the Grand Canyon Railway station. As for Battleship Rock, Clint may have been thinking about the ill-fated Maine which sank in Havana harbor at the start of the Spanish-American War; after all, the warship was named after his home state.

Throughout the summer, prospectors staked more and more claims in the Canyon, some on a copper ledge in Skeleton Canyon. Even Clancy Jennings, who everyone thought had given up prospecting and mining, filed two claims, one he called the Darby claim at the mouth of Dancing Ghost Canyon and the other he called the River Rat claim southwest of his boat crossing.

The Trails West Company, with its close Grand Canyon Railway connections, already had a monopoly on the tourist trade at the Canyon. In fact, the railroad became hostile to the pioneers and objected to the small stage line that Monte operated between Summit and the Village. Having relinquished his water rights to the Canyon Copper Company, Monte found himself forced to buy water from the railroad at ten cents per barrel.

To make matters worse, in reply to Monte's request for a telephone right-of-way from Grand Canyon Village to Summit, the Forest Supervisor, Everett Hostettler, reported that Monte needed a special permit granted by the Secretary of the Interior in Washington City.

Monte speculated, "Hey, Hostettler, you and I have known each other for a couple years now. You surely are seeing right through this like me. You and I both know the Railway and Trails West were readily granted their right-of-way."

Hostettler countered, "Bridgestone, all I can say is that the Secretary must have granted their permit when he granted the railroad right-of-way." He then had the gall to ask Monte to keep him informed of anything of interest in his vicinity of the Canyon. For many years, Monte Bridgestone served as the government's unofficial, uncompensated watchdog for the East Rim.

Under the Canyon Sky: Heart of Gold

***

The Federal government further heightened its interest in the Grand Canyon. It had already taken steps in preserving the Canyon by establishing the Grand Canyon Forest Reserve. Now, it dispatched Pierre LeMay, topographer for the U.S. Geological Survey, to the South Rim to begin the monumental task of mapping the Canyon. Assisted by Francois LaRue and Blake Jensen, he anchored his triangulations and elevation measurements at the Starlight Hotel and included most of the scenery at that point on his quadrangle maps. He used the miner's trails and river crossings to reach the otherwise inaccessible inner canyon.

After spending the spring months surveying on the South Rim, LeMay and his two assistants faced the need to reach the North Rim to continue their work. Skeleton Canyon presented itself as a direct corridor to the rim; but first, they had to cross the river. They selected LaRue Crossing. The survey party journeyed west along the rim to Cliffhouse Springs and descended the Powderkeg and Lakota Creek trails. LaRue offered the use of his boat as a ferry on the condition he gets to review the maps before they are finalized. They forced their ten pack mules and burros to swim behind the boat—easier said than done.

The surveyors led their livestock down to a rock platform, ostensibly for a drink, then pushed them into the swirling flood. One by one, they towed the animals behind their boat, but in the frenzy, some tried to swim back, and one tried to climb into the boat, putting the rower in danger of being dragged into turbulent rapids below the crossing.

After an exhausting two-day trek up side canyons, the survey party reached the North Rim, resuming mapping operations at Point Destiny. Here LaRue, who seldom said anything important to anybody, raised an interesting question.

"Monsieur LeMay, Point Destiny commands a wide view of the Canyon."

"So, what's your point?" asked LeMay, seeming only half interested in having a conversation.

"Well, first, I was thinking . . ." LaRue paused. "Seeing as we both have some French heritage in our backgrounds and seeing as we are working together for a substantial period of time, I propose we go on a first name basis."

"Yes, I agree Francois," showing a little more openness to their relationship.

Francois appreciated the change in attitude and returned to what occupied his mind.

"Pierre, now that there is a railroad to the South Rim, what do you think about a railroad to the North Rim? Maybe terminating right here on Point Destiny."

Pierre continued musing over his survey measurements and never answered the question. But Blake thought the idea worth pursuing, "Hm-m, rails to Point Destiny. I'll bet no one ever thought of that."

As summer turned to autumn, the time had come to leave the North Rim and return to the village, now well-known as Grand Canyon Village. In early November, Pierre LeMay's party started back, shuffling down into the Canyon and threading its way along the boulder-strewn Skeleton Creek, crossing it nearly one hundred times, and mapping it along the way.

They made camp just above the box canyon known as Dancing Ghost. The next morning, they woke to a view of a snow-covered North Rim. When the LeMay party reached the river, they again faced the dreaded task of crossing. Using a prospector's wooden scow, the men, along with instruments and maps, wrapped in oiled buckskin, made the opposite shore about two hundred yards above Six-Gun Creek Rapids.

They led the mule carrying the most precious burden—the notebooks and crude maps—with particular care. She lived up to her reputation and made the trip without a stumble. The other pack animals sensed being homeward bound and swam across without fear. The party then continued up the Pioneer Trail without mishap.

The next year, as LeMay moved eastward on his government surveys, Skeleton Canyon became his regular route to the North Rim. He used a sheet-metal rowboat, packed down to the river in two sections on mules. While working on the north side, LeMay learned that some enterprising citizens of Kanab, wishing to capitalize on future tourist travel to the North Rim, had started making plans to span the river with a four-hundred-and-fifty-foot suspension cableway, about sixty feet above the water. Crossing would have been a harrowing experience; they worried about a loaded cable carriage sagging between north and south abutments; so much so it would need to be winched along the second uphill half of its journey. The plan was sidelined for several years.

***

In time, the Canyon Copper Company ceased leasing any properties from Monte Bridgestone and his partners. Instead, it owned all mines, minerals, mill-sites, water rights, and trails that the partners had developed. Bradley Cooper not only orchestrated the acquisition of mines and associated real estate at Summit, he also managed the Canyon Copper Company. He amended the company's articles of incorporation to include the operation of hotels and livery. Its broadened charter also included constructing and operating toll roads, tramways and railways between its mines and plants. Monte became an agent for the company and the caretaker for its mining properties, while continuing to manage the hotels at Summit Point.

That winter, Monte, snowbound at Summit, had plenty of time to reminisce about the old days. All his years of hard work in the mines and on the trails led to little monetary reward. Gray clouds seemed to mirror his thoughts and feelings of despair. He agonized over his lack of creating any wealth. He pored over dusty ledger books and balance sheets, baffled, wondering where all the ore profits could have gone. Clint had often expressed similar frustrations about there being no money. Although the partners had negotiated sixty-five thousand dollars for the Grand Canyon Hotel, mines and trail, individual shares seemed to be far below expectations. Perhaps, Monte surmised, they had sold out too cheaply.

His brooding turned to the Shooting Star Mine. He had worked his crews hard, trying to meet Clint's endless demands for ore shipments. El Paso smelter records showed one year, they shipped three cars containing seventy-two tons, but he could not reconcile his own records of pack-train deliveries to the rim with those of wagon loads to the railyard at Flagstaff or Prospector Flats. He lived so close to copper bonanzas, but so far from prosperity.

Monte abandoned his attempts to reconstruct incomplete shipping records. But his suspicions lingered—perhaps someone squandered the profits; their canyon mining venture should have been a bigger financial success.

Chapter Six

MYSTERY LADY

A boldfaced lie will travel forty-five miles while the truth is still putting on its boots.

"You know, Hostettler, for much of the eighteen hundreds, the Federal government seemed hell bent on giving away land in the nation's public domain."

Forest Supervisor Everett Hostettler and Clint McCarty sat on the veranda of Clint's hotel, deep in a friendly conversation about government control at the Canyon. Normally they would lock horns on the subject but on this cool canyon evening, both gentlemen went out of their way to engage in peaceful dialogue.

Clint continued, "President Lincoln's Homestead Act allowed citizens to claim one hundred and sixty acres of public land for farming. And using the Timber and Stone Act, the government further encouraged the use of public lands by seizing land deemed unfit for farming and then selling blocks to citizens for logging and mining. And look at the railroads. To encourage westward expansion, the government gave them millions of acres. It seems to me any notion of setting aside scenic landscapes as national reserves or parks runs contrary to these acts."

"I'm impressed Clint. You know your history," admitted Hostettler.

"Even early government surveys, including those of John Frémont, avoided the Grand Canyon," said Clint.

It was Hostettler's turn. "Ah, but in time, the government recognized the Canyon as one of the greatest natural wonders in the country.

It took a U.S. Senator from Indiana, despite having never visited the Canyon, to start the government's long custody pursuit."

"Having seen early photographs of the Canyon, Senator Benjamin Harrison sponsored legislation to establish Grand Canyon as a public park, but with opposition from Arizona miners and cattlemen, it faltered. He reintroduced legislation two more times but again did not rally sufficient support. If I remember my history correctly, in his last two weeks as president, Harrison declared the forested region encompassing the Canyon as a national forest reserve. By issuing a presidential proclamation, he placed limits on livestock grazing, logging and, you won't like this, mining too."

Hostettler continued, "I believe subsequent administrations will create a national monument, and eventually a full-fledged national park. You prospectors and settlers will be able to file claims on national forests, but not on lands withdrawn as national monuments or parks. That Grand Canyon Forest Reserve proclamation outlawed private occupation in a forest reserve except through a mining or homestead claim. So, here at Grand Canyon, you can dig and settle, even though some northern Arizonans resent the new federal restrictions placed on land in their territory."

"Well, you know your history too, Hostettler, but here is what I predict is going to happen. As the government attempts management of national forests, it is going to find itself hampered by miners filing numerous claims. Our long-standing national mining laws threaten the integrity of any new national forest policies you establish."

Clint became more forceful. "Right here on the South Rim, trailblazing pioneers like Monte Bridgestone and myself have claimed possession of the land based on current laws. Unfortunately, some government officials already regard us as trespassers upon the public domain!"

"Well Clint, we will not settle this matter tonight or next year for that matter. And eventually we will also have to address the matter of illegal mining claims. I believe the courts will need to debate alleged fraudulent claims and the General Land Office will be charged with passing on the validity of claims. They may even feel obliged to examine some troublesome mining claims at will, without waiting for applicants to seek a patent or deed."

Clint interjected, "Dang it, Hostettler, that's not right! You best keep your hands off my canyon holdings. The courts will uphold my property rights because of my steadfast compliance with annual assessment requirements. Speaking for all canyon miners, we believe in the rights of individuals to gain title to lands in public reservations, including the Grand Canyon Forest Reserve. Now it's getting late, and I declare this discussion over before we both lose our temper."

As he stood up to leave, Hostettler made sure he put in the last word. "The government will prevail, Clint. It will forever secure the Grand Canyon for the people of the United States."

Some canyon pioneers found it difficult to support McCarty's defiance of authority; that is, making false claims and flagrant attempts to control canyon access. Jack Keystone, for one, proprietor of the Starlight Hotel, denied McCarty's right to collect tolls on the Pioneer Trail and only made payments under protest, pending court action. No doubt, McCarty saw a fight brewing, and to prepare for pleading his right to the Pioneer Toll Road in district court, he solicited affidavits from most of the canyon pioneers confirming his ownership of the trail.

***

For several weeks, Governor Alexander Brodie had been making final arrangements for an impending visit to the South Rim by his former commandant, now the President of the United States, Teddy Roosevelt.

As a Major wounded during the Spanish American War, Brodie commanded Arizona's Rough Riders. Promoted to Lieutenant Colonel, he succeeded Roosevelt as the unit commander. In appreciation for his service, the president appointed him Governor of Arizona Territory.

Roosevelt rested in his private car as the westbound presidential train steamed through Flagstaff in the predawn hours of May sixth, nineteen aught three. After a brief water stop at Williams, the special five-car train chugged north on the new line to the Canyon. Meantime, a second five-car train carrying three hundred passengers left Flagstaff at sunrise.

Two weeks earlier, the President had visited Yellowstone with naturalist John Burroughs—part of a rigorous grand tour of the American West, with hundreds of whistle-stops and public speeches. On his way to California and an eventual meeting with another naturalist, John Muir, in Yosemite Valley, he looked forward to this side trip to the Grand Canyon.

The presidential train arrived at the Grand Canyon station about mid-morning. Roosevelt received several local honors and gifts, then met the second train and prepared to give his speech from the south balcony of the Starlight Hotel. A secret service agent, his right hand on his holstered gun and mindful of the recent McKinley assassination, sat on the balcony corner, watching the restless crowd of eight hundred Arizonans—among them a contingent of Rough Riders—on hand to hear the President.

With so many veterans of the celebrated Spanish-American War in attendance, a spirit of unity prevailed between the national president and the territorial governor. The president started his address with a salute to members of his old regiment:

"I am absolutely thrilled to be in Arizona today. It was from Arizona that so many gallant men came into the regiment which I had the honor to command. Arizona sent men who won glory on hard-fought fields, and men to whom came a glorious and an honorable death fighting for the flag of their country, and as long as I live it will be to me an inspiration to have served with Troop A Captain Buckey O'Neill."

The crowd cheered. The President complimented Governor Brodie and then admonished America to preserve Grand Canyon as part of her natural heritage, to keep it unmarred by any of the coarser works of man.

"In the Grand Canyon, Arizona has a natural wonder, which, so far as I know, is in kind absolutely unparalleled throughout the rest of the world. Keep this great wonder of nature as it now is. I was delighted to learn of the wisdom of the railroad people in deciding not to build their hotel on the very brink of the Canyon. I am also pleased to see that the train station and railyard are set back in a low spot so as not to spoil the view. I hope you will not have a building of any kind, not a summer cottage, a hotel, or anything else, to mar the wonderful grandeur, the sublimity, the great loneliness and beauty of the Grand Canyon. Leave it as it is. Man cannot improve on it. The ages have been at work on it and man can only mar it. Keep it for your children, your children's children, and for all who come after you."

The President wanted to see nothing constructed by man at the Grand Canyon. Ironically, the Canyon Copper Company had just announced plans for a three-story annex next to the Grand Canyon Hotel at Summit. Also, the Santa Fe announced plans to build its magnificent Canyon Queen Hotel on the rim above the train depot. It planned to assign management responsibilities to the Trails West Company.

The crowd included many seasoned pioneers: Clancy Jennings, Cole Campbell, Francois LaRue, Clint McCarty, Monte Bridgestone, and Kirby O'Brien. Hiding in the background, Sabrina Jaffa risked discovery but could not resist seeing the President of the United States in person.

Many Northern Arizonans favored Grand Canyon becoming a national park because of the publicity and tourism that would come with national park status. But many of the old-timers—miners, stockmen and settlers—voiced their opposition to anything that threatened their mineral and grazing rights.

The prospectors and miners had been pushing for years to get a railroad to the rim to serve their mining enterprises. Instead of railcars for hauling rich copper ore, the railroad brought aggressive corporations hell bent on making a buck.

Teddy Roosevelt advocated conservation as a national policy, and, for the Grand Canyon, he advocated a national park. While the forest reserve allowed continuing land use and development—including mining, grazing, hunting, and timber cutting—it did not provide as much protection as the President wanted. He promised to work toward this in the coming years. In his famous speech that day, he added, "Keep the forests. Use them so they will not be squandered; so that they will be of benefit to future Arizona generations."

After his canyon address, the President galloped out to Summit Point on horseback, accompanied by Governor Brodie, a cadre of aides and secret service agents, and Monte Bridgestone. Bradley Cooper had arranged to serve the presidential party regular miner's fare at the Grand Canyon Hotel. Monte, always brooding over not making any money in his mining ventures, took advantage of the President's visit and opened a discussion about the plight of canyon miners and homesteaders.

"Mr. President," exclaimed Monte, "It is an honor to have you visit our corner of the Grand Canyon. My name is Monte Bridgestone. I came here fifteen years ago and have had success in mining below the rim, establishing a tourist enterprise, and homesteading in the forest reserve. I thank you for signing my homestead certificate."

"What's on your mind, Mr. Bridgestone?" asked the President.

"Sir, I feel I speak for all the prospectors and pioneers who came here with me. We see the Federal government overriding our claims to the Grand Canyon by designating national forest reserves on the North and South Rim to gain the upper hand on the Canyon itself."

"Upper hand? I hope to live long enough to see it become a national park," interjected the President, seeming rather gruff, even perturbed.

"For now, you folks can file legitimate mining and homestead claims but when we withdraw the Canyon from the public domain, private ownership must end."

"But Mr. President, we are the ones who opened this country to mining and tourism. We built the roads and the trails. We built the first accommodations, including the Grand Canyon Hotel where we have prepared a special lunch for you. We should not be deprived of all for which we have worked so hard," argued Monte.

"I note that you fellas continue to file mining claims as we attempt to administer the forests, almost as if you hope to stop this grand place from becoming a national park. No doubt, Mr. Bridgestone, you have accrued certain advantages for all your hard work and I'll admit that we have work to do in Washington City to set up forest management policies that can operate without jeopardizing the Mining Laws. You have claimed possession of public land on the rim and below through mining and homestead claims. However, I fear that a future administration will regard you as a trespasser—or worse—a squatter," stated the President.

"What do you mean, sir?" asked Monte.

"My staff tells me that some of you have filed locations for purposes other than those intended by the Mining Laws. I plan to direct the

General Land Office to investigate the validity of those claims. Good day, Mr. Bridgestone."

With that, the presidential party finished their private lunch, exited the hotel and stood in awe of the amazing canyon view for a few moments. For the first time, the president had a glimpse of the Colorado River. He and his entourage then mounted their horses and headed west along the rim.

On the return to the train depot, the president encountered Clancy Jennings with a crowd gathered around him on the rim. The place, known as Inspiration Point, offered one of the best views of Skeleton Canyon, Haunted Mesa and Dancing Ghost Canyon. The president dismounted, handed his reins to an aide, and stood unnoticed behind the crowd.

"There used to be a saloon right here on the edge of the Canyon," Clancy boasted. "In fact, I was the proprietor for a while. All the prospectors and miners stopped by after a hard day's work below the rim. Why I remember one time, we served beer to burros!"

"Burros?" questioned a wide-eyed, incredulous tourist, "Everyone knows burros don't drink beer."

"Sure, they do—I remember when a hunch-backed prospector wandered into the Road-to-Ruin Saloon, right here where yer feet are now. He was accompanied by two burros!" Clancy had the crowd's attention.

"The animals moseyed along behind their master even though they were not led by so much as a light rope around their necks. Everyone in the saloon stopped talking and looked astonished; even the rowdy faro game in the corner came to a halt, and patrons cleared a path as the prospector and his burros sidled up to the bar." Clancy looked around at his listeners and assured himself he still had their rapt attention.

"As entertaining as it was," Clancy continued, "I just could not allow such a ludicrous display detract from my fine saloon, so I ordered the prospector to leave his burros outside."

'The name is Lucas,' the prospector countered, fixing his blurry blue eyes on me, 'and this here burro is Chester, and this is Otis, my two best friends.'

"I explained that I didn't care who or what he was, animals just aren't allowed in saloons!"

Clancy by now had attracted passersby, and his audience doubled in size. With their attention fixed, he did not let on that the President of the United States and his party had taken up a position within hearing distance behind the throng. And in his story, the crowd around the bar also doubled as they waited to see what would happen next.

"Ol' man Lucas, ignoring my complaint, asked, 'Ya serve beer, don't cha?' I had to say yes and before I could go on, the old timer interrupted, 'Great, a beer for me, and another for Chester and Otis to share,' the old man demanded, slapping two five-cent coins on the bar."

"Seein' as everyone was enjoying the show, I decided to have some fun with this feller so with a wide grin I asked, 'Do I serve theirs in a glass?' The crowd roared with laughter but ol' Lucas, detecting a hint of scorn, or was it just good-natured banter, was not amused. 'Don't mock me, mister,' he admonished. 'There ain't no way burros can drink out of a glass. Put their beer in a pan.' "I chuckled, shook my head and obliged his request. 'Chester,' the old man said, 'I been promisin' you and Otis a treat all them months down in the Canyon. Even when you both were mean, ornery, and wouldn't do what I asked. After this, just you two remember I always keep my word.' The crowd watched Lucas lecture his burros."

"Wal' Chester and Otis stood stone-still; then their ears perked up when I placed the pan of beer at their feet," Clancy explained, "as near as I could tell, the burros were waiting for some sort of signal."

He explained that Lucas ignored the snickers and jokes from the crowd and raised his glass high, saying 'Here's mud in your eye, Chester, you too Otis,' but he was congratulating himself on his good fortune while prospectin' below the rim. After a few noisy gulps by his master, the burros joined in. Clancy then laid claim to the mud-in-your-eye expression, explaining that it was in reference to his string of burros on a muddy canyon trail, with the feet of each burro slinging mud into the face of the one that followed.

"The old man guzzled the remaining beer in his glass, slammed it down with a thump, and wiped his mouth and straggly beard with the back of his dirty shirtsleeve," Clancy continued, "and then propping himself against the bar, Lucas turned his gaze toward his burros."

'You jacks ready for another?'

"Chester did not raise his head until the last of the beer was gone. Otis belched several times, then both burros answered in the affirmative by twitchin' their ears."

"Lucas flipped two more five-cent pieces onto the bar. He and his burros emptied another glass and another pan of beer as the patrons watched in awe. Seeing as everyone was in high spirits, I decided this amusing display was good for business, and ordered a round on the house."

"Lucas appreciated the gesture and with a half-hearted wave, said 'That's right kind of you, sir—I thought you was downright unfriendly when we first straddled in here. But me and Chester and Otis are happy to accept your apology—and your beer.' By now everyone was joining in the fun. We lost count of the number of beers consumed by the old prospector and his four-footed companions," Clancy explained, then continued, "feeling rather woozy, Lucas called it quits. He looked down at his burros, 'Drink up, you two; we ain't got all night, ya know.' Wal as those ol' burros turned to follow his master to the door, they stomped all over the beer pan. Lucas and both burros teetered as they weaved through the crowd and disappeared into the forest."

Then came a booming voice from the back of the crowd at Inspiration Point. "Now Mr. Jennings, I've been informed that is your name; I don't believe a burro would drink beer. How can you expect us to believe a story like that?" asked a distinguished gentleman. Everyone turned around, startled to see President Teddy Roosevelt in their midst.

"Look right behind that tree, Mr. President," Clancy retorted, somewhat miffed that the President himself came across as a doubter in his audience. "See that crumpled pan? That's what Chester and Otis were drinkin' outta—yep, that's proof right there in plain sight."

The presidential party remounted and resumed their ride to the train station. Sabrina, who had been hiding under a slouch hat, as she had done at the President's address in the Village, slipped away unnoticed as the crowd dispersed. After hearing about the beer-guzzling burros, folks did not know whether to believe the wild tale or pity Clancy for his loss of good senses.

It bothered Clancy to hear grumbling as his crowd dispersed. A man shouted, "You know Clancy, a boldfaced lie will travel forty-five miles while the truth is still putting on its boots." No one else even turned to look back.

At a rushed late afternoon reunion with his Rough Riders in his private car, Roosevelt expressed his appreciation for their service during the Spanish-American War. Even the loner Sam Thornton dared not miss the opportunity to visit with his fellow troopers. "I have a mind to propose annexing Arizona and New Mexico as one state—as a tribute to the two great American territories that produced hundreds of Rough

Riders." While the president favored joint-statehood, Governor Brodie and the vast majority of Arizonans did not. Back in Washington City, the idea fell flat, and the two territories continued to go their separate ways in pursuit of statehood and admission to the Union, just like the two Dakotas during the Harrison administration.

After the Rough Riders reunion, the presidential train steamed towards Williams for a brief stop. An eastbound freight, upon which several hobos rode, remained on a sideline at Ash Fork to allow the passage of the presidential party. Roosevelt delayed at Ash Fork for a short time, and the hobos lined up with the rest of the townspeople to shake his hand. As the hobos then ran to catch their freight to Williams, Roosevelt resumed his western tour.

The next day he gave speeches in Barstow and San Bernardino, California. He enjoyed seeing his Rough Riders again and even greeting the hobo citizenry, but one question kept nagging him—did the Grand Canyon ever have a Road-to-Ruin Saloon on its South Rim?

***

One day Cole Campbell and Francois LaRue met on the Pioneer Trail. "Bonjour Monsieur Cole." Francois enjoyed greeting fellow canyon pioneers in French. "I have not seen you for quite some time. I trust you are doing well. I'm headed down to Poverty Gulch—or what you call Six-Gun—for a little prospecting."

"Francois, it's good to see you. You know, if you have a few minutes, I've always wanted to discuss something with you. I believe we both hail from eastern Canada," announced Cole, with a strong measure of pride. "I'm from Nova Scotia."

"I'm from Quebec, Cole, and I understand we have had similar paths through life. Who would ever think two Canadians would meet here at America's Grand Canyon?"

"I came through California as a very young lad looking for adventure, and California sounded exciting, even though the goldfields had long played out by the time I arrived," said Cole.

"California? I've never been there. If there was no gold left, what lured you there?" asked Francois, with a questioning smile.

"My uncle was the millwright at Sutter's Fort and it was he who ignited the California Gold Rush. Except for pocketing the first nugget, he had bad luck at every turn. His life became a series of disappointments. I heard he died in poverty."

"How did you get from Nova Scotia to California?" asked Francois, remembering many Forty-Niners sailed around the Horn.

Cole continued, "Being on the Atlantic seaboard, I guess it was just natural for me to select passage on a sailing ship rather than a prairie schooner. Going overland by wagon train was just not for me. But I did not sail around the Horn like so many before me. I think I paid about two hundred dollars for passage to Panama, and another twenty-five dollars for train fare on the American-built Trans-Panama Railway. I understand President Roosevelt wants to build a canal across Panama so that ships can move freely between the Atlantic and Pacific. Oh, I'm straying from my story."

"Let's see, when I was in Panama," continued Cole, "there was a month-long wait for California-bound ships. After paying one hundred and twenty-five dollars for passage to San Francisco, I had depleted my entire money stash. I was as destitute as my poor uncle," explained Cole. "I was never driven by the glittering promise of gold, but could have used some good-sized nuggets when I walked down the gangplank and planted my feet on that San Francisco wharf."

Francois did not divulge how he found his way to the Canyon, but he offered some background on his life in Canada. "In Quebec, I made a living as a woodworker and furniture craftsman. I was good at making tables, chairs and cabinets but it was long hours in a dusty building that got me down. I too was looking for something more adventurous and challenging," reported Francois, as his mule shuffled his feet.

"I found work in the forests of northern California, first as a lumberjack and then as a sawmill operator. After a year or two in the logging industry, with its high risk of serious injury, even death, I moved on," Cole said.

Cole dismounted and hitched his horse to a cedar. Francois stayed on his mule. "I eventually made my way to Arizona, settled down, raised a family, and built up a decent cattle ranch. And as you know I spent many months prospecting in the Canyon with the late Stuart Casey."

"Ol' Casey, he was a good man," Francois volunteered.

"I agree. I soon did less ranching, less prospecting and more community service work in Flagstaff, like serving as a member of the volunteer fire department. But with a wife and two children, I still needed to make a living, so I became a jack of all trades. Recently I operated a blacksmith shop from a cabin near the Starlight Hotel. And I served as a mine foreman for the Black Diamond Development Company. I still keep my hand in some mining operations down here but now I am taking the lead on developing Flagstaff's first public water system."

"Well, we have much in common, Cole," commented Francois, "besides coming from Canada. We've both worked with wood, me on a small scale in a workshop, you on a grand scale in the logging industry. And we both selected prospecting and trail-building as new adventures; and we could not have picked a more out-of-the-way place to do it than right here at the Grand Canyon."

"Ah, you are much more of a prospector than me, Francois. In fact, you look the part, sitting astride your mule, outfitted with a pick, shovel, trail-making tools, rope, canteen and what looks like an old model Winchester—ready for the next prospect hole. But your bearing of confidence and dignified presence telegraphs a touch of the mystique."

"And that's the way I want it. I prefer to keep folks guessing," emphasized Francois.

Cole concluded, "I daresay I like to think we exhibit frontier virtues—friendship, hard work and loyalty—and I see us as men of calm demeanor and gentle disposition, slow to anger, and not all that talkative."

After an awkward pause, Francois confided, "As for me, I'm not so sure about that last part. I may leave this Canyon if the Santa Fe doesn't stop harassing me. I'm getting angrier by the day."

"Well, my friend, government bureaucrats are registering undeserved disdain over us early pioneers. If we stick together, we can endure their harassment and prevail. We should be able to resolve problems with reason and diplomacy . . ."

". . . and sometimes an old Winchester," interjected Francois, as he patted his long gun.

"Good luck to you down at Six-Gun, or Poverty Gulch as you call it."

And with that, Cole mounted his horse and continued up the trail as Francois headed down, having enjoyed his conversation with a fellow canyon pioneer, and a fellow Canadian at that.

***

After the president's visit, Kirby O'Brien went to work for the Canyon Copper Company. He supervised the day shift, a team of four miners at the Shooting Star Mine and thought of himself as acting foreman. He pitched in and worked underground with his team but for variety he also performed various odd jobs.

One of those jobs involved hauling water from Arrowhead Spring. This involved leading a string of burros, each with two empty barrels strapped to its back, down the east wall of Windsong Mesa and filling the barrels from the spring. On a bright sunny day in late May, as Kirby approached the Redwall opposite Windsong, he spotted a lone rider rounding the northern tip of the red-stained limestone formation. Being the curious sort, he decided to follow. He dismounted his mule, hitched the burro string to a post and climbed back into the saddle. For the next hour, he trailed the lone rider, staying back some distance until he could determine the stranger's intentions. He wondered how this rider got by the mine without discovery.

Kirby paused when the rider paused, then resumed when he resumed. The slow pursuit along the Tonto, skirting deep side canyons and hugging the Redwall, continued for another hour. Kirby forgot about filling water barrels at the spring. When the rider rounded another protruding red formation, he lost sight of him. With a nudge to the side of his mule, he quickened his pace, hoping to regain sight of the mysterious rider. He hung back too long.

Kirby paused. Except for shadowed areas close to the cliff, he could see the meandering path through sagebrush, with no one in sight. Then a soft but firm voice from the shadows asked, "Mister, are you following me?" Kirby almost fell out of his saddle as an attractive woman, astride a chestnut mare, moved into the light. She dressed like a male rancher. Her right hand hovered over her holstered six-shooter. Her left hand gave an extra tug on her slouch hat to cover her features. A long brown braid hung down her back. Kirby figured she must be the mystery woman prospectors have encountered on rare occasions.

Kirby gulped, "Ah, yes, I've been following you ever since you showed yourself east of Windsong Mesa. What is a pretty woman like you doing way down here?" He felt positive that he had finally met the Canyon's mystery lady, but asked anyway, "Who are you?"

"I should ask who you are first and why am I being followed?" Her hand still hovered over her holster. "I do not like being followed. Not long ago, two drifters followed me but I managed to lose them in a side canyon." Just like her unpleasant encounter with Morton and Sykes, she sensed a touch of nervousness in her new stalker, but waited for an answer.

"I apologize if I have frightened you or offended you. My curiosity got the best of me. My name is Kirby O'Brien." He gave himself an official-sounding title to make himself appear more important than the average mine worker.

"I'm the foreman at the Shooting Star Mine."

"Well, Kirby O'Brien, let me introduce myself. I'm Sabrina Jaffa. I've been doin' some prospecting down here, on and off, for years. I don't think we've crossed paths before, but I have encountered other prospectors and miners during my wanderings."

Kirby's jaw dropped. "Sabrina Jaffa! the mystery lady? I think you know Monte Bridgestone. I used to work for him before he sold the mine. Now I work for the Canyon Copper Company."

"Yes, I've met Monte several times. Mystery lady? Is that what you fellas call me?"

Sabrina felt different about this chance meeting. She usually exchanged brief greetings and parted ways. Her right hand relaxed on top of her holster.

"Sabrina, what are you looking for down here on the Tonto?" asked Kirby.

"Well, not so much on the Tonto but all these side canyons. I'm looking for that metallic glitter that all prospectors look for. So far, I'm not finding much; in fact, I have not staked a single claim yet."

Sabrina caught herself being more forthcoming with information than ever before. She enjoyed the conversation with another human being, and thought to herself, this Kirby fellow is rather intriguing, and the feeling seemed mutual.

"Sabrina, I'm glad you intercepted me. I've got a pack of burros back at the spring where I'm supposed to be hauling water for the mine. I need to get back, but will I see you again?"

Kirby hoped she would be receptive to another meeting.

"Well Mr. O'Brien, you need to head back and Serendipity and I are heading east. It seems we both spend time below the rim. I'm sure we'll cross paths again, but right now it's time to part ways."

And with that, she turned her horse around and trotted off. Kirby watched her for a minute or two, wishing he could get to know her better, but then turned his mule and headed west. A minute later, he halted, turned around and chased after Sabrina.

"Sabrina, hold up, I don't want us to lose contact," shouted Kirby. She heard him and stopped.

"What is it now, Kirby?" somewhat pleased for another opportunity to get to know him better, and allowing a bewitching smile while being careful not to encourage him too much.

"I would like to see you again. Where do you live when you're not gallivanting below the rim?" Kirby thought she might regard him as being too forward, but the risk seemed worth it.

"Oh kerflooey, Kirby, I've told nobody this but I'll share it with you. I board with the Klostermeyers at Little Springs. In exchange for room and board, I help around the ranch." Sabrina looked like she just delivered a confession.

"Ah, that explains why we never see you in Flagstaff. Could I meet you at the ranch sometime?" pleaded Kirby, hoping she would set a date.

"No, not the ranch. I'll let you know when and where."

With that she resumed her eastward trek. Kirby, smitten by this bewitching woman, also started back, confused about how she would let him know.

Sabrina defied what one might first imagine a female prospector would look like—rough-and-ready, a muscular, large frame body, flanked by shooting irons on each hip, bacon grease-stained buckskins, and with a rather grim countenance. Instead, here came along a good-looking slender woman, maybe five-foot-five, with delicate feminine features and a sunny disposition.

While filling water barrels, Kirby realized how they would meet again. *"Got it! Sabrina will find me and this is the logical place where that could happen. From now on, I need to make all the water runs."*

Kirby sat back and rested before starting back up to the mine. The Canyon made no sound, except for the steady dribble of the spring and the buzz of insect wings. He repeated Sabrina's name over and over as if it had some magical meaning. He even liked the sound of her mare's name. Serendipity has a mystical ring to it. Soon he dozed off, dreaming about his next encounter with the mystery lady.

Chapter Seven

STUMBLING BLOCKS

Nothing destroys one's respect for others more than greed, dishonesty and defiance.

With canyon exploration, prospecting, and trail-building complete, and with mining operations proving to be too difficult to be profitable, the pioneers found themselves in dire straits. Federal bureaucracy further compounded their dilemma—the government siding with business monopolies and early tourist enterprises being overtaken by outsiders. By opening Grand Canyon for all to see and experience, the pioneers lost what they worked so hard to establish.

One day in June, a month or so after Teddy's visit, Clint McCarty and Monte Bridgestone sat on the veranda of the Grand Canyon Hotel gazing at the geologic wonder spread before them. Monte opened the conversation.

"Clint, the General Land Office maintains a contradictory policy in the matter of forest reserves and agricultural homestead entries. I understand reserves are needed to protect the forests from devastation—already rampant in the Appalachian Mountains—by preserving timber resources and water supplies for future needs. But the government also encourages settlement by home-builders and ranchers."

"Yeah, Monte, I think you're talking about homesteaders. The Land Office guards against exploiting and scavenging of the land by those who have no permanent attachment or interest, or by those who do not build homes or maintain continuous residency, yet it accords reasonable protection for settlers within the forest reserves. Personally, I'm more interested in mining in the reserve."

"I'm interested in both mining and homesteading. As you know, Clancy Jennings and I filed homestead claims here in the Grand Canyon Forest Reserve."

"Ah yes, I understand your homestead on the rim encompasses the Navajo placer claim, a section of the wagon road to Grand Canyon Village, and an access road to Summit Point," said Clint.

"My one hundred and sixty acres joins the Summit mill-site on the north and overlaps about half the area of the patented Shooting Star mill-site on the south which includes this hotel. Pat Wyatt, the forest ranger at Tusayan Well, says I'll be able to apply for permits to graze horses and operate a roadhouse, general store, livery stables and feed yard here on the forest reserve. He came out here to examine my agricultural claim and found no sign of fraudulent use but noted the problem of overlapping claims. He recommends a survey for my claim, followed by granting full title to the land." Monte stopped talking as he felt he might be bragging.

Clint added, "There's talk in Washington City about a proposed Forest Homestead Act that will allow citizens to settle on land better suited for agriculture within national forest reserves. By the way, what is Clancy's plan?"

"I'm sure he'll continue doing what he enjoys most, guiding tourists below the rim while regaling them with wild tales. He has neither the capital nor desire to operate a full-fledged mine, even though he serves as an agent of the Jennings Asbestos Mining Company."

"You're probably right on that, said Clint. "As for me, with the tourist season well underway, canyon visitors are arriving by the trainload, and creating brisk business for that dang Trails West Company. I'm also capitalizing on train arrivals with my hotel. I put Francois

LaRue in charge of daily operations—including collecting tolls on the Pioneer Trail and managing my outfit at Canyon Gardens."

Monte and Clint spent another hour discussing tourism, federal control and government bureaucracy, wondering what new stumbling blocks the government will impose upon the canyon pioneers. They both recalled simpler times at the Canyon.

***

The Canyon Copper Company, hoping to increase the tourism side of its business, installed Stephen Herrington as the new hotel manager and updated its plans for a major expansion. At the terminus of the old stage road, the Summit complex remained cut off from the tourist trade the railroad brought to the Village. To combat the gross imbalance in the tourist accommodations, the company started construction of a first-class, three-story annex to the Grand Canyon Hotel that would rival the Starlight Hotel.

While watching another wagonload of lumber being offloaded at the annex, Monte spotted one of the regular summer guests of the Grand Canyon Hotel, Dr. Roberto Torrez. "Hello Doc, when did you get in?"

"Good morning Monte. Just after dark last night."

"Vacation or business?" asked Monte, suspecting both. Torrez became fascinated with the Grand Canyon and fell in with a group of Vermonters who had drifted out to Arizona. They invested in Monte's collection of copper mines on Windsong Mesa and enjoyed staying at his rustic hotel on the rim. Doc Torrez, never very impressed with the mines as a money maker, always looked forward to summer stays on the South Rim. Year after year he pitched his old khaki tent near the hotel.

"Just a vacation this time, Monte. How are things going?"

"Mining no longer looks to be a good investment since the bottom dropped out of the copper market. And to make matters worse, the Santa Fe is building that big fancy hotel where its line ends. They hope to freeze us out. Maybe Herrington can turn things around."

Later that afternoon, on the Grand Canyon Hotel's veranda, Torrez invited Monte to join in a friendly conversation with Herrington and Cooper.

"Bradley, I see you are still palming off those villainous cigars," said Torrez. Bradley, with a smile of satisfaction, took his place in the circle. Monte often caught Bradley chomping down on a cigar with his tobacco-stained teeth. "And Monte, we remember you with your big boots covered with red dust, up from the mine, or in your slicker down at the reservoir, puddling muddy water with a hoe. Ah, those were the good ol' days."

"And you, Doc, in hungry from a wild chase after runaway stock out beyond the Coconino Wash." added Bradley.

While construction of the annex seemed slow, the tourist business at the Grand Canyon Hotel seemed even slower—only one or two guests per day. Monte's Summit Hotel saw only the occasional guest. Matters would get worse when the Grand Canyon Railway opened its regal hotel and turned over its management to the Trails West Company.

"Herrington, what do you know about that new hotel in the Village?" asked Torrez.

"Well, I happen to have a news report that Ryan Perkins wrote last month. Here it is." Herrington read the report for the men. "The Santa Fe designed the Canyon Queen Hotel to look old but to last more than a century, to blend in with her surroundings, not dominate them. It will exhibit frontier austerity with bulky ponderosa logs imported from

Oregon by rail, rough-hewn rafters and a massive native stone fireplace in the lobby, while still presenting an air of dignity and nostalgia. Her majestic character will prevail as daunting but simple, her hardwood floors strewn with Navajo rugs, her creaky stairs leading to elegant lodging, her rambling passageways narrow, her balconies and verandas sprawling, and her hammered tin ceilings high."

"That's quite a description, Herrington," said Doc.

"Wait, I'm not finished. The Canyon Queen will boast over seventy rooms and premier suites, fine dining and a cozy lounge that welcomes guests with southwestern hospitality. She will stand within forty feet of the rim, remote, yet the epitome of luxury. Well that far exceeds anything we can offer canyon visitors." Herrington tossed the report on a side table.

"I met Perkins a few times. He's a good writer; has a way with words," said Monte. After sitting silent for a spell, the men parted ways; all but Torrez, having chores to tackle before sundown.

***

The American people reelected Teddy Roosevelt, deciding he had enough popular support to challenge Congress. He lobbied for stiffer regulation of big corporations, including railroads. Roosevelt wanted more protection of the poor and the working class. He wanted Americans to be free from the abuses of powerful industries and influential corporations. Perhaps reverting to his days as Assistant Navy Secretary in the McKinley administration, he wanted America to become a global power. With all that, his favorite cause became his legacy—preserving America's natural heritage.

Famous for his uncanny ability to sense and express the feelings of the common man, William Jennings Bryan served as the nation's self-appointed conscience in opposing special privileges for favored organizations, a practice that had been rife at the Canyon. That summer, Francois LaRue guided the Bryan party down the Pioneer Trail. Bryan had reached a low point in his political career. His trail ride offered a refreshing change from Washington politics. Twice defeated by William McKinley, Bryan lamented about ever running for president again.

In the simple life of LaRue and other canyon pioneers, Bryan saw hard-working citizens who resented flagrant federal interference and government-by-injunction. He believed these frontiersmen personified the American spirit and a sympathetic cause for the common man.

By mid-July, the Grand Canyon Hotel had opened its new three-story annex for business. The new frame building featured forty rooms with many modern conveniences, including steam heat and bathrooms, and connecting rooms on all floors. It planned a telephone line connection with the telegraph office and railroad station at the Village. On the canyon side, the hotel's three dormers and dozen windows offered a panoramic view of the curving amphitheater of the eastern canyon. Beyond the temples and buttes, one could see the Painted Desert, the irregular abutments of Echo Cliffs fifty miles distant, and the slate-blue mound of Navajo Mountain brooding one hundred miles away.

The Canyon Copper Company hauled drinking water from Arrowhead Spring for its tourist cabins on Windsong Mesa and its hotel buildings on the rim. That task became Kirby O'Brien's responsibility. No one figured out why he enjoyed hauling water so much; perhaps it provided a way to stay out of the dusty mine. The company offered saddle animals, overnight lodging, and hearty suppers at its Windsong Camp. On days when the mines operated, tourists could watch the loading of pack burros in the rock corral or tour the underground workings. After supper, they could ride to the edge of Windsong Mesa for a view of the western horizon ablaze in all its golden glory—and, when nightfall washed the colors out of the Canyon, watch the grays and blacks well up from the darkening Granite Gorge.

***

Kirby, on an old grey mule, and his string of burros showed up at Arrowhead Spring around mid-morning. With ten burros, each harnessed to carry two wooden barrels, he faced a time-consuming chore to fill each barrel and load them on the pack train. That sultry morning found Kirby dipping into the pool, ladling spring water into barrels, trying not to spill. This time, about halfway through the tedious operation, he looked up and saw Sabrina Jaffa astride Serendipity with Jenny close at hand!

"Sabrina! I've been wondering how we would connect up. Every day I hoped this was the place where you'd show."

"I'm on my return, hoping my timing would find you here. I've been far to the east, exploring side canyons beyond Redrock Canyon."

"Sabrina, how did you get past Doubtful Canyon?"

"Where's that?"

"You know, it's that part of the trail, if you want to call it that, where it hugs the Redwall as you skirt around Doubtful Canyon. It's barely wide enough for a horse or mule. It got its name because there is considerable doubt one would live long enough to get to the other side," explained Kirby, trying to imagine Sabrina with a horrendous drop at the tip of her boots. "It ought to be called Turn-Around Canyon."

"Oh that; I just dismounted and led Serendipity along the ledge," said Sabrina, not willing to disclose her harrowing experience under a precarious overhang during a rockslide, not to mention harassment by two no-good drifters. "I'm concentrating on the eastern part of the Canyon now and hope to go down the Jackson Trail next. How have you been Kirby? You're looking well and trim." Sabrina wanted to jump off Serendipity and give the handsome workman a little hug, but she held back, hoping he'd make the first move.

Kirby finished filling his eleventh barrel, stood it on end, and stepped towards Sabrina, tripping on the reins to his lead pack burro, and falling into Serendipity.

"I see you like my horse better than me," said Sabrina, with an impish smile and her arms crossed.

"Sabrina, I've missed you. I helped ol' Levi Jackson build that trail. I've been dreaming, I mean thinking, about you ever since the day I followed you."

That's not all Kirby wanted to say. He felt flustered, searching for the right words. Just then, an ore cart emerged from a dark opening in Windsong Mesa and a booming voice broke the canyon stillness.

"Kirby O'Brien, what's taking so long? Get that water train moving. We're out of water here at the mine and the hotel is waiting for you to refill its tanks."

"Kirby, I thought you were the boss man. Anyway, why doesn't the hotel draw water from Summit Tank?"

"It's been dry for months now so there's no water on the rim." Good question, Kirby thought, but not what he wanted to talk about.

"Maybe all that water leaked into this spring," Sabrina guessed, trying to suppress a grin. Kirby did not know what to say.

"I best go," Sabrina explained, "I'm going back up Clancy's old Whiskey Trail. See you next time." She turned to leave.

"Dang it, Sabrina, you're taking leave of me already? The mine can just wait a little longer for water," Kirby declared. "I'm coming with you, at least part-way. We need to talk." He unhitched his mule, mounted, and quickly caught up to Sabrina.

They rode until they were out of sight of Windsong Mesa. Both dismounted and sat on a rock in the shade.

Kirby wasted no time. "Sabrina, maybe I could go with you when you go down the Jackson Trail. I know it well."

"Sorry, I prefer to prospect alone." Kirby assumed a mournful look. "Do you know about any waterfalls here in the Canyon?"

Kirby, taken aback by the question, tried to recall where he had seen waterfalls. "There are two falls on the lower part of the Whiskey Trail, but there's not much water flowing there. Oh, but there are some big ones in Cataract Canyon. I've never seen them but I hear tell the water is turquoise blue. Why the sudden interest in waterfalls?"

Sabrina answered, "Just wondering. I'm fascinated by waterfalls. I find them rather mesmerizing. I've seen the trickle on Clancy's trail, not much to look at. So, I'm always looking for others."

Kirby changed the subject. "Sabrina, I am hoping we can get to know each other better."

"Well, it's your turn to tell me your story. I've already shared my secret life with you."

Sabrina actually had revealed very little about herself. With a glint of mischief in her sparkling green eyes, she turned into a tease for Kirby. For a defiant loner who had long been avoiding human contact, she had a playful side.

"I have no secrets," Kirby started in, "I'm thirty-seven and I came to the Southwest from Joplin, Missouri. My parents were Irish immigrants and raised me on a farm but, like you, I wanted more adventure in life. I met Levi Jackson in southern Utah and traveled with him to the part of Grand Canyon where the Little Colorado meets the Big Colorado. I never married—just never found the right girl." Kirby wanted to say he had fallen for her but held up.

Sabrina volunteered more about herself. "I've been married twice. I lost my first husband in a terrible ranch accident—and my second marriage really was an accident!" Kirby now assumed he could court Sabrina.

"I see the question in your eyes; yes Kirby, I'm divorced."

"I'm still amazed to see a woman down here prospecting—don't get me wrong, Sabrina, I admire your pioneering spirit." Kirby seemed befuddled over Sabrina's determination to move on.

"Kirby, I and my team here need to start back to Klostermeyers' ranch and you need to get back to hauling water. When I get back from my next escapade—the Jackson country of the eastern canyon—I'll come find you. I assume you'll still be working as the boss man at the mine."

"Fair enough—and good luck in yer prospectin'—here's hoping you find a fortune."

Kirby watched her head for Clancy's trail. She sat straight in the saddle, her ribbon-tied hair swishing from side to side. While pleased with their meeting, he wished he had tried harder to express his feelings for her. Could the glint in Sabrina's eye and the lilting tone of her voice be signs of good things to come?

Sabrina, satisfied that she kept up her air of mystique, thought about their meeting; by asking about waterfalls, she introduced more confusion to keep everyone guessing about the real reason she roamed the Canyon.

***

One autumn day, Clint McCarty encountered Monte Bridgestone in the Village. "Hello, Monte, you might be interested to know I'm planning a trip to Washington City where I hope to lobby against a new park bill."

"And I presume you are most concerned about protecting your mining interests," said Monte, with a measure of sarcasm. Clint's self-interests had driven a wedge into their friendship.

"Well, just in case Teddy's scheme to make Grand Canyon a national park works, I plan to sell some of my canyon holdings. I've already interested a Boston buyer." Instead of cash payments, and with an eye towards a future in national politics, Clint seemed eager to assume ownership of some prestigious properties in Washington City in exchange for certain canyon properties.

Monte, highly skeptical, asked, "Clint, how are you going to produce valid claim titles?"

"I'll figure something out. Meantime, I'm still hassling with the Trails West people. Those rascals are not only operating the Starlight Hotel establishment, but the Grand Canyon Railway has just entrusted them with its newly completed Canyon Queen Hotel."

Monte had the last word. "You know Clint, I think the Trails West Company's foothold on the South Rim is now stronger than yours."

***

While he hoped to capitalize on the increase in tourist activity on the rim, Clint McCarty constantly locked horns with the Trails West people. In fact, the bitter commercial rivalry between the Trails West Company and McCarty's Hotel and Camp grew worse. Jack Keystone and Canyon Queen manager Charles Brentwood considered revising their livery charges to counter McCarty's rates.

"It is astonishing," complained Brentwood to Keystone, "how our guests gain information on McCarty's livery charges compared to ours before arriving here."

"I suspect someone has paid a scoundrel to post notices at the station in Williams or on the train between Williams and here," surmised Keystone.

Later, Clint McCarty bragged that he had men on the trains distributing cards which advertised his hotel. Whenever the Grand Canyon Railway discovered this, they would stop the train and eject the men, sometimes many miles from the Canyon. McCarty also bragged that he cut his rates for lodging. The Railway retaliated by undercutting McCarty's prices and refusing his men access to the depot, now relocated further down the track, effectively bypassing the McCarty Hotel.

***

Teddy Roosevelt urged Congress to create the U.S. Forest Service, a new agency to manage federal forest reserves. He appointed fellow conservationist and strong ally, Gifford Pinchot, as Chief Forester. In effect, Roosevelt transferred forest control from the Department of the Interior to the Department of Agriculture.

During the President's first visit to the Grand Canyon, he realized its vulnerability to being spoiled by its burgeoning tourist industry, being littered with the scars of mining, and its forests being trampled by free-grazing cattle and sheep. He recognized the right and duty of his generation to develop and efficiently use the natural resources of our land. He did not recognize the right to deprive future generations of their use. Roosevelt and Pinchot believed in using our natural resources for the benefit of all Americans and not monopolizing them for the benefit of a few. Roosevelt exercised existing presidential authority to designate public lands as national forests, placing them off-limits to commercial exploitation of tourism, timber, minerals, grazing and waterpower.

Rangers exercised their authority as the Forest Service assumed administrative control of the Grand Canyon. Although protection of the Canyon began with its designation as a forest reserve, miners could still file claims on land within the reserve. But officials found management of the forests hampered by numerous lode and placer mining claims. They appealed to the General Land Office, upon which rested the responsibility for determining the validity of claims, requesting immediate examination of those claims to determine if they contained valuable minerals. Forest officials suspected many mining claims to be invalid, but did not have the authority to interfere.

Although Monte Bridgestone had sold most of his mining properties to Canyon Copper Company, forest rangers continued to harass him. They felt obliged to protect and manage forests at the Grand Canyon—forests that contained the world's largest stand of ponderosa. On one occasion, the forest service ordered Monte to vacate or face prosecution for trespassing. Another time, forest service officials from Washington, Albuquerque and Flagstaff, accompanied by a representative of the Trails West system, visited Summit. Monte resented this intrusion and in an unusual display of anger and frustration, let the forest service entourage have it with both barrels.

"I suppose it is like it has always been in this forest reserve since you let the big interloping corporations in here," Monte shouted, then continued to lambast these unwanted visitors. "You people get information more suitable to the corporations from their representatives than you do from the poor man like me that blazed the trail to make it possible for you to find your way in here in the first place!" Monte became so upset he left the men standing aghast at Summit Point. The Flagstaff representative followed Monte.

"Monte Bridgestone, stop," called Bernard Weinstein, the local Forest Ranger. "I need to say something to you in confidence." Monte waited for Weinstein to catch up.

"The Trails West people are seeking a concession on Summit Point. You need to understand that, as to enforcing the rules, it makes a big difference to the Forest Service if a man has plenty of money."

"What are you saying, Weinstein? Sounds like bribery," Monte charged.

"No, it is not bribery. I'm trying to explain the Santa Fe Railway is extremely powerful, and by association, some of that power extends to their captive Trails West Company. These monopolies have the financial means to get what they want. I'm a government official, but I'm talking to you as a friend who recognizes and respects your position."

"Again, Weinstein, what are you trying to say?" Monte became more upset and frustrated.

Weinstein tried to explain. "I think the problem stems from when the two houses of Congress favored transcontinental railroads. The government offered generous compensation to railroad companies for construction and to individuals displaced or hampered by lines crossing their land."

"You are talking about eminent domain. It is downright condemnation. The government takes over private lands for public use, against the will of the landowner, often for far less compensation than the owner would demand."

Monte clenched his fists, his nostrils flaring. "I'm not giving up my Summit holdings!"

Weinstein's jaw dropped. "You're unwilling to entertain a Trails West offer?"

Monte shook his head, still glaring at him. "No, and that's final. As for homestead and mining claims, toll roads or tourist enterprises, those scoundrels have no authority, call it eminent authority, over the pioneers who have settled here at the Canyon." Monte slowly simmered down.

"I agree, Monte, but they act like they have a free rein because of their close association with the Santa Fe, and sadly the government looks the other way. I don't like what they are doing any more than you do. But I'm here to administer forest policy. The fight between these interloping corporations, as you call them, and you pioneers is out of my hands. All that being said, my friend, I appreciate your services as our unofficial guardian of the East Rim."

"Weinstein, you should be a politician. That long tirade about railroads and eminent authority is a lot of gobbledygook. The Forest Service clearly favors big business over the little man. Dagnabbit, your superiors have called us trespassers!" Monte stomped off, leaving Weinstein feeling ashamed about working for the government.

While Monte struggled with the Forest Service, and with subtle actions taken by the Trails West people to make life difficult, Clint watched as the Trails West people diverted most of his tourist business. As his hotel floundered, he schemed of ways to fight back. He found a way of controlling, with a vengeance, the South Rim. Using a loophole in the mining laws, he filed more and more mining claims, many in strategic locations—not just the head and foot of his Pioneer Toll Road and Canyon Gardens, but vast portions of prime real estate on the South Rim.

McCarty served a two-year term as Chairman of the Coconino County Board of Supervisors and another term as a board member. By controlling access to the Canyon, and wielding his authority as board chairman, McCarty became a dominant force in developing the South

Rim. Longing for greater influence, he entertained thoughts about becoming a member of the House of Representatives for Arizona Territory.

The Railway contested the validity of McCarty's claims, and considerable controversy arose from his alleged flagrant abuse of the mining laws. At the heart of the matter lay McCarty's two twenty-acre claims on the rim—the Battleship Rock encompassing the Pioneer trailhead, and the Cliffrose encompassing the train depot and yard tracks.

In a lawsuit where the federal government joined as an interested party, Grand Canyon Railway alleged McCarty's lode mining claims did not occupy land containing veins of precious mineral, assessment work had been inadequate to warrant patenting, and mill-sites had not served their intended purpose but instead comprised a miner's camp and blacksmith shop. Just before the first hearing, McCarty ordered a pack train of ore from his Concord and Rainbow claims transported to Canyon Gardens and piled up on the Lightning and Thunderbolt claims.

At the hearing, McCarty described his mining operations. "Thunderbolt at Canyon Gardens is for reducing ore from my Rainbow mining claim." He did not divulge that it just happened to encompass a part of the Pioneer Trail known for its sharp switchbacks. McCarty continued, "Lightning, at the head of running water in Shadow Creek, is also for reducing ore at Canyon Gardens."

McCarty also defied the Grand Canyon Railway with his Boxcar claim next to the railroad right-of-way, but it looked like he would lose direct control of the Pioneer Toll Road. As his franchise expired, he insured that control of the trail reverted to Coconino County. The Railway applied to the Forest Service for a permit to operate the trail. But the County Board of Supervisors had the ultimate power of refusal, and McCarty, as a member, used his influence to defeat the Railway's application and ensure the County Sheriff had the authority to protect the

County's property against encroachment. While the County held the franchise, it allowed McCarty to lease the trail and continue collecting tolls on its behalf.

To further complicate matters—and to challenge the government—McCarty filed more claims on the Pioneer Trail and many more along the Colorado River contiguous with his Lightning claim. He located a three-mile string of thirteen adjoining lode claims so as to span the river. He connected three more claims to the Rainbow, and seven more to the Lightning mill-site near Grand Canyon Springs. He also located five claims just east of the Canyon Queen Hotel.

This time, Monte felt his old partner had gone too far. Standing on the balcony of McCarty's hotel, with the great expanse of the Canyon before them, Monte confronted Clint on the matter.

"A string of side-by-side lode claims spanning a 400-foot-wide river squeezed between vertical granite walls? Have you been relieved of your senses, Clint? How can you justify any valid mineral claim under present law? You may as well claim control of the Mississippi while you're at it!"

Monte worried that Clint's flagrant actions might tarnish the reputation of all their fellow mining associates. He continued, "Ten more claims surrounding Canyon Gardens? That's a blatant attempt to control tourism in one of the most popular parts of the Canyon. You and I know there's little mineral value there. Right now, I'm embarrassed to be associated with you!" He took a deep breath and looked Clint in the eye. "Our fight with the Forest Service is all about holding onto assets we accrued, not to control the whole Canyon. Nothing destroys one's respect for others more than greed, dishonesty and defiance."

"Monte, you are overstating the situation. You'll see everything will work out in our favor. Go back to Summit and relax. I'll handle matters with the Forest Service and the Santa Fe."

"Clint, do you know what they are calling you? 'Vandal of the Wilderness'!"

With nothing more to say, Monte left in a huff. Not long ago, the two pioneers reminisced on the Grand Canyon Hotel veranda. But that day's confrontation, with all its sharp-pointed words, signaled the crumbling of a long-standing friendship.

For another year, McCarty ignored Monte's warnings and continued his rampant claims to ever bigger tracts of canyon land. Instead of locating twenty-acre lode claims, he resorted to large placer claims, most of which encompassed one hundred and sixty acres.

Over a three-month period, McCarty added five thousand acres to his canyon holdings. His twisted interpretation of the mining laws netted him thirty-two more claims. He tried to dilute any image of greed by using the names of family members, friends, and business associates on claim filings. He overlaid thirteen placers on his earlier Canyon Gardens lode claims. He blanketed Six-Gun Creek with four placers and located five more on Windsong Mesa to encompass his former holdings.

On his earlier river-spanning lode claims, he superimposed ten placers as a series of tangent quarter-mile-wide strips from Skeleton Creek to a point three miles upstream. He also appropriated most of the flow in the Colorado River, amounting to thirteen million miner's inches of water.

Clint recorded these claims just as Augustus Holloway completed plans to install a four-hundred and fifty-foot cable with suspended cage across the river, near where Skeleton Creek spilled into the Colorado, no doubt on one of McCarty's placer claims. That suited Ernst Bergner just fine. He had tried to finance a cableway across the river but then lost interest when north-side mining proved to be an unprofitable proposition. For many years, this cableway and connecting trails would serve as a canyon crossroads linking the two rims.

McCarty had an ulterior motive for blanketing the Canyon with placer claims and appropriating most of the water flowing in the Colorado River. The Peabody Company of Boston, with the newly passed National Reclamation Act on its mind, had been considering a plan for a seven-million-dollar dam to generate hydroelectric power for mining operations in northern Arizona. Current legislation allowed federal construction of dams and reservoirs in the West.

Peabody's plan called for a six hundred-foot wide, two hundred and thirty-foot high dam at the foot of the Pioneer Trail to impound water fifteen miles upriver, not high enough to reach the so-called bathtub ring, that dirty white band of rock, but enough to flood the Canyon and create a giant artificial lake. With McCarty holding claims to key points on the river, Peabody needed an agreement. The company offered an option to purchase these properties pending proof of title. However, the deal collapsed just as the copper market once again collapsed, leaving McCarty and others with devalued holdings.

Chapter Eight

LADY LUCK

Even without colorful rainbows, in the end there can still be pots of gold.

Sabrina Jaffa found the Jackson Trail, which descends a tributary canyon, to be easy-going. While she saw no signs that anyone had traveled the trail for months, perhaps years, she saw evidence of rockslides and storm damage. Serendipity and Jenny had no difficulties stepping around jumbled rocks and broken junipers. Having journeyed halfway to the river, she set up camp for the night.

She no sooner started cooking over her campfire when a dull kettledrum rumble across the Canyon caught her attention. Looking up, she noticed dark gray clouds building on the North Rim and a series of lightning flashes that split the sky. "Well, girls, it looks like we may be in for a wet evening." She checked the lines tethering her horse and mule to a stout cedar and tightened her tent lines. She ate her traditional supper of beans and tinned beef and drank her fresh-brewed coffee under a canvas tarpaulin she had stretched between scraggly junipers in front of her tent. At first, the campfire, with its mesmerizing flicker, cut her off from the dark stormy night and only a few raindrops plummeted into the fire and sizzled out of existence.

Within seconds of a flash of lightning, there came a piercing crack of thunder that shook the ground. And then the random drops hitting her canopy and campfire became large splats, then a raging downpour, sheets blown sideways against Sabrina's tent. She congratulated herself on selecting high ground for her camp, a spot with good drainage and diversion on the uphill side. With each lightning flash she could see a stream building beyond where she tethered her animals. For the next hour, rain pounded her campsite, with no sign of diminishing or moving on. She murmured, *"Sabrina Jaffa, you picked a fine time to explore in the eastern canyon. I reckon you're in for a rough night."* She snuggled up in her bedroll but at the peak of the thunderstorm, sleep came in irregular intervals.

It rained all night. At one point, she awoke to the sharp pungent smell of wet sage. It sounded like the storm had moved onto the South Rim and yet she still heard rushing water outside her tent. She sat up. "Flashflood!" she shouted, but no one heard her except her horse and mule. Sabrina did not climb out of her bedroll until the first glimmer of morning light.

With a chance to assess her situation, she ventured outside. Two streams of raging muddy water rushed by on either side of her camp. Sabrina found Serendipity, dripping and shivering, but still hitched to the cedar; however, the storm must have spooked Jenny and caused her to break free. Repeated calls failed to bring her back.

The sun never showed itself that morning, although the eastern sky brightened to a dull gray. It would be tough going, but Sabrina felt she needed to get away from the gushing water, hunt for Jenny and resume her journey down the Jackson Trail—assuming it had not washed out. She skipped her morning coffee, bacon and flapjacks, collapsed her canopy, tent and bedroll, and tied them behind her saddle. With Jenny gone, Serendipity would have to carry the load.

Erosion had gnawed and scoured the trail, a mass of slick mud and rock. Water still gushed along the trail, eager to reach the river. Sabrina found better footing on talus slopes where Serendipity experienced less mud but more rock, some being new arrivals from higher ground. She heard the clatter of hoofs behind her. Jenny came galloping down the trail. "Jenny! Where did you run off to? Thank goodness you're back." Sabrina reloaded Jenny with her normal pack and the Jaffa party resumed its canyon expedition. The day remained gray and overcast, with intermittent showers. And it seemed the storm had parked itself on the rim as water continued to pour from overhangs and rock-cluttered gullies.

The weather finally cleared, and she resumed her careful examination of side canyons. At one point, she caught sight of the river—a muddy brown flood. After two days of prospecting, dark brooding clouds again formed on the North Rim. It looked like another thunderstorm brewing. She scouted for a campsite, not as exposed as the one during the last storm. This time she found an alcove with a wall between her and the river to serve as a shield from the approaching storm. Better yet, this site had an overhang to deflect water rushing down from higher elevations. With no trees for hitching Serendipity and Jenny, she stretched a tether line between rocks.

This storm raced across the canyon and again the rain came down in heavy sheets. Lightning flashed close by, and thunder echoed in the side canyons. By late afternoon, the sky darkened with heavy gray clouds. Sabrina watched one lightning bolt strike a high rock pillar, setting several boulders crashing into a ravine. Hunkered down under her canvas canopy, she waited for the rain to stop.

It continued pouring for another two hours. She could not tell if she heard river rapids or waterfalls but water poured down around her camp on all sides. "Waterfalls!" she shouted to herself, "this storm is making waterfalls where there are usually none!" She looked up at the rock overhang and saw dirty water spilling off the edge and pouring into a bed of shattered rocks at the base of the falls. "*I wonder,*" she thought to herself, "*could this be the place? Could this be the hiding place for Lee's fabled lost gold?*"

Sabrina had to look, heavy rain or not. As water and debris swirled around her camp, striking the shield wall and turning as it raced to the river, she made her way to a point behind the waterfall. To her sheer delight, she spotted five large rusty tin canisters that looked like they had not seen the light of day for decades. Someone had pulled the hinged lids back, when they once contained coffee, then pressed them back down. Water had washed away rocks and gravel, exposing a possible treasure. A rusty rifle barrel lay next to the canisters, its hardwood stock partially gone. A crushed canteen lay several feet from the rifle. Sabrina surmised that water and fallen rocks had invaded this treasure's hideout many times over the years.

Already soaked to the bone, she crouched under the falls and reached for the closest canister. The sides crumbled in her hands, revealing the glint of yellow metal as gold nuggets spilled into the mud. "Gold!" she shrieked. Sabrina Jaffa had found the legendary lost gold behind the elusive waterfall. Drenched, she sat back on a rock shelf, her heart pounding, long hair plastered to her back, her clothes dribbling brown water. "I need to be careful here or I'll lose the entire cache down the ravine. I don't dare try to move these canisters in all this rushing water." She waited for the rain to stop and the waterfalls to turn into a trickle.

Another day passed before the rain subsided and the waterfall became a sporadic drip from the overhang. While waiting, she devised a plan to retrieve the gold from their decrepit containers. Assuming the other tin canisters contained gold nuggets, she filled her coffee pot with the precious pieces. She picked the loose nuggets out of the mud as a long strand of light brown hair, still darkened by rainwater, fell in front of her face, and she swung it around to her back. She swished the nuggets in a puddle, dropped them in the coffee pot, then turned to the remaining nuggets in the canister, carefully removing them and, one by one, dropping them into the pot.

Kirby had wished Sabrina good luck and hoped she would find a fortune. He thought she had been searching for minerals worth mining but all along she had been hunting for lost treasure. She indeed found her fortune.

After hours of tedious work, Sabrina had recovered all the nuggets from the first canister. When she peeled back the lid on the second canister, she found saturated gold dust—more like gold mud—instead of nuggets. This called for a different method of containment. Saddlebags came to mind. She emptied Serendipity's bags in her tent, and returned to the waterfall, now just a random drip. Using a spoon and a steady hand, she carefully moved wet gold dust, mixed with some gritty sand, from the canister to the saddlebag. She peeled the rusted walls of the canister away as she worked to remove every grain of gold. With one side of the saddle bag full she switched to the other. There remained three canisters and no way of telling whether they held gold dust or gold nuggets until she bent their lids back.

The descending call of a canyon wren signaled break time! She stepped out of the shadows and into the noonday sun. Sensing she was making history, she called out to Serendipity and Jenny, "Hey girls, it's a beautiful day. Wait till you see what I found!" The free-wheeling Sabrina Jaffa had struck gold!

She found the next canister filled to the brim with gold dust but found the remaining two stuffed with gold nuggets, larger than the first canister. The rest of the gold dust fit into the other side of her saddle bag and she soon topped off her coffee pot with nuggets, but she could not budge the pot. Where else could she stuff nuggets? Her boots! She switched to wearing her lace-up ankle boots. Again, the canisters disintegrated as she plucked nuggets and dropped them into her taller boots. Sabrina giggled, "This brings a whole new meaning to bootlegging."

Finally, her boots had equal loads, about half full. She folded over the open ends and cinched them tight with leather straps. Each boot felt as heavy as the coffee pot. She would not start back until the next morning, so she left the coffee pot, saddle bag and boots behind the waterfall, now just a series of drips.

At sunrise, Sabrina awoke and set about breaking camp. To her surprise, she could barely move the coffee pot and saddlebags and could only drag her boots a short distance. She would need to move her gold in smaller quantities, distributing the load in smaller bundles she could lift and Serendipity and Jenny could carry. She sat and pondered her situation.

"The tent! I could cut up the tent and with strips of rawhide or twine I could bind up small pokes of gold dust and nuggets." With her jackknife, she shredded the lightweight canvas into one-foot squares—a slow process consuming half the morning. When she had moved half the nuggets in her coffee pot to her makeshift gold pokes, she found she could move the pot. She wondered how anyone could have man-handled five full canisters.

By sundown she had reduced the saddlebag contents to half, to a point at least where she could lift and balance them astride Serendipity. She needed more time to deal with the boots. She would need another evening and part of the next morning to finish the job.

Surveying her huge collection of canvas bundles, it became clear that she would need three trips and considering the heavy load, three days per trip. It would take two weeks for Sabrina and her sure-footed animals to transport her newfound treasure to the rim and cross-country to the Klostermeyer homestead.

After stashing her remaining bundles under rocks and weeds, she started on her first long climb to the rim. It took two full days trudging on foot through slippery mud and loose rocks to reach the trailhead, leading her faithful animals along the damaged trail. After a day of rest in a secluded clearing, she started again on the long trek to the ranch, hoping she did not encounter another human along the way. Sabrina contemplated her future, her next move with Kirby and whether she should tell anyone, even Kirby, about her great find.

Unbeknownst to Sabrina, another human did see her, in fact, another woman. Teresa Cordova, who had worked as a driver for the Grand Canyon Stage Line, now made official U.S. Postal runs from the train depot at Grand Canyon Village to tourist camps and residents at Summit and Clancy's Ranch, as well as way stations along the upper stage road. Teresa ran a tight schedule and did not slow down to observe the slow-moving pack train. Being too far away to identify what appeared to be a prospector, she thought nothing more of the encounter.

The smell of rain-washed sage still lingered on the Coconino as Sabrina, Serendipity and Jenny made their way with their heavy payload. When a lone Navajo horseman emerged from a muddy gulch, Sabrina and her girls stayed out of sight until he passed. She spotted a lone coyote trotting across the stage road, the only other encounter on her first return trip to the ranch.

After two more round trips, she succeeded in moving her gold to the barn at the Klostermeyers. She rewarded Serendipity and Jenny with extra oats. Sabrina seemed well satisfied that no one had seen her. No one would ever suspect she had made a great discovery. As she rested at the ranch, she wondered how much gold weighed, how many pounds had she hauled from the elusive waterfall, how could she determine the going rate for gold? For a while, she planned to do nothing but revel in her secret for a spell. She said to herself, "Even without colorful rainbows, in the end there can be pots of gold."

***

Still on her mail run, Teresa Cordova just happened to find Clancy at his ranch. "Hey, Clancy, I was hoping you were out here instead of hanging around the Village this week. I've got a letter for you from Bill Cody, postmarked in Wyoming!"

"Buffalo Bill?" Clancy took the letter from Teresa and tore it open.

Teresa, in a low, melodious voice, asked, "I've got time, Clancy. I never met Buffalo Bill. Would you read the letter out loud?"

"Sure, let's see what ol' Cody's got to say. It seems to be about buffalo hunters."

"Okay, let's hear it," urged Teresa, already enjoying her respite from mail delivery.

Clancy read the letter aloud. "Clancy my friend, I hope you are doing well there on the South Rim. I ran into a young cowboy from the Goodnight Ranch in the Texas Panhandle named Kurt Ritter." Clancy paused for a moment and gave a quizzical look to Teresa, "Why do I need to know about this fellow?" He continued reading.

"He seemed real interested in my visit to the Canyon and asked a lot of questions. I sense he has a hankering to start some sort of buffalo enterprise. I mentioned an area just north of the Canyon that might be suitable for raising buffalo. Just thought you should know."

Clancy sighed, "Well, sure good to hear from my friend Buffalo Bill."

"Thanks for sharing Cody's letter with me. Now I need to get moving." Teresa started to unhitch her horse.

"Oh, Clancy, before I go, let me tell you something. On the way over here I saw a prospector, walking slowly, leading a horse and a pack mule, both heavily loaded, on the old stage road, headed for town, I presume. I only got a quick look, but I got the feeling the prospector was not a man, but a woman. Have you come across such an outfit?"

Clancy stroked his beard and thought for a minute. "If you think it was a woman, it could be the mystery lady. She tends to avoid others, even goes out of her way to stay out of sight; strange that she was walking and not riding."

"There's a mystery lady hereabouts?" asked Teresa.

"Yeah, if I remember right, her name is Sabrina, yeah, Sabrina Jaffa. She hijacked my Whiskey Spring camp a few years back. Could be that's who you saw."

Teresa shrugged, "I don't rightly know. I never heard of her. I'll be on my way. Thanks Clancy and take care."

***

One hot summer day, Sabrina Jaffa and her trusty mare plodded along on the old stage road, thinking about Kirby and whether there could be a future for the two together. In past sojourns, she avoided encounters with other travelers, but this time it seemed to matter little. So, when she crossed paths with an elderly man leading a small pack train, she initiated a friendly conversation with the stranger.

"Hello, mister, are you getting along okay?" Sabrina asked, noticing he seemed tired and haggard. "I'm Sabrina Jaffa, headed up to the Canyon for a few days of camping."

"Good Lord, lady, you should not be out here alone. There's been horse thieves and outlaws hereabouts lately," warned the old man. "Camping you say?"

"Yes, I'm meeting a good friend of mine at the Canyon. Kirby and I plan to camp below the rim and take in the scenery." Sabrina surprised herself in being so open with a stranger.

"That wouldn't be Kirby O'Brien would it?"

Sabrina perked up, "Yes! Do you know Kirby?"

"Why certainly, he used to work for me during my mining and trail-building days; hardest worker I ever had. We made a great team back then. Dagnabbit, where are my manners? I should introduce myself Miss Sabrina. I'm Levi Jackson."

"Levi! I've heard all about you and always wanted to meet you. Where are you headed?" Sabrina could not believe her luck in meeting the venerable Levi Jackson.

"I've been trading with the Havasupai and now I'm heading to the Hopi villages, and then home to my ranch south of Joseph City. Kirby was always gabbing, a non-stop talker as I recall, and quite an inquisitive fellow. He loved to hear my stories of hunting bears, living with the Hopi and Navajo, oh, and lost gold," sighed Levi, his raspy voice trailing off.

"Lost gold?" asked Sabrina, playing it coy as she dared not disclose her discovery.

"Yeah, there's been rumors circulating for years about Lee's gold stashed somewhere in the eastern part of the Canyon. Some say it's buried in an old prospect hole; others say it's lost forever under some rockslide; still others talk about it being tucked behind a waterfall. Probably no one will ever find it, if it exists at all, and that's what I used to tell Kirby." Levi stopped rambling.

"Well, I'll tell Kirby we crossed paths, Mr. Jackson, and I bid you farewell and a safe journey." Sabrina patted the side of Serendipity's head as they prepared to move out.

"You too Miss Sabrina, and you be careful on this stage road. It's seen more than its share of unsavory characters. And please pass my best regards on to Kirby."

And with that, Levi resumed his eastward trek. Sabrina watched him for a few minutes, listening to Levi alternatively taunt and praise his mules. She then resumed her own journey, still bubbling over her chance meeting with the legendary Levi Jackson.

She arrived at the head of the Whiskey Trail, having followed her usual route on the old stage road across the Coconino. A group of tourists occupied Clancy's place, so she camped at a nearby seep. Serendipity needed the water break and some oats, and the location allowed Sabrina to ponder her meeting with Levi. At one point she almost blurted out she found the gold cache behind a temporary waterfall. She wanted to put Levi's mind at ease by telling him the lost gold legend turned out to be a true story. But then she thought better of the situation; she would not make her discovery known to anyone, not even Kirby.

***

Very early the next morning, before anyone stirred at Jennings' place, Sabrina made her descent into the Canyon and contoured over to Arrowhead Spring to wait for Kirby to show. She did not have long to wait, a half-hour at best. She watched the pack-master maneuver down the Redwall with a cavalcade of six burros, the trail dust billowing up behind the swishing tails, suffocating the unfortunate trotters that followed. Kirby looked like he was walking on limestone marbles.

"Howdy, stranger," she said, startling Kirby.

"Dang-it, Sabrina, I never know when you will show up here," he blurted, but then followed, "I've been thinking about you for weeks, hoping you'd come by when I'm here. You'll never know how much

I've missed you. Uh, I need to stop babbling!" Flapping his wide brim hat free of dust, he asked "Any luck on the Jackson Trail?"

"Well, it was a good trip but very rainy," she responded.

"Yeah, it rained here too. Say, I'm on my last water run for a few days and I have some time off." He wanted to suggest they spend a few days together.

Sabrina read his mind. "I'm thinking we might go down to the river for a spell," suggested Sabrina. "Maybe we could sit and watch Whiskey Rapids and have that talk you've been hounding me about."

"And I suppose you want to do some prospecting along the way." That didn't matter to Kirby. He had wanted a long talk with her for quite some time. An excursion down Whiskey Trail might provide the perfect opportunity.

"I've prospected every inch of that side canyon. Besides, I'm not interested in looking for pay dirt anymore. Can we leave after you have filled your water barrels?" Sabrina hitched Serendipity to some sagebrush and sat in the shade.

"I only have twelve barrels to fill this time but then I need to get them up to the mine. Can you sit there for about two hours while I finish my chores? In the meantime, you can tell me about your Jackson Trail adventures."

"There were two big thunderstorms so everywhere I went there were rockslides and mud. I'm sure you and Levi built a good trail, but it's in terrible shape now." Sabrina vowed not to divulge anything about her happy discovery and may not even mention yesterday's chance encounter with Levi, at least not yet.

Speaking flatly, she explained, "Conditions were just not right for prospecting. It took several days to dry out and get back to firm ground on the rim. That was about three weeks ago."

"So that has discouraged you from prospecting?" Kirby asked, thinking nothing would deter this ambitious woman.

"You know Kirby, if we do all our talking now, we won't have anything else to talk about on the Whiskey Trail. That's when I'll tell you how I met Levi. Now get back to work," she teased, "I hope you have a mule or horse at the mine."

"You met Levi? When? Where?" Kirby, caught off guard, wanted to know details before they hit the trail.

"I'll tell you later, now get back to work," she again teased.

Kirby finished filling barrels, cinched them up on his ornery burros and led the string back up to Windsong Mesa, then hurried back down on his mule. After filling their canteens at the spring, the two rode east, intercepted the trail, and started down, winding their way down crumbling talus slopes, at least as far as their animals could go.

As promised, Sabrina described her meeting with Levi Jackson. They hitched Serendipity and No Name, Kirby's mule, to a stand of shady willows, with enough lead to reach the stream for a drink. Then, with knapsacks and full canteens, they continued to make their way to the river, navigating through overgrown thickets of brush and willows, downed cottonwood branches and logs, tangled vines and matted weeds in the creek bed. They climbed down trouser-splitting rock steps that took the place of rope ladders that Clancy Jennings had once dangled over rough spots. At first, the roar of the Colorado seemed muffled by mesquite among the sand dunes.

"I've never been to the river on this trail, have you Sabrina?" asked Kirby, hoping to stimulate some conversation.

"This is my third time, maybe fourth," then changing the subject, "Kirby, what do you want in life?"

Sabrina waited for an answer, but Kirby appeared mesmerized by the fast-moving water. Standing waves exploded into a riot of whitewater. The roar drowned out any conversation, so perhaps he did not hear her question, or perhaps he did, and this seemed a good way to avoid answering.

The late sun played on talus slopes, setting brilliant red shale afire. Bats and swallows darted in the inner glow of a canyon sunset. Two figures silhouetted against the last golden glow of a sinking sun watched the wild rapids. The river at one moment seemed to panic and surge ahead, then the next moment its rapids seemed to be celebrations of freedom.

"Kirby, I guess you did not hear me back there, what do you want in life?"

"Well, for sure I don't want to be a miner the rest of my days. I'd like to settle down, do some ranching, perhaps raise a family." Kirby felt a little uncomfortable with where Sabrina might take the conversation. Pointing upstream, "Let's move to where it's quieter in those sand dunes."

"I'd like to settle down too. For me, I should say settle down again, maybe get back to ranching, I mean running my own ranch, not working for others, and no more canyon prospecting for me. It sounds like we share the same interests."

Sabrina tried to draw him out. She picked up two rocks and threw them into the river—kerplunk.

"You never know just how big a splash two middle-aged rocks can make!"

"What?" Kirby did not understand what that meant.

Sabrina tried to explain, "Kirby, I'm in my mid-thirties and I'm guessing you're in your late thirties. We still have half our life sentences to serve. Let's spend them together!"

Kirby, still thinking about what else he wanted in life, missed her last statement. "Kirby, are you fixin' to say something? If so, let's have it."

"Sabrina, you are an extraordinary woman and by now you must have an inkling about the way I feel about you."

"I can guess," she mumbled, figuring this conversation may eventually lead to a marriage proposal.

Kirby seemed to be only half listening to her. He yammered on, "Sabrina, I don't know how it happened, but I've fallen for you. I go to sleep every night in my Windsong shanty imagining I am hugging and kissing you. I dream I'm making love to you. It's a blaze of emotion, but then I awake and wonder if I have a chance with you at all."

Sabrina looked up to return his gaze, deciding to be a tease. She had a cryptic smile on her face, her green eyes carried a curious glint, and her long auburn hair, back-lighted by the last yellowing rays of the setting sun, swayed in the light breeze. It seemed like five minutes had passed since Kirby announced he had fallen for her.

She contrived to form a blank stare. "Uh, I wish I could say the same."

That caught his attention. Kirby slumped into a state of being crushed, speechless, dismayed. Had she led him on? Did he misread her interest? Was this just his fantasy? A long moment passed, then he mumbled, "Oh—that is not the response I hoped for."

"Just kidding!" Sabrina displayed one of her characteristic broad impish smiles. "I guess you did not hear me suggest we spend the rest of our lives together. I too have fallen in love—with you—there, I said it."

"Sabrina, talking with you has not been easy for me. You exasperate me beyond measure," Kirby declared, still not listening to her.

"Well, I gave you enough hints!" Something perverse in her nature caused her to refuse to make things easy for Kirby.

He stared at her for a time, then he knew the moment had come for him to take action. He reached for her hand and pulled her toward him. With an arm around her, Kirby felt her hair cascading to her slender waist. She sighed in relief and pleasure as she yielded to his embrace.

"For the record, I love you too, Sabrina. Will you marry me? I promise the moon and stars, I will love you forever."

"And for the same record, I love you, with all my fluttering heart," she replied, "so yes, I will marry you. But you don't need to promise me the moon and the stars; just promise me you will stand under them with me forever."

Kirby felt like dancing a jig. His dream had come true. He kissed her for the first time. They spread a blanket on the soft sand. Sabrina returned his kiss with such passionate depth it left Kirby shaking and tingling—rousing pleasure at river's edge as night seemed to well up from the river itself until their waterfront camp became engulfed in blackness.

***

One quiet afternoon at Summit, while Monte sat alone on the veranda of the Grand Canyon Hotel, a stranger dismounted and hitched his horse to a post. "Howdy, mister, my name's Ritter, Kurt Ritter. Would you happen to be Clancy Jennings?"

"No sir, name's Monte Bridgestone—say, looks like you've come a long way. And I see you are wearing moccasins—new in these parts, are you?"

"Moose-hide moccasins and I see yer wearin' boots," Ritter countered, adding with a grin, "Dad-blame it, the kind of shoes you folks wear out here are about like sheet-iron for comfort and warmth."

"Okay, meant no offense, it's just that we don't see moccasins or moose here at the Canyon. How 'bout some coffee?" offered Monte.

"Don't mind if I do; it's been a long ride."

"Anna, we've got company," shouted Monte, "please bring the coffeepot and two mugs." Turning to the stranger, "She'll be along in a few minutes. Anna started out being our housekeeper here," volunteered Monte, "but we've since become close companions. We got married with no fanfare, just wanted to make things legal."

Ritter smiled as Anna emerged with the coffee and left the pot, plus a tray of fresh-baked cookies. "Anna, this is Kurt Ritter from . . . I didn't catch where you're from, sir."

"Pleased to meet you, Anna. I'm from Texas."

"You too, sir," said Anna as she left the men to their business.

"Any way to get across the canyon here?" questioned Ritter. "Buffalo Bill didn't think so; told me he had to skirt around to the east for days back in ninety-two, perhaps there's a ferry or a bridge now?" Monte answered, "Some fellas up on the Kaibab are building a cableway of some sort across the river, but you can bet your boots on this—it won't be ready for months yet."

"I don't wear boots, remember?" reminded Ritter with a smile, being careful not to offend his host.

"That's right, you told me your feet prefer moccasins. Anyway, there is a plan to span the river with a cable system and suspend a carrying platform on it. I think they're still trying to figure out how to move it along the cable, considering it will sag in the middle and the second half of the ride will be quite a climb," surmised Monte.

Ritter, not quite ready to leave, asked, "Monte, if I can use your first name, what are you doing at this quiet, lonesome outpost?"

"Well Kurt, it hasn't always been lonesome and quiet. See that red butte down there? That's where my copper mine is—well, I don't own it anymore—with prices down I had to sell it. Anna and I have been operating this hotel—built it myself but had to sell it, too. No one comes out here anymore on account of tourists being corralled in the Village—used to be they all came here but the Grand Canyon Railway and Trails West monopoly has just about put us out of business. How in tarnation did you find your way out here?"

"Ol' Buffalo Bill suggested I see a fella named Clancy Jennings—that he would help me out."

"That old geezer?—he hangs out in the Village now—regaling tourists with his outlandish stories. Why do you want to get across the river?"

"Buffalo Bill suggested that a place called House Rock Valley, just off the edge of the Kaibab Plateau, might be suitable for grassland grazers like buffalo."

"Well, I wouldn't know about that," Monte confessed, "don't know much about buffalo either."

"Well, I need to be moving along."

As Kurt mounted up, Monte suggested the long way around to the Kaibab, advising against a solo river crossing or waiting for cableway construction.

"Say goodbye to Anna for me, Monte," shouted Kurt as he rode away.

***

The Canyon Copper Company hired a Prescott mining engineer to assess the company's copper properties—and a most favorable report resulted. The engineer seemed complimentary of the development work on Windsong Mesa but noted the operation could be more profitable. He suggested an aerial tramway and a smelter on the rim to allow recovery of large bodies of copper ore and yield good profits. He recommended the owners sink the main shaft to a depth of six hundred feet to reach deep-seated copper sulfides believed to be resting on top of the granite bedrock. The engineer predicted high returns on these investments if the owners used good management practices and followed his recommendations.

Just when the optimistic Shooting Star Mine report buoyed the owners, another national financial crisis dashed their hopes. It came on the heels of the worst natural disaster in the nation's history—the San Francisco earthquake and fire that leveled the city. The quake rumbled through the city for less than a minute, but its aftermath lasted for years. Its greatest destruction came from fires ignited by broken gas lines and toppled cook stoves. The three hundred and fifty-million-dollar cost of devastation in San Francisco drew gold out of the nation's major financial centers and served as a catalyst for an economic recession.

To make matters worse, several New York City tycoons tried to corner the market on United Copper Company stock by buying up shares, driving up share prices, and causing a frightful six-week run on banks. Several banks and trusts failed, leading to a crisis of faith in the nation's banking system. Across the country, vast numbers of panicky people withdrew deposits from their regional banks, regardless of any involvement in the stock market.

The financial panic caused copper prices to plummet. The Shooting Star Mine, in which Monte Bridgestone and Clint McCarty had worked so hard, closed down—having produced its last copper ore.

Despite the recession, Clint vowed to control the commercial development of the South Rim on his own terms. Through political maneuvering, mining law manipulation, and obstructionist tactics, the irrepressible McCarty succeeded in his plan to control the rim, the trails, the water sources, the river accesses, and the regions suspected of containing high-value mineral. He grumbled about the federal government siding with large corporations to the detriment of private enterprise and local government. While satisfied he had levied a troublesome barrier for the Grand Canyon Railway-Trails West coalition and the Forest Service, McCarty knew his barriers would not hold—that, in the end, he would not prevail—but he would continue his fight for as long as he could. Before long, the General Land Office denied McCarty's patent applications—first the Rainbow and Concord mining claims and the Thunderbolt and Lightning mill-sites, then the Battleship Rock and Cliffrose applications. The government vowed to rule all of McCarty's mining claims invalid.

Chapter Nine

A NEW TRAIL IN LIFE

When your cause is right and just, never surrender to despair.

With the unfortunate closure of the Shooting Star Mine, Kirby O'Brien lost his job. He and Monte both saw the end coming for canyon mining. The two sat on the hotel veranda talking and reminiscing about better times. They could not recall the last time they saw the Canyon so crystal clear and quiet—no breezes, no tourists, no workers. South Rim activities reached a virtual standstill.

"Kirby, with Canyon Copper Company's announcement it can no longer keep you and your crew engaged in mining at the Shooting Star, what are you going to do? You've been a dependable worker over the years, loyal to the bone, and I'm proud of our long and rewarding friendship, but with national park status in Teddy's gunsights, mining here is coming to an abrupt end. I know you make friends easily and I'm guessing you keep them for life, but do you have a plan?" Monte seemed overly concerned with Kirby's welfare.

"I'm switching to ranching, Monte," answered Kirby rather matter-of-factly, "so don't worry about me. I'm more worried about you. I'm not going far. I'll always be around to help an old friend."

"Oh, never mind about me," Monte said, trapped in his own pride. "I settled here at Summit because it is the closest point on the South Rim to the stars. I have no place else to go. I have always had a deep-seated love of canyon life, of mining and of trail-building. I've never relished the prospect of knuckling under to big corporations, but that's just the way things have played out. What we accomplished below the rim, and up here too, is commendable but all for naught, lost in a swirl of chaotic controversy."

Kirby had never seen Monte so downtrodden and emotional. He tried to reassure his friend and mentor. "When your cause is right and just, never surrender to despair." For several long minutes, Monte seemed lost in thought, then he blurted, "Ranching, you say? Where are you going to do that?"

Monte, surprised about Kirby's sudden change of occupation, could not picture him as a rancher but he needed to do something. Just then, Anna appeared with two cups of coffee. "Thanks, Mrs. Bridgestone, much appreciated," said Kirby.

"Little Springs," answered Kirby, "You asked where I plan to do ranching." He took three slow slurps of coffee, let his uneasiness melt away, then opened to his old partner.

"I need to confess something to you Monte. Well, it's not a confession, more like a secret. Do you remember the mystery lady, Sabrina Jaffa?" Monte tipped his hat back and nodded.

"Well, for the past year or so we'd been meeting secretly. She made a habit of intercepting me at Arrowhead Spring during my water runs. At first, she stopped by every two or three months during her so-called prospecting trips, then more frequently." Kirby let that news sink in before continuing.

"I could never figure out that woman," argued Monte. "She is certainly a good-looker, but as a prospector she didn't seem to know what to look for. She never dwelled long on any of her diggings, or should I say scratchings. Prospecting is more of an art than a science. So, you two got to know each other, did you?"

"Better than that, we got married in Flagstaff several months ago!" Kirby watched for Monte's reaction. They both burst into infectious grins.

"Well, I'll be a horned lizard—you rascal. Congratulations! Where is she?"

"Little Springs. She is buying the old Klostermeyer homestead. Augustus and Martha Klostermeyer are getting up in years. Sabrina had been boarding there for a long time, in exchange for doing ranch chores. The Klostermeyers are moving into town and now we are working the ranch. With no mining work anymore," allowed Kirby, "I'll be able to do more of my share of the work."

"So, all this time she's been operating out of Little Springs. No wonder we never crossed paths in town," Monte concluded, shifting his weight in his rocking chair.

"She'd hide in the barn hayloft whenever the stage made its brief stops," added Kirby. "But wait till you hear the rest of the story." Kirby sported a wide grin and Monte suspected he had a bigger surprise coming. "Her prospecting trips were just a ruse!"

"She was spying on us down there?" Monte asked, "Maybe scheming ways to jump our claims?"

"No, Sabrina is not a claim-jumper. She was searching for lost gold," explained Kirby. "It wasn't till after we got married, she told me she found it!"

Monte leaned forward, "Found what, Lee's fabled lost gold?"

"Yes, she found Lee's gold."

Monte leaned back in his chair. "That was just a legend, an entertaining story bandied about at evening campfires and around saloon tables, told and retold with just enough plausibility to keep everyone guessing and to keep the legend from diminishing with passing time. That legend was real? Where did she find it?"

"It was during a bad storm. She was camping near what turned out to be temporary waterfalls off the Old Jackson Trail. I probably trudged by the spot many times when I worked for Levi. It was dry then—no storm, no waterfalls. Yup, Sabrina found the legendary lost gold—five decrepit tin canisters full to the brim—gold dust and gold nuggets, after hordes of treasure hunters had spent years searching canyon nooks and crannies, my Sabrina hit the jackpot!"

Monte could not believe Sabrina's and, by association, Kirby's good fortune. He knew Levi Jackson, Clint McCarty, Clancy Jennings, even ol' Lucas Randall and his burros, had been hunting for that gold cache for decades.

"Kirby, I've got to tell you about a wounded horse thief on the Jackson Trail. He shot it out with the sheriff but escaped and arrived right here at the hotel. Before he died, he confided that there was a cache of gold nuggets in a stone crock covered with a flat rock at the foot of the Jackson Trail. I often dreamed of getting some of us old-timers together to make one more trip below the rim to recover the loot. You probably heard such wild yarns while working with ol' Levi. Sorry, I've interrupted you—I'm acting like Clancy in my old age—regaling folks with wild tales. So, Kirby, what's your next step?"

"You are the only one who we have told, and we think it best we do not tell anyone else, at least for now," Kirby said, as he looked around.

"Why tell me?" Monte asked, with a quizzical look.

"Because I trust you and we need your advice. How does one convert gold to ready cash?" Kirby knew the next question would be how much gold do they have.

"Here's what I suggest." Monte, firm but brief, always gave good advice. "Go see Jesse Parks—the most trusted banker in Flagstaff. He can determine your gold's value in today's market, and deposit it in a special account. But don't be in an all-fired hurry, take your time and think this through. Ol' Jesse can guide you in the right direction."

"That's what we'll do then," stated Kirby, "and right now I need to skedaddle back to the ranch. Thanks for the coffee and the advice; I'll be back again soon." Kirby stepped off the veranda and ambled over to his horse at the hotel hitching post.

"Oh, there's one more thing, Kirby. When you come back, bring Mrs. O'Brien with you. I've just got to meet this lucky lady again. It's been years."

Monte lingered a while on the veranda. He sighed, "Kirby O'Brien, rancher—and the husband of the prettiest woman in northern Arizona—with a golden future ahead of them." Monte mused, "Good for them."

***

With continuing developments on both sides of the river, canyon pioneers realized their greatest worry—increasing government control. President Roosevelt declared the Grand Canyon as a national monument—ostensibly to further safeguard the Anasazi cliff dwellings from pilfering and destruction. In setting aside Grand Canyon as a pristine wilderness, the president hoped to preserve natural landmarks, Colorado River tributaries, vast forest resources, and the titanic gorge that may reveal some of our planet's oldest geologic secrets.

To raise public interest and concern, the president used the power vested in him by the Antiquities Act to reserve from appropriation and use all public lands within the Grand Canyon Forest Reserve. With this order, the president intended to protect the region from encroachments under the mining and land laws, while still allowing use of national forests.

He withdrew the Grand Canyon, contained within the forest reserve, as an object of unusual scientific interest—one of the greatest examples of erosion in the world. He declared Grand Canyon National Monument the dominant reservation, barring the location of new mining claims. The order limited further mine development to valid claims already in existence. While signing the presidential proclamation, Teddy noted that it carried strong language regarding future settlement: "Warning is hereby given to all unauthorized persons not to appropriate, injure or destroy any feature of this National Monument or to locate or settle upon any of the lands reserved by this proclamation." The president believed views of the Canyon should hold nothing that is manmade.

With the Grand Canyon becoming a national monument—a kind of purgatory between a forest reserve and a national park—it seemed inevitable within a few years it would, through an act of Congress, attain park status. The government took two more actions to tighten its grip on the Grand Canyon. It enlarged the Game Preserve to include the entire Grand Canyon Forest Reserve, outlawing hunting, trapping, killing or capturing game animals on both sides of the Canyon without a permit. And Teddy issued another proclamation which divided the Grand Canyon Forest Reserve into two parts. The region north of the Canyon became known as Kaibab National Forest and that on the south as Coconino National Forest.

One day, while sitting on the rocky edge of Summit Point, Monte tried to explain the dilemma to Kirby. "As a national monument, Grand Canyon came under administrative control of the Department of Agriculture," stated Monte, "but mining came under the Department of the Interior. I remember reading in the paper how the President spoke about the obvious solution, making Grand Canyon a national park and placing it under one federal agency—Interior."

"Yeah," said Kirby, "that would ease the difficulties of administering Grand Canyon as a national forest, a game refuge and a national monument."

"Agree, but I believe park status may remain out of reach for another decade. While stockmen will issue a sigh of relief, knowing they can graze their cattle on the reserve, mining men will continue to complain about the new restrictions."

***

The summer remained deathly quiet at Summit Point. Unable to compete with either Trails West at the Village or the Grand Canyon Hotel owners there at Summit, Monte agonized over closing his small struggling hotel. Humbled and desperate, he continued managing the Canyon Copper Company's hotel complex. He and Anna served meals to the tourists that the Trails West rigs brought out to Summit Point on day trips, but the number of overnight guests continued to dwindle. Trails West used Summit Point as a way station, and floated offers to buy the outpost hotel, hoping to add it to its monopoly.

While Clint continued his fight for his mining claims, he also waged a successful campaign for Congress. He defeated the long-time incumbent democrat and became Arizona's new delegate to the House of Representatives. During his term, Clint lobbied for statehood and urged his fellow congressmen to pass the bill to admit Arizona into the Union.

As the government tried to improve management of the Grand Canyon, it found McCarty's old lode and placer claims as threats to enforcing its policies. Congressman or not, the government would make him an example. Eager to have the Canyon developed for the benefit of the public, the Forest Service appealed to the General Land Office, responsible for judging the validity of claims.

Assuming it had the authority to investigate the character of a mining claim, the Land Office did not believe it had to wait for the claimant to seek a patent. Annoyed by the claimant's ability to keep his rights alive for many years through annual assessments—rendering the government incapable of interfering with a claim, whether valid or fraudulent—the Land Office announced it had the right to examine such claims.

The government found that McCarty's widespread claims presented a troublesome obstacle to its administration of Grand Canyon National Monument. It judged some of his claims contained no mineral value and planned to cancel them when the judicial system overturned the entire policy of the Department of the Interior with a new decision touching the question of holding private claims on public land.

A similar case challenged the use of certain claims for purposes other than intended by the mining laws. The Land Office examined these claims, ruled them fraudulent, and cancelled them. When lawyers appealed the cases, it became clear the Department of the Interior had no authority to interfere with a claim until the claimant sought a patent. In effect, the ruling placed the rights of private individuals to gain unconditional title to lands on public reservations paramount to the rights and welfare of the public or to the responsibility of the Department to protect those rights.

It took several years to render this landmark decision. In the interim, Clint and the government continued to argue. He took time out of his push for Arizona Statehood to seize the advantage offered by the decision on a similar case, and threw his own case into court in Washington City—and won! Because of the gravity of his canyon claims being upheld, the Interior Secretary allowed the case to go to appeal to test the Department's policy and to settle the question once and for all.

Another case involving McCarty concerned ownership of the Pioneer Trail. This case saw its twentieth court action, as a Flagstaff judge argued for McCarty and Coconino County in the Supreme Court in Phoenix. Trails West attorneys viewed the toll road act of the last territorial legislature as unconstitutional because it favored one interested party over another. The judge countered that the railroad prosecuted the case solely in its own personal interest. One party being favored over another backfired on Trails West and the court ruled in favor of McCarty, allowing the County to take possession of the Pioneer Trail.

Monte had read about Clint's court cases and, during a chance meeting in Flagstaff, the two estranged pioneers caught up on each other's news. "Clint, while I still don't like your trying to claim most of the Canyon for yourself, I must congratulate you on winning the Pioneer Trail case." Monte described how Trails West continued its efforts to freeze him out, as they had done with the Grand Canyon Hotel the previous fall. "Clint, I was in town here about a month ago. Everybody was kicking about it being dull. They were all asking me how business was out at the Canyon. I said, 'better than expected for the winter,' Actually, we served only three meals in three months."

Clint reported, "I understand your opposition to this, but I need to fight or lose my mining claims." He had appealed the decision by the Department of the Interior to cancel his patent applications. In fact, the Department rendered its final decision to cancel the applications, as President Roosevelt's second term drew to a close.

Just before parting ways, Monte said, "Clint, you know me. I don't want to see Grand Canyon Railway and Trails West get all the canyon country. As our Congressman, you need to do whatever is necessary to prevent that. As for your lust to claim the entire canyon for yourself, you know how I feel about that. On a lighter side, Anna wants you to get the scenic railroad for her."

Clint had introduced a bill in Congress to grant a right-of-way for a scenic railway along the East Rim. In late spring, the Grand Canyon Scenic Railway, backed by eastern money, appeared before the Public Lands Committee of the House of Representatives. The legislation called for building a railway spur from the Grand Canyon train depot to Summit Point. It also called for constructing an incline from the rim to the brink of Granite Gorge, and a traction railway to reach Canyon Gardens. The company seemed willing to settle for just the incline but everyone viewed the project as doomed from the start. Chief Forester Gifford Pinchot remained as opposed to a railroad below the rim as much as one along the rim. With such strong opposition, the bill died in committee. Meantime, construction outfits arrived by rail to work on the road from Promontory Point across McCarty's claims to Sunset Point.

In Washington City, Congressman McCarty telegrammed Monte that the President cringed when he heard about the railroad proposals and worried whether the next administration would allow such outlandish development to proceed along and below the rim. The President handpicked his own successor, William Howard Taft, a progressive who he thought would continue his legacy. Taft won on the strength of Roosevelt's popularity. In effect, Roosevelt handed the presidency to Taft.

With Teddy's concurrence, Pinchot altered public land policy from one that dispersed natural resources to private corporations, like the railroads, to one that maintained federal ownership and management of public land for the collective public good. More conservative forces opposed these, even when Congress, dumbfounded by actions of the Roosevelt Administration, forbade creating more forest reserves in the West. That is when Roosevelt reinterpreted the newly passed

Antiquities Act to allow him to create more protected sites, adding to the nation's inventory of forest reserves before leaving office.

But with Teddy out of the picture, the Taft Administration undermined Pinchot's authority. The new Secretary of the Interior, unsympathetic to Pinchot's views, favored private development of lands over withdrawing sites for public use. After considerable political haggling, Pinchot believed the new president would soon fire him for his conservative views, lack of cooperation, maybe even insubordination.

Despite Washington politics, the canyon pioneers exchanged mutual assurances that all would be well but—in reality—it seemed certain Clint would lose his claims, Francois would continue bearing the brunt of government harassment, and Monte would be run out of business.

Clancy Jennings, on the other hand, happily allowed himself to be adopted by Trails West. He earned twenty-five dollars per month as a canyon character and, under Forest Service special use permit, lived in a small cabin near the entrance to Sunset Rim Road.

***

Clancy took great pride in knowing all the hard facts about the Canyon, but also took great liberty with them. He would weave fact into light-hearted fantasy, tweak the truth according to his bent, and spin tales to delight his audience, not knowing what he would say until he said it. Clancy sought crowds in daylight hours, but on rare occasions, he would conduct an evening session. On one such dark night, Halley's Comet wrapped its tail around the planet like a giant sky monster, or so reported several national newspapers.

While most reporters depended on astronomers like Percy Lowell at his Mars Hill Observatory for their facts, Clancy pursued the comet story in a more fanciful way, at the risk of fueling fears among his impressionable listeners.

"Folks, I suppose you've heard Halley's Comet is about to brush Earth with its tail of poisonous cyanide gases," said Clancy, intending to capture the attention of canyon visitors. "The South Rim here is a great viewing station. You should be safe here, assuming you took your comet pills for protection, even though a big piece has broken off." A bright evening star hovered above the western horizon.

"That's enough doomsday talk Cap'n Jennings; look at that beautiful array of bright stars up there. Say something cheerful about stars, especially the bright yellow one," said a young woman, sweeping her hand across the Milky Way.

"Those are not stars," Cap countered, "those are holes in the sky. You realize that the sky is no higher than a rifle shot, don't you? Those could be bullet holes." With this response, Clancy tested the gullibility of his evening crowd.

"Then how do you explain the moon?" the woman challenged.

"Simple, just a bigger hole, perhaps a shotgun blast," Cap answered. "Anyone got another question?" The young woman shook her head in disbelief, perhaps even in pity for Clancy slinging such hogslop.

An elderly gentleman piped up, "I visited Lowell's observatory yesterday. There's a team of astronomers there using glass-plate photography to capture historic images of Halley's Comet and planet Venus all in one picture. I suggest, Mr. Jennings, that you take time to visit with Percy Lowell about comets, planets and stars. That bright star near the comet is not a star at all, nor is it a piece that has broken off the comet. It's the planet Venus!"

Another gentleman had a question. "I noticed when you pointed to the moon, it appears you lost the tip of your right index finger. How'd that happen, Cap?"

"Wal, you know how the Canyon sometimes looks like a giant canvas mural but sometimes dingy and blurry like a mirage? I plumb wore off the end of my finger touching up all those rough edges on painted buttes and rocky ravines. Had to be careful I didn't press too hard and poke a hole in the scenery. Next question; by the way, you folks in the back, I appreciate all the snickering and giggling I can get."

"Captain Jennings, why did you build such a long trail into the Canyon?" asked a young girl. He had a quick answer. "Oh, I can explain that. I didn't have time to build a short one." Several in the crowd groaned.

"Are there any rats here at the Canyon?" asked the girl's concerned mother.

"Yes, I don't want to alarm you folks, but mind yer valuables—we have trade rats hereabouts. They do all their trading at night."

"What? oh, you mean pack rats," the mother countered, gathering her children a little closer.

"No, trade rats," said Cap. "They deal in good faith, mind you, and in fact do not steal. They believe in fair trade. Sometimes they trade among themselves, just to stay in practice. Most times they remove somethin' of yours and leave somethin' in return."

"Like what?" asked one of the snickering men in back.

"Oh—like a pocket watch or a penknife or a fork or something they removed from someone else," answered the captain.

"Next question? Come on folks; what good are answers if there are no questions?"

A fellow standing off to the side said, "Here's one Captain Jennings. Have you written your biography yet?"

"Why would you want my biography while I'm still alive and kickin'? It would be incomplete!"

"Aw right folks, if there are no more questions tonight, I'll leave you with this little gem to think about. Ya know how old glass windows have ripples in the panes? One in my cabin facing north is so rippled it is telescopic. That's right; if I stand behind it just right, I can see deer and visitors on the North Rim."

With that, the crowd dispersed, with some grumbles rising from the non-believers. One man commented, "I always thought ol' Clancy Jennings had a dim view of the North Rim. I was right."

"He has me worried about Halley's Comet," said another departing guest. "I wonder if he can see it coming through his telescopic window."

***

"Kirby, I don't know Monte very well, but you seem to have a lot of respect and admiration for him," Sabrina offered, as the two rode up the old stage road to the rim.

"We were both raised on farms in southwestern Missouri, but we did not know each other then. I've worked for him on and off here at the Canyon for about twenty-five years," answered Kirby. "He's under-appreciated by most. He dreams of prosperity but realizes life is passing him by and, knowing there is no way to beat the clock, he sees the chances of improving his life's standing dwindling away."

"How sad; he sounds like a man with a lot of regrets."

Sabrina tried to recall the few times she met Monte below the rim. To her, he seemed anchored with sound knowledge and strong commitment. Yet a disconcerting awkwardness hovered about him.

Kirby continued, "Until recently, he never wanted to admit his predicament—that there was a fortune in good ore but it cost a fortune to get it to market—pack burros and mules were just not the answer. History may lose a thrilling story because of Monte's reluctance to talk about himself. He would be the last one to inflate his many achievements. The best record of his life's work lies written in the trails he built, the mines he developed, the tourist enterprises he started; enterprises like the one coming up on our left."

"Is that Monte whittling a stick?" asked Sabrina. When they got closer, they noticed he sat on a wooden case labeled Giant Powder.

"Yes, that's him," answered Kirby, sounding a little jittery. "And that's high-grade dynamite! I hope that case is empty!"

Kirby and Sabrina dismounted, hitched their horses to a perimeter fence, walked past a long pile of cordwood and stopped at the front of the infamous Grand Canyon Hotel. Sabrina had dressed for comfort rather than style. She sported a long, divided khaki skirt designed for trail rides, a light blue blouse and her signature floppy hat and long hair cascading down her back. She clasped Kirby's hand as she leaned against him for support. Monte stood up and extended a hand to Kirby, saying, "I heard you two mumbling about something," but his eyes remained fixed on the attractive Sabrina Jaffa, now Sabrina O'Brien.

"Sabrina, it is so good to see you again." Monte could not recall the last time they crossed paths on the Tonto. "We used to call you the Mystery Lady. Now I understand we should call you the Lucky Lady."

"Mr. Bridgestone, it's good to see you too, and you can just call me Sabrina. I'm no longer a mystery but I am lucky in that I married your old partner here."

"I meant no disrespect Sabrina. I congratulate you both on your recent marriage." Monte directed the couple through the hotel lobby and onto the veranda with the stupendous canyon views and the warm swirling updrafts from below the rim.

Kirby noticed Monte still had a hitch to his get-along. "I see you're still favoring your right foot, Monte. I guess it never did heal properly."

Monte did not want to talk about old injuries. "Kirby, did Jesse Parks help you two through the various issues surrounding ownership of gold? You know about five years ago, Congress passed the Gold Standard Act establishing gold as the only standard for redeeming paper money, so I assume the reverse is true."

Sabrina, picking up the narrative, responded to reinforce that she controlled her fortune.

"Jesse consulted with his gold dealer regarding the process of converting native gold to dollars. I learned a lot about gold. For example, native placer gold is never pure; there can be other metals like copper or silver mixed in, reducing purity and value. I also learned native gold is graded by size, with nuggets commanding a higher premium than what the dealer called flour gold, what I call gold dust. It's rather complicated, but we put our trust in Jesse Parks. And we thank you for recommending him."

"So, what's the verdict? How much gold did you have and what's it worth?" asked Monte, who then apologized for prying into their private lives.

Kirby reached into his vest pocket for a folded paper and explained, "The dealer weighed Sabrina's gold." Reading from some scribbled notes, he reported, "The nuggets weighed four hundred and thirty-three pounds and the flakes weighed five hundred and twenty-nine and a half pounds, for an amazing total of just over nine hundred and sixty-two pounds or fifteen thousand, four hundred ounces. At the average market rate of twenty dollars per ounce, Sabrina's fortune is worth three hundred and eight thousand dollars. After banker and dealer handling fees, she netted an even three hundred thousand in cash, which remains secure in an account in her name at Jesse Parks' Arizona Central Bank."

"I'm impressed, not just in the value, but Sabrina, how did you haul nearly a thousand pounds up the slippery, washed-out Jackson Trail?"

Sabrina had a quick answer. "My two girls—Serendipity and Jenny—did all the work. I hitched Serendipity to your fence out front. Jenny is my trusty mule back at the ranch. They made three trips, each girl carrying a load of over one hundred and fifty pounds on each climb up the trail. I walked."

"If I'm not being too personal, what are you going to do with the money?" asked Monte.

Again Sabrina, with an intriguing smile on her face, had a quick answer. "First, we plan to buy another dozen sacks of oats for the girls!" Monte chuckled.

"Sabrina, do you think you can afford that?" teased Kirby.

Smiling again, Sabrina added, "Then we will complete the purchase of the Circle K Ranch from the Klostermeyers, including the old stage stop at Little Springs."

"My turn," signaled Kirby, looking at Sabrina as he prepared to pitch an idea involving Monte himself.

"Monte, you have often talked about the industrial revolution of the nineteenth century and the way it has led so many to believe anything can be achieved through good ol' American ingenuity, creativity and hard work. I remember hearing how thrilled you were when you accompanied Martin Griggs on his return trip aboard a steam-powered automobile to Flagstaff, a trip that took you back down the stage road, through Red Horse, Cedar Ranch and Little Springs, where we now live, and into town."

"Kirby, where are you going with this? Sabrina, I'm sure you have noticed that Kirby here can be rather long-winded."

Sabrina jumped to the punch line. "Monte, our idea is to buy a fleet of autos so you can compete against Trails West's fancy touring cars." She let that idea sink in. Several minutes passed. "Say something, Monte, what do you think?"

Monte took a deep breath, "You know, when Clint McCarty and I discovered copper on Windsong Mesa, we considered ourselves millionaires in the morning, but lowly prospectors in the afternoon, sitting on the ragged edge of poverty, feeling as blue as the blue limestone we were digging. That's the way it's been through all my days of prospecting and mining. In my later years here at this rustic hotel, hope has given way to despair. Now I have no money, no job, no pride. Your proposal breathes new life into an old prospector."

"Now look who's being long-winded," interjected Kirby, followed by Sabrina.

"No pride? Mr. Bridgestone, you have plenty to be proud about, which brings me to one more idea, and that is to establish a museum of turn-of-the-century life on the South Rim—a place where visitors can feel the pioneering spirit, experience the life and times that men like you endured on the frontier, and take pride in this magnificent place. No one more than you, sir, knows the Canyon is richer in history than it ever was in copper." Sabrina thought she noticed a tear trickling down Monte's cheek.

Kirby added, "Monte, you told me once that hope begins in the dark where you are looking out at the light. We envision that light to be a Grand Canyon Pioneers Museum to inspire exploration, discovery, and achievement through experiences that engage visitors in the history, geology, and natural resources of the Canyon. It would be a tribute to all that is grand, which is far greater than the scale of human intervention."

"See what I mean about Kirby being long-winded, Sabrina?" interjected Monte. Then turning to Sabrina, "Why would you do all this for me?" The downtrodden pioneer rarely showed his emotional side.

"Because you are an upstanding public-spirited citizen; because you maintain high principles and sterling honesty; because you are stronger than a keg of two-penny nails; because you have the steely resolve to fight the double-barreled stupidity of federal control; and because you deserve a break," Sabrina insisted, placing her hand on Monte's arm, "And because Kirby and I can afford to make some of your dreams come true."

"Well Kirby, you have quite a firebrand in this woman. Never let her go. As for you Mrs. O'Brien, I reckon I'd like very much to travel this new trail you are offering me."

"Mr. Bridgestone, I look forward to working with you on these projects. We can discuss details later, but right now let me say with all my heart it will be an honor and a privilege to help you preserve the human history of Grand Canyon while providing an alternate means for folks to visit this grand place."

Chapter Ten

ADMISSION TO THE UNION

Grand Canyon is a sacred place that tugs at the heart and touches the very soul.

In June, Ranger Pat Wyatt escorted Grand Canyon Railway and Trails West officials on a special survey for a new trail and road at Sunset Point. They visited Francois LaRue's camp at Cliffhouse Springs and the site of a proposed hotel near Sunset Creek. Congressman Clint McCarty, seeing Trails West scheming to shut out the Pioneer Trail as it had shut out the Summit Trail, hoped the Forest Service would refuse to grant Trails West a special use permit. Such an operation interfered with valid, though still undeveloped, mining claims on the road to Sunset Point. The Congressman questioned the Forest Service's right to issue permits within a national monument when the intent of that designation is to preserve existing natural conditions.

Although McCarty had his hands full in matters of Arizona statehood, he took the time to draft a strongly worded letter to Chief Forester Pinchot, with a copy to the Interior Secretary. McCarty wrote: "You have refused to grant permits to individuals for similar enterprises. It would not square with the dignity and good faith of your office to grant a permit to a monopolistic corporation."

McCarty continued, "To show the insatiable greed of the railroad and its subsidiaries, I wish to advise you that for some time after Grand Canyon Railway secured control of the right of way to the Canyon, private individuals maintained an excellent hotel at Summit Point. Through various manipulations of the railroad, which desired no competition in the tourist and sight-seeing business, it discouraged everyone from making the trip to Summit and with such success it compelled the owners of the Grand Canyon Hotel to discontinue business."

With President Taft working on his replacement, Pinchot referred the matter to local officials. Meanwhile, Forest officials, agitated by McCarty's stance and opposed to his scenic railway plans, retaliated by issuing a special use permit to the South Rim Improvement Company, a subsidiary of the railroad. The Forest Service authorized construction of an eight-mile rim road, a trail into Sunset Basin, and tourist facilities at Sunset Point and near Sunset Creek. Ranger Wyatt filed the permit in the Albuquerque District office.

Trails West planned to operate the new road as a free public highway for horse-drawn carriages, equestrians, and pedestrians traveling between the Canyon Queen Hotel and a rest station at Sunset Point. Plans called for boardwalks and hitching posts at Promontory Point and Pinnacle Point. The company received permission to construct the Sunset Trail to the river and a camp on the Tonto Plateau.

The permit allowed maintenance of the county-owned Pioneer Trail as a free public highway! McCarty considered this action hostile and discriminatory. He fought back by blocking construction where Sunset Rim Road crossed his mining claims. He secured an injunction against construction across his Old Timer and Evening Star placer claims. The road ended at McCarty's old Wrangler and Muleshoe lode claims at Pinnacle Point. McCarty gloated over the road degenerating into a rutted quagmire in the spring. For the time being, he remained in control—able to interfere with government-sponsored development at the Canyon. But he faced a formidable adversary in the heartless Grand Canyon Railway empire.

The Forest Service became concerned that the public would get the impression that Grand Canyon Railway had masterminded control over the Canyon. It became sensitive to accusations it favored the railroad, but when the subject of the Grand Canyon Hotel's temporary closure came up in ranger meetings, they blamed the hotel's ill prosperity on competition in the tourist trade at the Canyon.

Francois LaRue worked hard to remain on good terms with the Forest Service, which regarded him as a man of notable courtesy. However, when it favored the Grand Canyon Railway and allowed developers to enter Sunset Basin, LaRue became disheartened. Not only did the Railway ignore McCarty's protests, but it intruded into LaRue's "private" canyon domain. Adding insult to injury, Ranger Wyatt offered LaRue ten dollars per month to maintain his own trail to Cliffhouse Springs for Trails West tourists. The disgruntled canyon pioneer saw the proposition as an underhanded attempt to further the interest of the Santa Fe.

The Forest Service viewed the Frenchman as a mighty fine old gentleman, though somewhat peculiar in his views and mannerisms. When LaRue complained about unfair treatment, the Forest Service suggested he may be mentally unbalanced. Disparaged and heart broken, LaRue abandoned his Cliffhouse Springs camp, trails and mining claims, and left Grand Canyon for parts unknown. As he left, the South Rim Improvement Company signed contracts for road improvements to the Sunset Point rest station, trail improvements to Sunset Rapids, and construction of Sunset Creek camp.

The downtrodden pioneer visited the District Forester in Albuquerque. At that meeting, the official said, "Francois, I hope you understand there has been absolutely no attempt to deprive you of the advantages which have accrued to you in constructing your trail to Cliffhouse Springs."

LaRue responded, "Sir, I do not believe you. Ranger Wyatt all but told me Trails West planned to guide their tourists on my trails. I built them. They are mine. Check the records at the County Courthouse! Mine, do you understand, mine!" The mild-mannered old-timer could no longer control his temper.

"Well, that's just the way it is going to be," said the District Forester, "But to counter any hard feelings from this unfortunate incident, I am giving you a letter of introduction to the forest officer at White Springs, Colorado. I suggest you look him up." LaRue tore up the letter, threw the pieces on the floor, and stomped out of the building.

The District Forester turned to his secretary to say, "Whatever offense the old man feels is because of his own fantasy rather than to actual facts. No, I take that back; the fact is he's a squatter and needs to clear out." The secretary rolled her eyes and resumed filing papers.

Learning of LaRue's fight with the railroad and the Forest Service, Monte became more disappointed in his old friend McCarty. Still new to Washington politics but with a seat in Congress as Arizona's territorial delegate, Monte expected Clint to show more concern for the plight of his fellow canyon pioneers. However, Clint wished to bask in the glory of statehood. Created from the western half of New Mexico Territory, Arizona had been knocking at the door of Congress longer than any other territory. Arizona and New Mexico's Rough Rider volunteers in the Spanish-American War would help bolster both statehood causes. Clint cautioned statehood could take several years, but he expected strong support from the Taft Administration.

Trails West scheduled separate daily round trips from the Canyon Queen Hotel to the river, and to what the pioneers called Plateau Point on the Tonto. Another popular trip carried tourists from the Canyon Queen to the river via Sunset Rim Road and the Sunset Trail. The Forest Service seemed to contradict itself by advocating the Pioneer Trail as a free public highway while at the same time sanctioning the collection of tolls.

Having already validated McCarty's rights to the Pioneer Trail, the Arizona Supreme Court sustained his protest. For the time being, the Forest Service withdrew its attempts to exercise any jurisdiction over the trail. It also resolved to approach the congressional delegate more diplomatically, as it needed his consent to use Promontory Point for a proposed memorial to Colorado River explorer John Wesley Powell.

As the years passed, the Grand Canyon Railway and its attendant Trails West Company gained control of most tourist facilities and trails. The government played a major role by discouraging—and eliminating—nearly all other private land holdings and concessions at the Grand Canyon. The men who came first—lured by promises of valuable minerals—found themselves at odds with the government-favored Railway-Trails West consortium and the Federal government itself.

These powerful commercial and institutional forces denied the canyon pioneers and miners their long-sought rewards. To many, the conflict symbolized the classic struggle of the little man against big corporations; history would one day judge the efforts of the frontiersmen just as important as those of the Grand Canyon Railway and Trails West Company in the development and exploitation of the Grand Canyon.

***

One day in mid-March on the rim, a stranger approached Captain Jennings and asked about deer hunting in the vicinity. "Why, it's fantastic," Jennings replied. "I went out this morning and killed two bucks. Right now, the Starlight Hotel kitchen is turning them into venison steaks and stew."

"Well, that's really something," exclaimed the stranger. "Do you know who I am?"

"No, sorry, I don't," admitted Jennings, "a first-time tourist, I presume."

"No, I'm not a tourist. I am the new Coconino game warden here in the president's forests, and it looks like you've broken a few of the game laws!"

"Do you know who I am?" asked Jennings.

"No, I can't say I do," replied the game warden.

"Well, I guess you are new around here. I'm one of the biggest so-and-so liars in the territory!"

"And I'm the other one," jabbed the stranger.

Caught rather flat-footed, Captain Jennings walked over to the train station to meet Teddy Roosevelt. On this visit to the Canyon, Roosevelt and his party would venture down the Pioneer Trail on mules with the Captain as the guide and newcomer Chad Sherman as the photographer.

Chad Sherman longed to travel, and perhaps become a professional photographer. Deciding to capitalize on tourism at the Canyon, he purchased cameras and processing equipment in Flagstaff and started to take pictures of canyon visitors.

"Good morning, Mr. President. Your timing is good. We have very little snow or ice on the upper trails."

"Morning, Clancy; it's good to see you again. It's been about eight years since my last visit and that quick run out to the eastern canyon. This time I've got time for a leisurely trail ride below the rim."

They walked to the Canyon Queen Hotel where the party settled in. An hour later, they mounted mules and prepared to ride. Teddy turned in his saddle and addressed his fellow riders, seven men and three women. "Folks, I'd like to introduce you to the best trail guide and storyteller of the Grand Canyon, the venerable Captain Clancy Jennings. He's been here since the early eighteen-eighties so you can ask him anything."

Clancy loved to wield his authority as a canyon guide, so he issued some stern words of caution. "Ladies and Gentlemen, your mule is very sure-footed and knows the trail better than I do. Mules tend to walk on the very edge but that's so's you get the best possible view. Now, there will be no lollygagging on the trail. No gaps between mules. If you lag behind, your mule will run to catch up. I do not recommend running downhill on a steep canyon trail with tight turns. When your mule comes to a sliding halt at the rear of the mule in front of you, it could catapult you out of the saddle. You'd become a footman instead of a mule rider." Several members of the party chuckled.

Clancy continued, "You men snickering in the back, any questions before we get started? Okay, there being none, let's head over to the trailhead and begin our descent. After the first few terrifying switchbacks, you and your mule will get along just fine."

Teddy, resplendent in his signature knickerbockers, vest and watch fob, astride his mule, enjoyed the trip, grinning all the way, pleased with the actions he had taken as President to set aside Grand Canyon for future generations.

About thirty minutes into the descent, the trail party stopped at a switchback. Teddy traded places with Clancy so that Chad could get a picture of the former president at the head of the line.

"Clancy, in your own words, as Clancy the canyon pioneer, not Clancy the storyteller, what is it about Grand Canyon that makes you want to spend the rest of your life here?" The group waited for their photographer to stow his gear and remount.

"Mr. President, this is a very sacred place that tugs at the heart and touches the very soul. Living here on the ragged edge, or in the rocky depths as I have, reveling in the canyon's sheer immensity and its rugged beauty, has convinced me that there is no place on Earth where I would rather be."

"Well said, Clancy. You have given me further assurance that Grand Canyon will become one of our greatest national parks."

***

Kurt Ritter found his way to the North Rim and settled there. Except during the winter months, he lived in a cabin near a spring in a secluded forest clearing, where he posted a sign: "Ritter's Camp, Guiding and Hunting Parties. Specialty Mountain Lions—Affordable Rates." With snow depths of six feet or more and brutal sub-zero temperatures, Kurt often wintered in Fredonia.

Kurt was somewhat of a recluse, but cherished memories of the few distinguished visitors who happened by. Sharlot Hall, the independent daughter of an ornery, tobacco-chewing buffalo hunter, and her wilderness guide, Seth Westbrook, aboard their heavily loaded Studebaker wagon harnessed to two Arabian ponies, reached the halfway point on her tour of the Kaibab Plateau and the Arizona Strip. They crossed the river at Lee's Ferry where a sign read, "If you want to cross, fire a single shot to get our attention. If you plan to swim, fire two shots so we know to look for your body downstream." They rumbled past shaggy buffalo in House Rock Valley and reached the Buckskin Forest—known for its plentiful deer.

As territorial historian on a seventy-day mission to explore the lands north of the Canyon, Sharlot planned to report her findings to fellow Arizonans. Her crusade aimed to keep the strip from being annexed by Utah. By the time she met Kurt, he was serving as the Kaibab Game Warden. Kurt spent a week showing her the lay of the land—land with its back to the Utah line. Sharlot tried her hand at tracking mountain lion with the legendary hunter but only managed to kill a bobcat, which they roasted for supper.

Kurt guided Sharlot to scenic points, one from which she could see prolific springs gushing from the walls of Skeleton Canyon, parts of the trail to the river, and, straight across on the South Rim, with field glasses, she could see the black smoke of the canyon train. They visited a great peninsula that jutted into the Canyon like a craggy cape on a rugged sea coast. Kurt called it Cape Royal.

From her meetings with stockmen of northern Arizona, and discussions with Westbrook and Ritter, Sharlot realized the importance of predator control. Kurt convinced her that killing mountain lions and wolves saved livestock and increased the deer population for sportsmen.

Her colorful descriptions, written at a time when Arizona statehood seemed imminent, helped convince legislators they should fight Utah's designs on lands north of the Colorado. Her crusade identified the vast timber and mining resources and the ranching potential of the North Rim. Due in part to her promotional efforts, the strip of north country remained part of Arizona.

As the territorial delegate to Congress, Clint McCarty became instrumental in steering Arizona down the long road to statehood. Territorial delegates seated in Congress could debate issues and could serve on standing committees but had no voting rights. Still, he campaigned hard for statehood and never hesitated to remind his fellow delegates that Buckey O'Neill gave his life for another star on the flag.

When the Senate unanimously passed the statehood bill, Clint wired the good news to the people of Arizona Territory. Flagstaff celebrated with bonfires, and citizens danced in the streets. Congratulations flooded Clint's Washington office. Arizona became the 48th state on Valentine's Day. Clint stood at the side of President Taft when he signed the bill. Throughout his two terms in Congress, he served on the House of Representatives' committees on mines, post offices, Indian affairs, and territories—all important to Arizona, and to Clint personally.

Two years after Sharlot Hall's sojourn on the Arizona Strip, the hard-riding Teddy Roosevelt and his two youngest sons returned to the Grand Canyon. They stepped off the train at the South Rim station and made final preparations for the next phase of their journey—a two-week hunting trip on the North Rim with Kurt Ritter as his guide.

On a stifling hot August day, the former president and his party reached the inner gorge. As their trail guide, Cole Campbell had the job of conducting the adventurers to the new cableway. Cole spent most of his time in Flagstaff so had not yet seen the new means of crossing the river but as an early canyon pioneer, he took great pride in being well versed on riding mules down steep trails.

"Mr. Campbell, no offense, but while I applaud your Congressman's hand in achieving Arizona statehood, I resent his rampant filing of mining claims here in the Canyon. He has exasperated the Forest Service and the General Land Office with numerous claims for purposes other than mining."

Cole had no response.

Teddy continued, "And further, I resent his continuing opposition to making Grand Canyon a national park. If you share his views, then we have nothing further to discuss."

Cole found himself in an awkward situation, guiding the Canyon's biggest proponent for park status while fumbling for a worthy response to the former president. Then he looked up at the darkening sky.

"Sir, I think we're in for a change in the weather. There's thunder rumbling on the North Rim and I just saw a flash of lightning." Teddy looked up to see a second flash.

The party had a fleeting look at the river coursing through the gorge, then it became obstructed as the trail contoured along rock walls. To Cole's relief, Teddy changed his line of questioning.

"What do you know about this cable apparatus strung across the river?" Teddy seemed apprehensive about crossing the river, especially during a thunderstorm.

"Sir, I have not studied it but there are two suspension cables between the granite walls supporting a wooden crate large enough to carry a burro or a human. They use a third cable to haul the carriage across."

Cole, about to add that the conveyance depended upon a system of pulleys, stopped short of any further explanation when the cableway itself came into view. The owners had constructed the so-called crate as a sturdy-looking oblong box, its sides and floor wrapped with heavy iron straps.

"Bully, that doesn't look too bad, even in this downpour," said the former president. "If no one else wants to be first, I'll go." His sons, Archie and Quentin, looked the other way, no interest at all in being first to cross the wide, swift-flowing river.

The party had halted at the south terminal. Teddy dismounted and entered the swaying iron-ribbed carriage as a bolt of lightning barely missed hitting the cables. Cole called over to the cable attendant at the north terminal to set the system in motion. Rain came down in wind-swept sheets as the cable sagged lower and lower but stayed just above the swirling current. The journey took only five or six minutes, although the uphill climb to the north side seemed to be a slow process.

"Good afternoon, Mr. President," said the attendant.

"What's your name, feller?"

"Jacob, Mr. President, Jacob Greenfield. How was your ride, sir?"

"Jacob, I'm not the President anymore, you can just call me Colonel." Stepping onto firm but slick ground, he answered Jacob.

"I'll tell ya; hanging out there with dark churning water not far beneath my boots and dark churning clouds above my hat reminded me of a submarine voyage I had in aught-five."

"A submarine, sir?"

"Yes, it's a submersible ship. I crossed the gangway that formed a bridge between a tugboat and a new Navy submarine named Plunger. I chuckle every time I think of that name—so fitting for a vessel that sinks on purpose. I stepped onto the only flat part of the deck while the round-bottomed submarine rolled and bobbed in violent waves that lashed Long Island Sound. I spent an afternoon inside that submarine, including an hour submerged."

"Submerged, sir, I mean Colonel?"

"Yes Jacob, and the crew delighted in having the President of the United States aboard a ship that sat on the bottom, out of sight, out of any means of communication. Ah, but I digress, thank you, Jacob, for not submerging me in the Colorado River."

Teddy watched the others cross until his entire party had landed on the north side. Cole started back up the slippery Pioneer Trail, leading a string of empty mules. Two of Ritter's men stood ready with fresh mules. The rainstorm subsided, and the adventurers journeyed up Skeleton Creek to the North Rim where they met Kurt Ritter.

"Greetings Kurt; I haven't seen you since our buffalo-hunting days." Teddy looked around, then in a low voice asked, "Say, any chance of getting a shot at the big white mountain lion spotted in the forest here?"

Many papers of the day had circulated the white mountain lion story but Kurt first pretended he had not heard about it. The Colonel carried the tattered news clipping in his vest pocket.

Kurt hesitated a moment, then in his ever-present Texas drawl, he responded, "Mr. President, I heard that yarn before too, and took no stock in it."

"Kurt, call me Colonel. I prefer it to President."

Kurt again hesitated as the Colonel guessed his thoughts. "There isn't any such thing, eh?" he said in his rather terse manner. "That news report wasn't true?"

Kurt cautioned, "Well, sir, I've been in this forest many years, and killed many mountain lions here and seen a lot more I didn't kill—and I've never seen a white one."

With that, Kurt, a storyteller in his own right, set the record straight by unraveling how the wild tale came about. "Mr. President, I mean Colonel, let me explain what happened."

"Earlier this summer, a hunting party's pack burro entered their tent in search of food. As the hunters lingered on the rim, watching the sun slip below the horizon, one of them returned to the tent for his pouch of pipe tobacco. Just then a white monster emerged. The startled smoker dropped his pipe and tobacco, and ran back to the rim."

"A white monster, eh?"

"Yes sir. To keep their flour out of reach of critters, the hunters hung the sack from the ridge pole. The burro nibbled a hole in the sack and then busied himself with other eatables, all the while being sprinkled white with sifted flour." Kurt paused a moment, then continued.

"When a newspaperman heard this wild tale, he could not let it go. The press copied the reporter's story of a great white mountain lion and perpetrated an innocent hoax."

Realizing no such animal as a white mountain lion ever existed, Teddy roared with laughter. As it happened, the success of the Colonel's North Rim hunt allowed his party to eat off the land. They found mountain lion meat to be as tasty as venison.

After his return to New York City, Colonel Roosevelt sent Kurt a rifle with an engraved plate that read: "To Kurt Ritter, with the thanks and regards of the Roosevelts." When he returned from his winter quarters in Fredonia, Kurt found that someone had broken into his cabin and stolen his souvenir gun. For the rest of his life, he regretted leaving that special rifle behind.

***

For many years, canyon pioneers talked about the need to replace the flimsy cableway across the four-hundred-foot-wide Colorado River with a suspension bridge. Cole Campbell, Clancy Jennings and Ernst Bergner raised the issue on many occasions.

"I held my breath when I watched Teddy and his two sons ride that rickety cage," explained Cole.

Clancy added, "Ol' Casey and I kicked around ideas before the cableway was installed but could not get past agreeing on a location. We decided a suspension bridge presented a better solution. Ernst, we hoped you and Otto might have had some ideas."

Ernst joined the conversation.

"You fellas came to us many times but the engineering and construction challenges, to say nothing about the cost, overwhelmed us. So here we sit, looking at this cableway, still with no plan going forward."

Clearly, with canyon visitation on the rise, the need existed for a system with the load capacity to carry more than just one animal and a man at a time, perhaps strong enough to carry an entire pack train and a line of backcountry footmen. A suspension bridge, literally a canyon crossroad, would provide the missing link needed to connect the rim trails on both sides of the river.

"Hey fellas," interrupted Clancy, "this is probably an impossible project. Pack animals can carry smaller bridge components but how are you going to get the cables, maybe five hundred feet long, down here? Certainly not by boat and maybe not even by the Pioneer Trail. And the anchorage in rock needs to be carefully engineered."

Cole added, "Another concern is such a bridge needs side rails and it needs to be narrow in case a mule has a mind to turn around midway across the river."

Ernst closed the discussion. "Fellas, we're getting nowhere. Maybe in a few years someone smarter than us will figure a way to bridge this ol' river."

Chapter Eleven

BLACK HUDSON

Follow your dreams; they know the way.

While a presidential proclamation can establish a National Monument, only an act of Congress can create a National Park. California Senator Frank Flint introduced a bill to protect the Grand Canyon in its entirety as a national park, serving all purposes intended by prior proclamations. His bill called for combining Grand Canyon National Monument and Coconino National Forest into Grand Canyon National Park. Flint hoped to preserve the Canyon's superlative scenery and surrounding wilderness for the American people.

Canyon pioneers charged that Flint's bill favored the interests of the Grand Canyon Railway, shutting out competing interests. In addition, they were furious about the Forest Service's plan to collect fees from them for use of trails they built, now encompassed within Teddy's National Monument. Flint's park bill died in committee and canyon pioneers breathed another sigh of relief when Congress shelved the National Park issue for a few more years.

Meanwhile, at Summit Point, forest rangers Bernard Weinstein and Travis Holmes laid out three acres for a rest house and stables. Holmes knew the canyon well, having worked as a Prospector Flats copper miner, a surveyor, and a canyon trail guide. The Forest Service planned similar improvements at Pinnacle, Inspiration, and Tonto Plateau points.

The railroad's improvement company applied for a special use permit for Monte Bridgestone's old Navajo claim at Summit Point. Forest

Service officials determined that the claim interfered with its administration of the forest and questioned its validity. The Canyon Copper Company considered the site as the terminus for a future aerial tramway in the event it reactivated its mines. Trails West, already using Summit Point as the turnaround for one of its most popular carriage drives, wanted the improvements for the traveling public.

A mining expert hired by the Forest Service found the Navajo claim to be non-mineral and, therefore, invalid; but the General Land Office ordered an independent mineral survey. Its inspector found no copper, but discovered enough gold and silver to allow the claim under the national mining laws. Case closed—for the time being.

***

Clancy Jennings became something of a fixture in the Village—a privileged guest around the Trails West hotels. To South Rim visitors, he was a canyon character—always ready with a story. The Trails West people provided him room and board in exchange for entertaining their guests with astounding whoppers. As the one canyon pioneer who quarreled the least with the railroad, or anyone else, Clancy had no concerns with government agencies or business corporations. He lived carefree, self-taught in canyon ways, in control of his own destiny and beholden to no one.

With a large bundle of stories upstairs, just struggling to get out, Clancy expressed himself in endless practical jokes and puns. As one who stretched the truth, indeed twisted it into outrageous tales, he had few equals and not one superior. One time in Flagstaff, while wandering streets lined with buildings butting up to one another, he encountered Otto Bergner.

"Clancy, what are you doing in town?"

He replied, "I'm trying to find my way out of these dang wooden canyons."

When Clint McCarty, ever vigilant, found the developers had cut and cleared six hundred feet of right-of-way through one of his claims, he served notice that the company trespassed on his property. After another two hundred feet, he posted a sign: "Trespassers will be shot, survivors will be shot again." He then sought an injunction because developers had taken it upon themselves to ignore his mining claims.

While McCarty continued to worry about trespassers and the intolerable encroachment on his properties, he considered Chad Sherman an exception, an enterprising man offering a valuable service. Finding his hands full running a photography business in the Village, Chad invited his younger sister to join him at the Canyon.

Heidi stepped off the train and into a bright sunny day on the South Rim. A fashionable straw hat with a dark blue band shaded her luminous violet eyes, freckles dusted her nose, a tight bun of blonde hair showed just under the brim of her hat, but the collar of her dark blue dress seemed to choke her without mercy. Chad, eager to show her the studio still under construction, emerged from the crowd.

"Well, you're finally here," exclaimed Chad, not knowing what else to say.

"That was a long journey from Scranton, Pennsylvania," sighed Heidi. Wanting to get right down to business, she said, "You wrote that photography as a profession required minimal investment to acquire the necessary equipment. But what about studio facilities to house our cameras and tripods and to serve as a place to process negatives?"

Chad hated to admit construction had progressed slower than expected, so he took a more positive approach. "I've got that handled. And I've got a good start on the studio; let's go look. We can come back for your luggage later." They walked over to the edge of the Canyon.

Heidi gasped, "My word, it's clinging to a cliff!"

"Yes, I am calling it Cliffhanger Photo Studio. It may look strange, but I have a crazy notion you will like my plan. There will be a window positioned so we can take pictures of dudes on mules as they begin their descent on the Pioneer Trail."

Chad explained the facility will serve as their photography studio, curio shop and residence. And with that, Chad, with a flourish, handed the keys to his sister.

"After Clint McCarty agreed to our occupying his Battleship Rock mining claim, I started building this multi-story frame building," said Chad, pointing to an imposing frame structure. Staking their reputation on the rim of the Canyon, and, with McCarty as their contentious landlord, the two siblings intended to build a very prolific photography business.

Heidi, quite the visionary, ambitious and intellectual, practiced taking pictures and became a famous canyon photographer hell bent on capturing history with her camera. In some ways Heidi came across as opinionated, but not combative or snooty. Although never married, her past became littered with broken hearts. At this point in her life, she no longer had room in her heart for intimate relationships. Instead, she devoted herself to photography. She produced amazing imagery of America at play—human adventures below the rim by foot and by mule. Some of the earliest views of the inner reaches of the Canyon and historic photographs of early canyon tourists, pioneers and entrepreneurs resided in her collection.

Most of the processing work fell to Chad, who hauled water from Tusayan Well for developing heavy glass-plate negatives. He used one of the Battleship Rock prospect holes in the Kaibab caprock as a darkroom and a place to store unstable processing chemicals.

Heidi, perched high in her studio, excelled in capturing mule riders with her large wooden box-camera. While the dudes explored below the rim, Chad developed the plates and sold prints as mementos for the returning mule riders—proof of the travelers' brazen accomplishments and the canyon's sprawling beauty, all captured on a single photographic print.

Chad and Heidi Sherman seemed destined to continue their thriving South Rim business, photographing trail parties and sharing canyon adventures with thousands of visitors.

***

In October, Monte and Anna Bridgestone, while guarding the Grand Canyon Hotel for the Canyon Copper Company, gave a millionaire an option to purchase their homestead. Publishing magnate William Randolph Hearst, on his way to owning and operating twenty-six newspapers, fourteen magazines, eleven broadcast radio stations, and a motion picture studio, raised considerable speculation. His interest in the Grand Canyon did not seem to fit with his journalistic empire.

Although the Hearst deal would not be closed for a year, Monte felt gratified in finally reaping a return on his investment while imposing a formidable financial empire in front of the Grand Canyon Railway, Trails West, and Forest Service organizations. He also served as sales agent for the Canyon Copper Company, which also offloaded its Summit properties, including the historic hotel, to Hearst. Speculation continued for years about how Hearst might exploit the Canyon. He had no interest in the mines; but perhaps inspired by the Santa Fe Railway, he entertained plans to capitalize on the tourist trade.

***

Despite winter storms, the Santa Fe's roadway construction advanced westward along the rim, and Francois LaRue returned to the Canyon for a visit. It may have been curiosity that drew him back to the South Rim, or maybe a desire to see his old friends, or maybe an interest in celebrating Arizona's impending statehood.

"Bonjour Monsieur Bridgestone; it's been a few years; Francois LaRue here, perhaps you remember me," catching Monte off guard.

"Francois, what a surprise! I never thought I'd see you again. You left the Canyon so suddenly back in aught nine." Monte, with a wide smile, hoped he planned to stay.

LaRue registered at the hotel and Monte assigned him a room with a canyon view, then added, "Francois, when you get settled in, come on down for some coffee and we can catch up on each other in front of the fireplace."

Monte knew LaRue had faced the same issues as he, with the Santa Fe-Trails West monopoly forcing independent entrepreneurs out of business, but he did not know many details of LaRue's situation.

"Monte, I can't say I didn't leave without regrets, because I did. I regret the way the Forest Service treated me. I regret not cashing in on my mines and tourist trade when I had a chance. And most of all, I regret not being able to live out my last days in one of the most revered places in America."

Monte nodded, "I share the same sentiments." Francois continued.

"I left here a disgruntled old-timer when the Santa Fe took over my trails and camps. From here I visited the Forest Supervisor in Albuquerque, a rather persnickety, steely-eyed federal bureaucrat. He had a personality about as prickly as barbed wire. The only consolation from that meeting was a letter of recommendation to a forest supervisor in

Colorado. Some consolation—I tore it into shreds and threw it on his office floor."

"I take it you had no interest in working for the Forest Service," volunteered Monte.

"No interest at all, but I did go to Colorado. Rode the train from Albuquerque with a brief stop in Las Vegas."

Monte interrupted him. "Oh, Las Vegas, I'm familiar with that town. There's a convent and boarding school just to the south, in a little village called San Miguel. When my first wife and I were going through troubled times, I placed my son Ben in the Sisters' custody. Ben is on his own now, working on a ranch in New Mexico. We stay in touch by letter." Monte surprised himself in disclosing so much personal information, then realized it had nothing to do with LaRue.

"I had no idea you had a son, Monte. Let's see, where was I? Oh, the train got me from Las Vegas through Raton Pass to Trinidad, a coal-mining town. I settled there for a while and that's when I developed a plan on how I might lure canyon visitors to the North Rim instead of always taking the train to the South Rim."

LaRue took a few gulps of coffee. "Say, I just realized I'm sitting in one of the oak chairs I designed and built years ago." Francois looked around the room and saw most of his handiwork. "These furnishings I built for you add real character and comfort to this grand hotel."

Leaning back, he continued, "From my canyon stomping grounds, I became intrigued by Point Destiny towering over Granite Gorge on the north side. In fact, when I helped Pierre LeMay, the French topographer, on his mapping expeditions, we went out on that great promontory to shoot survey lines."

"I've heard of Point Destiny, but never been there. In fact, Francois, I'm ashamed to admit that I've never been to your part of the Canyon."

"Well, no offense, but you have missed the best part. While in Trinidad, I advocated a one-hundred-mile extension of the Rio Grande Railway from Marysvale, Utah to Point Destiny. As of now, the developers have completed two surveys and detailed planning for a scenic narrow-gauge extension is underway." LaRue, smiling with pride, reached for the coffee pot.

"Francois, this is a huge undertaking! McCarty and I have been advocating a scenic railway along the East Rim from the Village to Summit Point but we're getting nowhere. Such a line would not only serve tourism but would help put the Shooting Star Mine back in operation."

"Ah, now you're catching on; that's what I'm thinking. With the aim of stimulating interest in the project and working with Union Pacific railroad officials, I've traveled several times between Trinidad and Salt Lake City to promote this great opportunity of interconnecting rail lines so that tourists could visit the North Rim."

"As upset as you are with railroad officials, I'm surprised you are promoting another railroad to the Canyon." said Monte.

"Yeah, I suppose that does seem strange, but I contend it is only from the higher north side where one can see the incomprehensible grandeur of the great gorge. From Point Destiny, well-named as a future rail destination, don't you think? From there, the view is so bewildering in its magnitude and so variegated in its colors and shifting shadows, that neither an artist's paintbrush nor a writer's typewriter can do it justice. Unfortunately, this north side view is now only accessible to the skilled mountain climber."

Monte grinned. "I can see you are very passionate about this concept and if your plan drew tourists away from the Santa Fe-Trails West operation, we'd both raise our beer mugs in celebration."

"And here's the real advantage. Just like your scenic railway idea of serving tourism and mining, the railway extension I have in mind would not only increase tourism in southern Utah and northern Arizona but would open the area for developing new iron and coal deposits. I have just come here from the coal mines in Utah."

Francois remembered something else, not related to his railway plans. "Monte, when I was living in Trinidad, I met an elderly prospector who claimed he lashed three or four cottonwood logs together and drifted through the Canyon two years before Powell."

"Francois, you and I know darn well a flimsy raft like that would come apart in the first set of rapids. I don't believe it is possible," said Monte.

"I didn't believe him either, Monte, but he showed me a tattered San Francisco news clipping proving otherwise."

That's not positive proof; it is probably an imaginative account of what he told a reporter."

Francois tended to agree and asked if his room reservation included supper.

"Ah yes," Monte responded, "and I hope you will stay long enough to help us celebrate Arizona Statehood. Clint McCarty's been working on it for a couple years and it looks like President Taft will sign the bill in a few weeks."

"Sorry friend, I cannot stay that long." LaRue felt he needed to get back to Utah. "When I came through New Mexico a few days ago, they were still celebrating their own statehood."

After a supper of venison stew and fresh-baked sourdough bread, Monte and Francois stepped out on the veranda for a breath of brisk night air. Looking up to the brilliant sky, where the Milky Way seemed to mirror the course of the river, a fireball streaked across the Canyon, turning darkness into light. Monte, pointing to the fading path of stardust, had just one more question. "Francois, do you reckon that fireball hit a government bureaucrat in the Village?"

***

An eastern syndicate, planning to extract placer gold from canyon sand, took over seven of McCarty's Canyon Gardens claims, and twenty-eight additional claims bonded to New York investors. Convinced he would convert his mining properties into a fortune, McCarty boasted, "I always said I would make more money out of the Grand Canyon than any other man."

However, the development scheme faltered when mining surveys showed his claims lacked sufficient gold or any other mineral. As with McCarty's hydroelectric power scheme, the deal completely collapsed when he failed to convey legal title to the claims.

McCarty kept possession of these claims and the whole canyon claim controversy alive by continuing to refile for a patent on Battleship Rock in the Village. This action became the test case whose decision would affect all other claims. The government rejected the Battleship Rock patent application, and sued to enjoin McCarty and other canyon pioneers from occupying, using, or interfering with the public use of land embraced by the Battleship Rock claim. A final ruling, in favor of the government, did not get handed down by the U.S. Supreme Court for a decade. However, with similar rulings in district courts, McCarty's tenuous world of canyon claims came tumbling down like a pile of boulders no longer able to keep their balance.

The hawk-eyed officials of the Forest Service attempted to pit canyon pioneers against one another. The Service continued its efforts to prove the Navajo claim an invalid mineral discovery, contending the real purpose for the filing had always been to control the approach to Summit Point. The claim obstructed the railroad improvement company's plans for tourist facilities under special use permit.

Since the Canyon Copper Company would not consent to any use, Grand Canyon Railway persuaded the Forest Service to contest the validity of the Navajo in court. The company contended that it had purchased the Navajo from Monte a decade earlier and kept the claim, even if it proved to be non-mineral, to protect its valid mill-site, and the improvements associated with the Windsong Mesa mines. Bradley Cooper testified his company began operations just after the turn of the century and eliminated a mile of the old trail from the mine to the rim by building a cutoff under Summit Point. The company then established a pack-train, with freighting headquarters at the Point where they built a log house and a corral.

As officials judged the Navajo invalid, the Interior Secretary overruled the former procedure allowing the Land Office to cancel mining locations before patent application. The Canyon Copper Company pleaded lack of jurisdiction and the Secretary agreed that the Department of the Interior could not annul a mineral location or rule on its validity without a patent application.

***

For several years, automobiles, at first Toledo Steamers but then other brands and models, visited Summit Point. Despite frequent breakdowns, they managed the five-hour drive on the old stage road.

Intrigued by the automobile ever since Martin Griggs' troubled run to the South Rim, Monte set his sights on establishing scheduled auto service to Summit Point. He secured county permission to repair several washouts on the stage road. He discontinued his stage line to Grand Canyon Station and purchased a Hudson touring car for nine hundred dollars.

Bradley Cooper commented to Monte, "Congratulations on your auto purchase. It may lead to increased business and prove the feasibility of an auto stage line."

"Thanks, Bradley, it's the first step in establishing auto transportation between Flagstaff and Summit Point. It will be a test to determine how the machine handles on dirt roads. I look forward to riding the rim road into the Village for the first time, a further test of my auto."

"Monte, follow your dreams; they know the way. And on your drive through the Village, toot your horn as you pass the Santa Fe's train depot, the Canyon Queen Hotel, and the Starlight Lodge. I'm sure you will delight in the reactions of those Trails West folks."

Monte still managed both the Grand Canyon and Summit hotel properties, and traded with the Navajo who drifted up from Coconino Basin, but he remained determined to start an automobile transportation service at the canyon. The Hudson Automobile Company in Detroit City transported his five-passenger roadster by rail to Flagstaff. The magnificent shiny black machine, with an open-air carriage, padded black leather seats and a portable rain-cover for inclement weather, waited for him at the railyard.

On his inaugural run from Flagstaff to Summit, he stopped by the Circle K ranch to show Sabrina and Kirby his new auto. "Well, look at that!" Kirby pointed as Monte chugged through an open gate and came to a stop in front of the O'Brien ranch house. Sabrina ran out to meet her dear friend and his new auto.

"It's beautiful, Monte!" Sabrina, drawn to the five-seat interior, noted the stylish back seat upholstery. "I might have known you would go for stitched leather in a black diamond pattern. It reminds me of the hard bedrock in the Canyon, and all the days and weeks spent scouring the black, diamond-studded granite walls."

"Nothing hard about the black diamonds in these seats," replied Monte, rather impressed by Sabrina's quick analogy.

Kirby, leaning over the hood, looked at Monte. "How's she run?"

"Just fine, and she looks nothing like that horseless carriage that Griggs had back in the big auto race. I'm still learning how to handle her three-speed gearbox and mechanical brakes. Look at this dashboard; I think that's what they call it, with a speed meter, clock, and temperature and pressure gauges. She even has electric head lamps and side lamps. I'm told she has a four-cylinder engine that produces forty horsepower. I wonder if that means it is equivalent to that many horses." Monte could not stop raving about his auto.

Sabrina interrupted the men's conversation. "Can we have a ride?"

Monte planned to motor up the stage road to Summit Point. "Sure, let's all go, but it will be dark if I needed to bring you back to the ranch. I'm not sure I'm ready for a night drive yet." Kirby suggested a short run up the road as their first auto outing. He and Sabrina climbed aboard. Monte made a wide turn and rolled back onto the dirt road. After a mile or two, Sabrina shouted over the engine noise, "Monte, get Heidi Sherman to take pictures of you and ol' Blackie here. Some prints might be useful in promoting your auto transportation company."

"Heidi who?" Monte paused halfway through his turn back to the ranch.

"The blonde photographer lady who has taken up residence in the Village, Heidi Sherman. She and her brother have a picture-taking business there."

"I'll look her up next time I'm over that way. Kirby, your lovely wife is venturing beyond the ranch more than ever now. She's even tuned in to what's going on in the Village."

Sabrina, lifting one shoulder in a shrug, confirmed, "I'm no longer in hiding, Monte."

As the screeching brakes brought the auto to a halt, Sabrina set her feet back on firm ground and broached the subject of a fleet of touring cars. "Monte, let us know when you are ready to order five more autos. Have you given any thought to finding drivers?" Then with a broad smile, "I'll volunteer Kirby to help you get started."

"I'm still working up a business plan. There's a lot more to think about than just the autos. I'll be on my way now. Come up to Summit for a visit soon." And with a double toot of the horn, Monte chugged out the gate and onto the road, grinning and gratified in having good friends like Kirby and Sabrina to cherish.

The couple, clinging to each other like newlyweds, watched the auto disappear in a trail of dust. "Monte seems so much like a loner. I know Anna is there for him, but—"

Kirby interceded, "but there seems to be little romance in their relationship. I know what you mean. Perhaps that's his choice. Perhaps it's mutual. Nothing like the O'Brien household. Shall we retire to our bed chamber?"

"Nice try, no." She contrived to look narrow-eyed and stern. "Let's sit on the veranda for a spell."

"Look at the great orange moon rising in the eastern sky. It's getting dark. Monte may get introduced to night driving before he's ready." Sabrina added, "Oh, but the full moon may help light the way." The only sound was a yapping coyote in the distance.

Kirby changed the subject. "Sabrina, you once told me an unfortunate accident killed your first husband at your Winslow ranch, and for that I am very sorry for your loss. But you rarely mention your second marriage, a different situation I presume."

"Oh, that. Wouldn't you prefer to just sit here and watch that spectacular moonrise?" Sabrina sensed Kirby wanted to know more. "I have told no one what happened because it is so embarrassing and regretful, but I suppose you have a right to know."

Sabrina took in a deep breath. "I was married to my second husband for a very short time. I was on the rebound but we were never passionate. At first, his manner was gentle and respectful, but then he began playing rough, and his advances were always ill-timed." Sabrina refrained from looking at Kirby as she agonized over how much detail she wanted to disclose. She struggled with composing her confession-like recital, but forced herself to continue.

"He was a heavy drinker, but at the same time a light sleeper, and one night after nearly emptying a bottle, he started to act strange, even paranoid, as if he had something to hide. That's when he confessed that he once killed two men in Texas and believed the Texas Rangers had trailed him to Arizona. At first, I thought it was just whiskey talking but his mood changed. Almost immediately he regretted telling me about his murderous deed. He must have thought I would tell the town sheriff."

Sabrina's voice faltered as she described her nightmare. "One stormy night, with raging fire in his eyes, he pinned me down and threatened to kill me if I ever told anyone about the men he killed. Abused and confused, my head throbbing, I could not think clearly. When I felt the knife poking my ribs, I promised to tell no one."

Kirby wrapped his arms around Sabrina as she worked through a long tearful pause. She wanted to shift the conversation away from her horrid past and back to the present, but finally regained her composure. "There seemed to be no end to the taunting, the threats, the misery, the drinking. I was being threatened by a wanted madman."

After another pause, Sabrina continued. "The more whiskey he drank, the worse the situation became. He never stopped threatening me, even during the few times he was sober. If I ever spoke about the

Texas killings, it would be the end for me. If I screamed for help, he promised to kill anyone who tried to rescue me."

"One morning he awoke dazed and dizzy. He staggered to his feet, then keeled over, hitting his head on the woodstove. Seeing this miserable drunk sprawled on the floor unconscious, I realized I could finally make my escape. I saddled up one of our horses and rode into Flagstaff. I filed spousal abuse charges and filed for divorce all in the same day. And that's enough about my terrible second marriage."

Kirby had to say something. "Sabrina, I had no idea you went through such an ordeal."

"Ordeal? that's putting it mildly! I fled to this ranch. The Klostermeyers are good folks and took me in. I worked for them on Saturdays and Sundays, and for Coconino County in the recorder's office on weekdays, staying at a boarding house in town. When papers were drawn up, I was so shaken that I paid little attention to what was written. It turns out I had a sleazy disbarred lawyer from Canyon Diablo. Instead of defending me, he flimflammed me, and I soon realized that he colluded with that rat of a husband, their wretched behavior beyond description. Together, they absconded with my Winslow ranch."

Kirby started to speak but Sabrina shushed him. "That dark nightmare—that harrowing torture in my heart—is over. I am no longer drowning in self-pity and this is the last time I ever want to talk about it. I've put it behind me and that's the end of the story."

They embraced. And the cheerful, playful Sabrina returned. As they entered the house, she added, "And as for you, Kirby O'Brien," wagging an admonishing finger in his face, if you ever—"

Kirby stopped her. They skipped supper and headed straight for their bed chamber. "Not so fast mister. Slow like a soft inner canyon breeze," she beamed. "How's that for setting a romantic mood?"

"How's this?" Kirby tried to outdo Sabrina's literary prowess. "Your eyes shimmer like the golden moon dancing on the Colorado."

"Kirby, stop talking, let's just float away on that ol' river."

***

While Bradley Cooper and Clint McCarty fought their separate wars with the Forest Service, the Trails West Company offered auto tours to Summit, and horse-drawn carriage drives over the Sunset Rim Road. Trails West guides conducted parties down the Sunset Trail, often visiting LaRue's abandoned camp at Cliffhouse Springs and staying overnight at Sunset Camp.

The Federal government, somewhat relieved that Clint McCarty lost his bid to remain in Congress, intended to show the mill-site at Summit Point not being used for its intended purpose. It would again prove the claim invalid. For several reasons, the Canyon Copper Company had not yet begun construction of its planned aerial tramway between Summit Point and its Windsong Mesa mines.

Monte accomplished the obligatory assessment work for the Canyon Copper Company, but he seemed more interested in settling his own affairs. He completed the sale of his homestead to Hearst for thirty-five thousand dollars, conveyance subject to paying off a small mortgage with Otto Bergner. Monte and Anna stayed on as rent-free caretakers.

Reports in the *Frontier Times* confirmed Hearst as the new owner of the one hundred and sixty-acre Bridgestone homestead and the five-acre Shooting Star mill-site, with its historic log hotel and more pretentious wood-frame annex. Hearst, riding in his private railcar, made several visits to the Village. He hired a driver to take him to Summit where he inspected the hotel, mill-site, and other patented land holdings on the rim. He never ventured below.

The Canyon Copper Company eventually sold its mining properties to Hearst for forty-five thousand dollars. Monte's caretaker duties included the hotel and the mines on Windsong Mesa. Speculation grew rampant about Hearst's plans for the properties—a palatial lodge and tourist resort, a private electric railroad, a cable car ride into the inner canyon, a museum dedicated to turn-of-the century life on the South Rim, a hydroelectric power project. Monte, buoyed by all the wheeling and dealing, and the wild speculations, hoped his plans for an auto transportation line would dovetail with Hearst's plans.

Chapter Twelve

A GREAT NATIONAL TREASURE

Strong American will and character always rise to overcome adversity.

The lure, lore and love of the Grand Canyon sustained the legendary canyon pioneers. But with increasing government control of the Canyon, and despite their persistence in the face of adversity, one by one, the pioneers lost their mining and tourism enterprises. As the Canyon transitioned from a National Monument to a National Park, they found themselves being run out of business. With one exception, the government allowed the Grand Canyon Railway and its captive Trails West Company to remain. Chad and Heidi Sherman's Cliffhanger Studio also survived on the rim as an independent enterprise. As for the men and women who opened the region, they lost everything—their claims to the land, their means to make a living, and even their pride.

But America soon gained a great national treasure—Grand Canyon National Park.

Clint McCarty, lying low in Phoenix as an investment company president, acknowledged that Monte had sold out: "I hope you will not leave canyon country; there are only a few of us old landmarks left."

Monte thought his comment rather odd since Clint himself, after allowing his burning ambition to ignite even more political fires, had left northern Arizona. The two had worked side-by-side below the rim but now they seemed worlds apart. Monte now looked with disgust and distrust upon this unyielding, unblinking opportunist with his grandiose plans and speculations for Grand Canyon. With their disagreement stoking discord, their long-time partnership disintegrated.

Far from the Grand Canyon, a major war brewed in Europe, and America, a nation of immigrants, many like Ernst and Otto Bergner who had strong German roots, found themselves in an awkward position. If the United States is drawn into the conflict, it could be fighting against the Bergner family's homeland. By late July, the Great World War had started but so far the United States remained neutral.

Meanwhile, the Grand Canyon Railway, as a common carrier of passengers and as the owner of the station grounds and hotels at the Canyon, filed an injunction against McCarty, Jennings, Bridgestone and others for soliciting railroad patrons. The railway asserted its agreement with the Trails West Company for the privilege of transporting patrons by wagon, carriage or saddle animals to and from points of interest, furnishing guides and offering comfortable lodging. It strongly objected to independents intruding in their business even though these independents built the roads and trails the Santa Fe monopoly used.

On a blustery September day, the Forest Supervisor in Williams received a directive from the District Forester in Albuquerque. The Forest Service had just cancelled six McCarty claims, including Cliffrose and Battleship Rock again. The outcome of a hearing on seventeen others hung in the balance, and at least twenty more still awaited action. The supervisor called Ranger Travis Holmes into his office.

"Travis, while our original instructions were to proceed against only those mining claims which interfere with forest administration, it is possible that having the matter well in hand, we may find it best to clean up the entire claim situation before turning the monument over as a park to the Department of the Interior."

The Forest Service interpreted its mission as the complete elimination of mining and miners at the Grand Canyon. Travis had no doubts about the contempt his supervisor held for so-called squatters, those who held mining claims, even legitimate claims.

"Sir, what would you propose we do?" asked Travis, wondering just how far his supervisor wanted to go.

"We have been challenging that ol' defiant McCarty for years and will keep the pressure on him. I now want to turn our attention to Summit; namely, Monte Bridgestone."

Travis, uneasy, twisted in his chair. "But, sir, you and I know he is not mining anymore. He sold out to that highfalutin' magnate in San Francisco, you know who I mean, Hearst. And Bridgestone has a permit to operate a roadhouse with a general store, livery stables, and feed yard on the forest reserve." Travis paused, wondering if that permit transferred to the new owner. "Anyway, the Canyon Copper Company is probably where we need to direct our attention but they also sold out to Hearst. Bridgestone is now just the caretaker for all the Summit properties. And I might remind you, sir, Monte has served selflessly for years as our unofficial guardian of the eastern canyon."

"Be that as it may, Bridgestone is the instigator out there. I don't care how you do it, but I want him off the reserve." Travis stood up, straightened his coat, and walked to the door.

"Yes, sir, I'll take care of it."

***

The District Court of Arizona refused McCarty an injunction against the Department of the Interior and denied that the courts had any jurisdiction in mining cases at the Canyon. The Court of Appeals of the District of Columbia upheld this view. Here, the court placed in the Department the responsibility of protecting the public against fraud. In effect, it restored the Department as the rightful guardian of public lands, allowing it to deal with fraudulent or annoying claims in the Grand Canyon.

McCarty, always scheming, resurrected his plans for a hydroelectric power generation project. He again sold his Grand Canyon Springs properties and mill-sites to Hydraulic Investment Corporation under a three-year lease-purchase agreement.

A year later McCarty transferred two mill-sites, twenty-seven placers, seventy-four lodes, and every inch of water in the Colorado River, including the Shadow and Sunset Creek tributaries, to his gullible business associates. The scheme collapsed when the eastern investors realized no placer gold existed to help finance the construction of a giant dam. Also working against the deal, authorities questioned the validity of mining claims in the Canyon, an unsympathetic government that shunned granting a right-of-way for power transmission lines, and the Grand Canyon seemingly destined to become a National Park long before the damming of the Colorado. McCarty kept his outrageous claims, unable to reap any monetary advantages as Monte had done with the Hearst Corporation.

Scheming again, McCarty raised working capital by selling his Pioneer Trail claims. Surely the railroad would pay cash to eliminate these long-standing obstacles to their own development plans. The railroad's land development company secretly acquired the Battleship Rock lode, the Thunderbolt and Lightning mill-sites with their precious water sources at Canyon Gardens, and many claims along Sunset Road and Trail. Reluctantly, the railroad paid forty thousand dollars to McCarty who retained all mineral and hydropower rights—in his mind, the rights to control the South Rim and to pursue his grandiose dream of converting his holdings into a fortune.

For many years, because the Grand Canyon Railway monopoly did not want to reveal its embarrassment or to appear as a pushover, this shadowy sale remained a secret.

In the meantime, the legal wrangling continued. McCarty blocked Forest Service plans to issue a special use permit to the railroad for a winter resort at Canyon Gardens and fought plans for a cottage community on the controversial Battleship Rock claim. Though irked by McCarty's continuing impedance to South Rim improvements, the Service stopped short of prosecuting him for trespassing. With local pioneer sentiment in McCarty's favor, the Service elected not to press charges.

With the Hearst Corporation not wanting to operate a tourist facility at Summit, the Grand Canyon Hotel sat empty and abandoned. Sadly, the dormant hotel closed its doors to the public for the last time. Monte, having no tourists to guide, abandoned the Summit trail. With winter coming, he and Anna continued as hotel caretakers. They spent countless lonely days with little outside interaction. But periodic visits by Kirby and Sabrina kept the Bridgestones apprised of any news.

"Monte, it looks like we're headed for war in Europe," exclaimed Kirby, as Sabrina joined Anna in the kitchen.

"What? What's happening?" Monte seemed shocked. "Keep your voice down, I don't want to upset Anna."

Kirby whispered, "I heard a German submarine torpedoed a British passenger ship, the Lusitania, with the loss of twelve hundred civilians, including one hundred Americans. That cowardly act is enraging the nation and propelling our entry into the war." Kirby stopped as Monte wanted to say something.

"This reminds me of the loss of the cruiser Maine in the Spanish-American War," said Monte.

"Yes, and there's a lot of speculation about a second explosion resulting from either igniting coal dust in the Lusitania's fuel bunkers or ammunition being smuggled in the cargo hold." Just then Sabrina and Anna arrived with fresh coffee.

"What are you fellers talking about?" asked Sabrina.

"Oh, I was just updating Monte on news from town," explained Kirby, while glancing at Monte.

"Here's the paper, Monte, with an article by reporter Ryan Perkins who interviewed Mark Warren about his mining days in the Canyon. With so much news dwelling on war and national politics, Ryan pushed for a peaceful human-interest story on the front page. I'll read it aloud."

"Well, I'll tell ya," confided Mark, "since my adventures on the north side of the Colorado, I've had no inclination to travel those trails again. Ol' Ernst Bergner and I are still great friends but we never talk about our mining days. But ya know, I really would like to know what became of those four Navajo mules. Until now I had not thought of them in twenty-five years."

McCarty still hoped he would profit from his canyon holdings, but complained of continuing trouble with the Forest Service concerning South Rim properties and the railroad's ability to manipulate government officials.

Monte, pleased about his own sale and the potential barrier it presented to the Forest Service, said to Anna, "These government bureaucrats may have to switch gears in their well-oiled machinery." Anna shrugged, not quite understanding Monte's statement.

Late one cold and blustery afternoon, Forest Ranger Bernard Weinstein visited Monte at his Summit residence. While still the caretaker for the Grand Canyon Hotel, he and Anna spent most of their time at home. Weinstein, known as a by-the-book Federal bureaucrat, sympathized with the plight of the canyon pioneers, often feeling ashamed of his association with the Forest Service.

Weinstein had become increasingly sensitive to accusations the Service favored the Santa Fe Railway and the Trails West Company, and worse, some government officials allowing themselves to be manipulated or bribed by large corporations.

"Monte, I've come here to warn you. It's Ranger Holmes. You remember him when we were doing a preliminary survey out on the point for rest houses and stables."

"Ah, don't remind me. I resented the intrusion; still do. The Trails West people were seeking a concession out there." Monte dreaded Weinstein bringing up the subject of Trails West's intent to develop Summit Point.

"Monte, I was just doing my job. I'm not here to fight or apologize. And I'm not on official business. I believe something bad will happen soon—something to help sway you to abandon your interests in Summit."

Anna overheard his warning. "Are we in danger, Mr. Weinstein?"

Monte interrupted before Weinstein could answer. "Anna, kindly bring us some coffee and maybe some of that gingerbread you baked earlier today."

Weinstein continued, "As you know, the Santa Fe Railway is a powerful and influential company. And that power extends to their Trails West partner. These monopolies have the financial means to get what they want."

"What has this got to do with Holmes? You know, I never liked him. When he delivered the bad news on our tank, he seemed to revel in lambasting me. I wonder what he is up to now."

"Monte, I don't know," confessed Weinstein.

"Well, what do you know, Weinstein?" Monte, on the verge of losing his patience, continued. "I do not own the mines and hotel anymore."

"Last night I saw Holmes talking to two middle-aged ruffians. When these motley men spotted me, one of them said 'Quiet Sykes' and they quickly scattered. One of the men dropped a piece of paper as they scampered away. I picked it up; here it is."

"Sykes, that name has come up before. I think the late Slim Broadway mentioned two drifters, Morton and Sykes, to me."

Monte held the paper to a lighted lantern. "It's a crude map showing how to get to Summit. What kind of shenanigans are these shifty scoundrels cooking up?" Monte looked at Weinstein with a wary eye. "I think it's time I had a talk with your partner. Care to join me?"

"He'll be at the Tusayan Ranger Station tomorrow. I'll meet you there, say ten o'clock." Just as Weinstein stood up to leave, Anna arrived with fresh coffee and gingerbread.

"Hold up, Bernard, you can't leave now, not without sampling Anna's baking. Better yet, we've got empty rooms. Why not stay overnight, our treat. I'd like to talk to you more about the government siding with large corporations to the detriment of private enterprise—a peaceful conversation, mind you."

"Monte, since it is getting late and I'd be traveling in the dark, I accept your invitation." He took a sip of coffee. "That is if you are not too hard on this frustrated bureaucrat."

"Bernard, nothing personal but my fight with the Forest Service has been all about holding onto assets that I had legitimately accrued. And that included this homestead where we now sit; well, I sold out, but it had been a real fight to keep our place. When President Teddy Roosevelt visited Summit back in aught-three, he was none too pleased with us pioneers. He must have had a change of heart because he signed the Forest Homestead Act allowing citizens to settle on land within national forest reserves. Ranger Pat Wyatt had encouraged me to proceed with a homestead survey and application, which I did. Teddy himself signed my homestead certificate."

"Oh, you know Pat? He's a good guy; serving in another district now." Weinstein paused. "Monte, this is really not about your old homestead. It's about the proliferation of mining claims and how they have interfered with our administrative control of Grand Canyon."

"I know, Bernard, I had to get that off my chest." Monte felt he and Bernard could be good friends.

"I must say Clint McCarty is not helping your situation." Bernard hesitated, trying to choose his words carefully. "That flinty troublemaker not only gives you pioneers a bad reputation, but he's trying to claim the entire canyon for himself!"

"Clint and I have had a falling out on that very subject. We've had several heated arguments. Everyone knows he's filing claims for purposes other than for mining and then trying to sell them! Strong American will and character always rise to overcome adversity, but he's so hard-headed I can no longer reason with him."

"Yep, that's McCarty all right. It is almost as if he hopes to stop this grand place from becoming a National Park. Even Teddy's presidential proclamation establishing Grand Canyon National Monument has made no difference. I wish you could reason with him, Monte."

"In one respect, Clint has a point. We do not believe the Forest Service has the authority to issue permits within a National Monument, the intent of which is to preserve the existing natural conditions."

"You got me there, Monte. I am confused about that myself. I've asked my supervisor about it and he shrugs it off as nothing important. And you probably noticed the Federal government is not perfect. We're at fault too. The General Land Office found out the hard way it has no right to examine mining claims before they are brought up for patent."

"I'd like to get back to the struggle of the little man against big corporations. Bernard, your agency is right in the middle of this conflict. You once told me it makes a big difference to the Forest Service if a man or a company has money. That's bothered me for years. I figured that's how Trails West could use Summit Point as a way station."

"I do recall saying that. I never liked the situation, but it was happening way above my level. I regret to say, it's still going on. Grand Canyon Railway and Trails West are in cahoots. They come to us strongly objecting to independents intruding in their business, even though it is you Monte, and your fellow pioneers, who built the roads and trails that those monopolies use today. Some say you are trespassers and could face prosecution. Perhaps it is the government that is the trespasser." Weinstein paused, then added, "I feel like I'm making a big confession."

"Bernard, I do not blame you. We've had a good discussion tonight but have solved no problems. At least we are closer to understanding each other. But it's getting late. I'll have Anna show you to your room. Let's meet for breakfast before riding to Tusayan Ranger Station."

***

With his squinty eyes and high-strung demeanor, and a six-gun on his right hip and a Bowie knife on his left hip, Sykes looked like an outlaw. Morton saw him as a bundle of nervous energy, jittery and edgy, as the two hung around the railroad depot.

"There they go," said Morton, pointing to several Forest Rangers boarding the train. "I see Holmes but no sign of Weinstein. I thought you said they were all required to attend an emergency meeting in Williams. Dang it, Sykes, I hope you have your information right."

Morton always ragged on Sykes. The easy-going Canyon Diablo train robber relished teasing his partner. It's a wonder the two drifters endured each other's company and traveled the same outlaw trail together.

"Let's head out to Summit, Sykes. Where's that map Holmes gave you?"

Sykes searched his pockets, hat band, boots. "You lost it? You fool. I should have taken it. All I know, we need to go east along the rim about fifteen miles. Let's get started."

***

Monte and Bernard Weinstein arrived at the ranger station about mid-morning. To their surprise, they found the building empty, except for Edna, the part-time secretary. Monte already felt he had made the trip for nothing.

"Bernard! There you are. Everyone has been looking for you but just could not wait any longer."

"Where are they? Why are they waiting for me?" Edna explained the emergency call for a meeting at the Williams office and the need to catch the morning train. No one knew about the meeting until early that morning. Bernard felt bad about dragging Monte to the Ranger Station and the lost opportunity to question Holmes about his meeting with the local riff-raff. He apologized to Monte, and they parted ways.

Monte started for the hitching post, shaking his head in disgust, not so much regarding Weinstein, but disappointed in the corrupt Forest Service.

He grumbled, "I guess this is a lost cause. No one will listen. The government will have its way."

Over all these years, Monte longed to take on the government, but now he could not even take on Ranger Holmes. Most regarded Monte as a common man, passive but passionate, chock-full of determination, with an extraordinary amount of heart trying to do something he strongly believed in.

Monte stopped in his tracks, looked back at the ranger station—a symbol of what government has become. He shouted, "Just leave me alone!"

Weinstein came to the door. "Just leave me alone, Mr. Forest Service. I have rights too. My life has value. And you will not take away everything I have worked for." Monte's emotions bubbled to the surface, a breakdown in the making. As if spouting fire, his scathing remarks sizzled on the Ranger Station doorstep.

Weinstein closed the door, sat down at his desk and penned his letter of resignation.

Monte, always willing to plod along in life, believed the government would eventually do the right thing. The missed meeting with Holmes, the long, fruitless discussions with Weinstein, the endless fight against government harassment—all amounted to nothing. Any agreements seemed to have the permanence of an early morning frost.

Monte felt tired, downtrodden and totally discouraged, but he made it back to Summit without incident.

***

Monte set another log on the fire. He glanced at the calendar on the fireplace mantle. "Anna, it's still September but already there is a chill in the air." Dark heavy clouds moved in. He and Anna sat in the rocking chairs of their cozy cottage near Summit Point; Anna knitted a sweater; Monte tried to read an old newspaper but could not concentrate. His dark mood matched the deteriorating weather. Restless ponderosas swayed and a lower branch scratched the roof. A lonely whistle sounded as the wind gusted across the cottage chimney.

"Anna, I think there's a storm brewing tonight. I'll check the windows and doors," said Monte as he left the room. Ten minutes later he returned to report the faraway rumble seemed diminished.

He seemed lost in thought. The crackling in the fireplace must have sparked his imagination as he rambled about how he regretted the government allowing big corporations to take over.

Anna piped up, "Monte, are you wallowing in self-pity again?"

"I reckon so. I feel like a relic of the distant past." The air seemed heavy with burning thoughts neither wanted to express. "I'll just spend my remaining days in dreams of yesterday and of what could have been."

Monte glanced over to a window on the east side of the house and seemed startled.

"What's wrong? Did you see something?" Anna stopped knitting.

"For a moment I thought I saw a yellow glow out the window." Monte got up to inspect.

"It's probably just the reflection of flames in the fireplace." Anna resumed her knitting.

Monte shouted, "Oh no, it's a fire! It looks like the hotel is on fire! Anna, stay here and pray for rain!"

Monte plunged his feet into his boots, grabbed his raincoat and hat, and rushed outside. Despite the dark, he knew the quickest route to the hotel. He arrived on the scene in record time and found the entire east end of the log hotel and two wood-frame sheds ablaze.

He first tried to bail water from Kirby's cisterns under the roof line, but he could not bear the heat while dipping buckets. He rushed over to the horse trough and made a dozen bucket runs. But his efforts seemed futile. The fire roared; giant flames curled around rafters and the cedar-shingled roof. The interlocked logs of both corners of the east wall glowed red. Flaming shingles dropped onto the upstairs floor and started the rooms and the easternmost dormer ablaze. Log rafters and burning debris dropped to the ground floor and set the thick planks on fire.

As Monte envisioned a total loss for the twenty-year-old rustic hotel, a thunderous cloudburst dumped rain on the fire. Log walls sizzled and puddles formed on the wood floor. The rain came down in windswept sheets. The system rumbled across the Canyon and parked itself over Summit, drenching Monte's old homestead and Hearst's log hotel. Fortunately, the storm spared the windward portion of the hotel. Confident that the storm had doused the fire, Monte slogged his way back to the house where Anna waited for some news.

"Oh, thank God you are okay. Has the hotel burned down?" asked Anna, holding the door open for her dripping firefighter.

"Not the whole building, I'd say about a third. I won't really know until it gets light. Some out-buildings are gone but I think the annex is okay. What I want to know is how did the fire get started; the building is vacant, and no one has been around here for weeks." Monte dropped his wet coat and hat at the door and moved to his rocking chair to remove his muddy boots. Anna handed him a steaming mug of hot chocolate.

Shortly after sunrise, Monte returned to the hotel to assess the damage. Heavy smoke still lingered in the air, diffusing the morning sunlight. The skeleton of Kirby's stone chimney marked all that remained of the east end, which once comprised several rooms, one dormer and the upper floor. The log walls, a burned-out shell, showed no signs of door and window frames. The fire reduced the oak tables and chairs of the east dining room to piles of smoking ashes. And in one pile lay a human body, blackened beyond recognition, and a Bowie knife sticking out of its chest. Monte suspected arson and immediately thought of Sykes or Morton.

He continued to survey the damage, stepping lightly around shattered window glass and charred shingles. A sour stench hung in the air as Navajo rugs and wolf skins lay smoldering on the floor. His private museum with crystalline stalactites and blue mineral specimens from the mines seemed undamaged. He stepped outside and noticed several badly singed ponderosas near the hotel. At one point the risk of a forest fire must have been high.

***

Postrider Teresa Cordova had started her mid-morning run to Summit. She made good time despite the wet rim road. Mail to the eastern part of the Canyon always seemed sparse and sporadic to Teresa, but she seemed determined to deliver the few letters and newspapers. Suddenly from around a bend came a rider slapping leather and pushing his horse to the breaking point. The distance between the two closed quickly. Teresa caught the stranger going for his six-gun. Before she could draw her own, he fired and missed. Her shot did not miss, and the desperado fell to the ground.

Teresa reined up, dismounted and ran over to the fellow, squirming in pain and bleeding profusely from his chest. "Who are you and why did you take a shot at me?"

"Help me, I'm shot. I need help." The man tried to get up but fell forward, grabbing Teresa as he went down.

"I'll ask you again. Who are you and why did you fire at me? I'm a Federal mail carrier and I want to know who I'll be turning over to the sheriff." With Teresa losing her patience, the wounded man seemed to fade in and out of consciousness.

"Morton, my name is Mor—" With one final gasp, the bushwhacker died. Teresa rounded up his horse and pulled the body across the saddle. She cancelled her mail run and headed for the old stage road, trailing the shooter behind her. The mail for Summit could wait another day. She needed to report the incident to the Sheriff's office in Flagstaff as a case of self-defense, a deadly encounter with a desperado running from something.

The cause of the fire remained a mystery. The coroner could not identify the body as Sykes but Monte had his suspicions. Ranger Holmes never returned from Williams and Ranger Weinstein, last seen boarding the eastbound express in Flagstaff, must have retired from the Forest Service.

Monte roped off the burned-out section of the hotel and outbuildings. The remaining two-thirds of the Grand Canyon Hotel lay dormant, a symbol of a bygone era when proud pioneers built trails, established tourist enterprises and tapped natural resources while preserving the awesome natural beauty of the Grand Canyon.

***

The legal wrangling over control of the South Rim stemmed, in part, from the government itself. Congress could have solved many of the problems and government inefficiencies if it had passed legislation elevating Grand Canyon from a national monument to a national park.

Even old "landmarks" like Monte Bridgestone and Clancy Jennings came around to the national park concept. A step in this direction took place in late August—the establishment of the National Park Service within the Department of the Interior, with a forty-nine-year-old, politically connected conservationist named as its first director. Like Teddy Roosevelt, he believed in protecting magnificent scenery from being developed for residential or commercial purposes, but unlike Teddy, he favored railroads for conveying visitors to remote parklands and rustic tourist lodges near the rim.

While the Secretary of Agriculture still questioned the location of mining claims and still maintained its charge of the National Monument, the newly created National Park Service seemed more reluctant to question claims.

One day, the Director, while touring the East Rim, commented to Monte, "It is not our custom to harass those owning private lands within a National Park. We fully recognize their rights just the same as if there was no park."

Chapter Thirteen

SPIRITUAL LAND WITH MAGICAL POWERS

Living at Planet Earth's Grand Canyon is like living in Heaven, which surely must boast another Grand Canyon within its environs.

As the United States declared war on Germany, Arizona's members in the sixty-fifth Congress introduced bills to set up Grand Canyon as a National Park. The state's first congressman, serving at-large, Carl Hayden, sponsored legislation in the U.S. House of Representatives. On the Senate side, the flamboyant Senator Henry Ashurst sponsored similar legislation. Former Tombstone attorney, Senator Marcus Smith, also supported the park bill.

Congress passed Senate Bill 390, steering Grand Canyon toward its rightful place with Yellowstone and Yosemite national parks. The legislative sponsors took care not to offend northern Arizona residents. They proposed a small park—encompassing the main canyon, tributary canyons and narrow strips of forest land on the rims—and tried to protect existing interests by allowing valid mining claims to stay in force.

Several years before the park bill passed, Monte's letters to his son urged him to join him in canyon country. Finally, Ben returned to Arizona and filed a one hundred-and-thirty-five-acre forest homestead claim in the Coconino Basin. With uncertainty hanging over Summit properties, Monte felt relieved to have family close at hand. Ben set about developing a ranch just outside the proposed park boundaries.

To channel labor toward the war effort against Germany, Congress suspended the need for assessment work on mining claims as long as claim-holders filed notices they intended to keep their claims.

The new park would encompass over six hundred thousand acres including patented lands—McCarty's twenty-five acres, Keystone's one hundred and sixty acres, and Hearst's one hundred and sixty acres. The bill included provisions granting concessions for hotels, camps and transportation in the park to the most responsible bidder—which turned out to be the Trails West Company. It stipulated any mining and hydroelectric power development required prior approval of the Interior Secretary. The bill allowed valid mining claims and protected the rights of individual property owners within the park boundaries. It also instructed the Department of the Interior to buy the controversial Pioneer Toll Road from Coconino County.

***

On the North Rim, Kurt Ritter drew several of his former associates from Texas to his canyon realm, especially during the summer months. Some of these young Texans had just returned from service in the Great War. They looked up to Uncle Kurt while growing up on Panhandle ranches and still held the pioneer in high esteem. Kurt considered all of them as adopted sons.

After his long years on the plains, Uncle Kurt developed a furrowed forehead, creased from constant squinting, and his skin was sun-beaten and leathery. The frontiersman lived like a spiritual descendent of Daniel Boone and the men of the long rifle—one of the last wilderness hunters.

***

In December nineteen-eighteen, Cole Campbell died in a Phoenix hospital, Levi Jackson died in the small Arizona community of Taylor, and the venerable Clancy Jennings entered a Flagstaff hospital.

Cole, still employed by the Flagstaff water department, had been ill most of the summer, but his sickness did not seem life-threatening. A few days before the end of the Great War, with no observed improvement, friends took the canyon pioneer to Phoenix for treatment. There, doctors diagnosed Cole as suffering from kidney disease in an advanced stage of development and offered little hope for recovery. Late one evening, with his wife Amanda at his side, Cole Campbell passed away.

Following funeral services, Flagstaff citizens gathered for a graveside ceremony in the Knights of Pythias section of Citizens Cemetery. They remembered Cole as an honorable man of a quiet, retiring disposition, a loving husband and father, a pioneer stockman of northern Arizona, a conscientious public official, and an early explorer of the Grand Canyon. He labored long and hard on early canyon mines, helped blaze the first wagon and stage roads, and shared his concerns about the government siding with the Santa Fe-Trails West coalition.

Monte recalled, "Despite his modest Canadian demeanor, he never faltered in his support of his fellow pioneers' fight against favored big corporations and government intervention at the Canyon. He devoted most of his younger days to blazing new trails, enabling those who followed to experience the Grand Canyon he loved and treasured."

Although not known at the time of Cole's death, within hours Levi Jackson also passed away. In his later years, his eyesight failed, and he became dependent on Molly for moving about. His family laid him to rest in the Mormon town of Taylor, about one hundred miles southeast of Flagstaff as the proverbial single-minded crow flies. His rewarding years of frontier life and his importance in the eastern part of Grand Canyon and the Little Colorado River Valley went unheralded by Flagstaff citizens.

The health of the canyon patriarch, Clancy Jennings, deteriorated as influenza ravaged the nation and reached pandemic proportions. The Trails West people cared for Clancy at the Starlight Hotel for as long as they could, but then felt it best to arrange transportation to Flagstaff for the frail and weak storyteller. After a month's stay at the Weatherford Hotel, he became helpless. In early December, he entered the County Hospital for the Indigent. On the same early January day, both Captain Clancy Jennings and Colonel Teddy Roosevelt died.

When Monte heard the tragic news about the former President, he commented to Anna, "Death must have taken Teddy while sleeping. If he had been awake, I'm sure there would have been quite a fight." The last trail ride for Teddy and Clancy together took place eight years earlier when they descended the Pioneer Trail on mules. The legendary canyon pioneer who cut the first trails along rock ledges and the American President who long advocated protecting the Canyon as a national treasure did not live to see Grand Canyon National Park become official.

Clancy Jennings had but a single wish that if he went to heaven, it would include a Grand Canyon within its environs. All his canyon friends paid their respects at the funeral service held under a shed roof near the Grand Canyon Railway station. Interred in a small plot east of the Canyon Queen Hotel, the site became known as the Pioneer Cemetery. The caretaker spaced Clancy's headstone and footstone ten feet apart to accommodate his tall tales. While Clancy rests in peace, his stories refuse to do so. The man devoted half of his life to the Grand Canyon. Unlike Clint McCarty, he claimed only a small part for himself, but the Canyon claimed all of Clancy Jennings.

Otto Bergner delivered the graveside eulogy. "Clancy was so outgoing it took him hours to stroll the short distance between the Canyon Queen Hotel and the Starlight Hotel. He stopped every few feet to chat with folks. He used to say he never met a person he didn't already know. He had an uncanny way with words, an infectious high pitch laugh, and an endless trove of wild tales. He was a free-spirited maverick and a trailblazer, but above all, a reckless storyteller. For Clancy's sake, I hope there are canyons in heaven."

In February nineteen-nineteen, President Woodrow Wilson, already responsible for creating the National Park Service, signed the bill making Grand Canyon National Park official. There were forty-four thousand visitors to the park that year. The National Park Service would forever exercise the administration, protection and promotion of Grand Canyon, under the Interior Secretary's direction.

Only a week after Grand Canyon National Park became official, Monte suffered an unexpected death in the family. The influenza pandemic claimed the life of his thirty-year-old son. Three months later, the government granted Ben Bridgestone's forest homestead. Monte had hoped that Ben would be there when he and Anna could no longer care for themselves, and could administer his estate when he passed. Instead, Monte had to administer his son's estate—the Coconino Basin Ranch—where he and Anna would later live out their remaining years.

Kurt Ritter—the North Rim's only celebrity—never filed for a forest homestead, but with permission from the government, he moved his buffalo from pastures in the forest and House Rock Valley to various places in the park, including the Walhalla Plateau. He presented a plan for a tourist camp on Walhalla's Cape Royal to lodge twenty visitors, with fifty buffalo nearby as a tourist attraction. The government denied permission since it had already contracted with the Trails West Company to offer such services, although the company had no plans for hotel, camp or trail development on the North Rim.

In the days of the Forest Service, Kurt could use discretion; but under the new National Park Service, decisions had to come from distant men in Washington swivel-chairs. The former Kaibab game warden, bounty hunter and guide retired in House Rock Valley where he tended his buffalo herd. While so many frontiersmen had grown hard and brash in their declining years, the seventy-year-old grew mellow and content as he reflected about his life journey. Kurt, with a droopy white mustache, twinkling blue eyes and a week's growth of stubble on his square jaw, conjured up treasured memories of the past. He spent his days smoking his pipe and gazing at his snorting buffalo, symbols of the frontier's glory days when great herds roamed free. In time, a nephew moved Uncle Ritter to his place in Afton, New Mexico, a lonely whistle stop on the Union Pacific railroad, halfway between El Paso and Deming.

***

Feeling well-settled in her photography business, Heidi Sherman ventured beyond her studio window at the Pioneer trailhead. With increasing concern about aging canyon pioneers after the recent loss of Clancy Jennings and Cole Campbell, Heidi became inspired to embark on a new photography mission.

A chance overhearing of their names caught Heidi's attention—just a snatch of a brief conversation between staff workers at the Starlight Hotel.

"Have you heard the curious story of two old-timers in a gunfight with only one gun?" asked one worker.

"I reckon not. I don't see how that is possible," answered the other.

"Well, it involved Clancy Jennings and Cole Campbell. The two got along fine until they launched into a heated argument about trail-building. They decided to settle the matter by shooting it out, but they had only one gun. So, they agreed to draw straws and take turns shooting. Cole lost and stood in the doorway of that cabin over there while Clancy, who had been drinking, and finding himself in a semi-liquid condition, fired a shot—and missed. When Cole took careful aim, Clancy turned tail and ran. From then on, Cole reminded Clancy of the bullet he still had coming."

Heidi giggled, "How ironic, the two legends had just passed away and Cole never took that fabled shot."

Such wild tales tend to get lost under dense layers of history. Although not a writer, Heidi could at least do her part in these waning days of the wild frontier. She could help preserve the lives and times of the canyon pioneers—with her cumbersome box camera. It bothered her there may not be much of a photographic record of several departed pioneers, not just Clancy Jennings, Cole Campbell and Levi Jackson, but Buckey O'Neill and Stuart Casey, who died years earlier, and the mysterious Francois LaRue who simply vanished.

With brother Chad taking over the daily task of photographing mule-riders, Heidi selected Summit Point as a logical starting place, before the historic complex became completely abandoned or destroyed. She borrowed a one-horse buckboard, loaded her camera and her box of heavy glass plates and headed east along the rim, hoping Monte and Anna still served as caretakers at the historic Grand Canyon Hotel. Heidi not only found them there but also Kirby and Sabrina O'Brien, who had arrived ten minutes earlier after a morning trail ride.

"Monte, here comes Heidi Sherman, the professional photographer I told you about a while back," said Sabrina, pointing to the buckboard.

Kirby greeted Heidi and introduced her to Monte.

"So, you're the famous photographer lady I've been hearing about," said Monte.

"I don't know about famous, but I am a photographer and I'd like to take pictures of you and Anna in front of the hotel with the Canyon as a backdrop." Heidi added, "Sabrina and Kirby, don't think for a minute you're going to escape my camera." Heidi planned her shots so as not to show the fire damage on the east end of the building.

After several group shots and a single shot of Monte leaning against his Hudson touring car, Anna served lemonade and cookies. Anna seemed her usual quiet and reserved self, but Monte seemed eager to engage in conversation. "So, I understand you are hoping to photograph all us old-timers while we're still alive and kicking."

Heidi explained, "That's my plan but I could use your help in directing me to the right people."

Monte turned to Kirby, "Does ol' Levi Jackson come around anymore? Last I talked to him he and Molly had settled over in Taylor." Glancing back at Heidi, "Levi may no longer be with us but if he is, you must set aside a few days to find him."

Sabrina answered for Kirby, "He's gone, Monte; we thought you knew. I had the good fortune of meeting him on the old stage road some years back. Later I heard from Molly that Levi, at age one hundred and one, had traveled his last trail."

Kirby interjected, "And Heidi, there's that slithering Clint McCarty, but he will not be easy. I believe he's still mired in Washington politics."

"And don't forget that ornery loner, Dan McLain. I saw him out this way a few days ago," Monte reminded Heidi.

"Well, I've got my work cut out for me," Heidi confessed. "I know nothing about McLain."

As Heidi packed up her camera and gear, Monte filled her in. "He lives in the Coconino Basin now, east of Navajo Point, in a cabin just off the road. The Village got too crowded for ol' Dan, and well, he is a loner like me. However, also like me, he was interested in capitalizing on modern-day life. Being a roadbuilder, Dan took a liking to automobile transportation and even established a motor court at Tusayan Well. But he was in for a fight with park officials."

"It's worse than that, Monte," offered Kirby. "Dan told me he built most of the roads around the Village, but with Grand Canyon becoming a national park, they fell under the unfriendly scrutiny of the Park Service which barricaded some of them. They took the position Dan's roads diverted tourists away from South Rim enterprises like the Starlight and Canyon Queen hotels. That's when Dan, seething with anger and feeling unappreciated, moved out here on the East Rim."

"But Monte, you saw him recently?"

"Yes Heidi, he's running several teams with road scrapers and a Navajo crew for pick-and-shovel work to build a passable county road between Grand Canyon Village and Navajo and Hopi villages. In fact, the new road goes right past my son's homestead."

"Your son, oh Monte, I was so sorry to hear he passed away at such a young age. Please accept my belated sympathies." As Heidi finished packing up her equipment, she thanked the group for their cooperation and encouragement. Sabrina walked her back to her buckboard. The two lingered in conversation, women talk no doubt.

"You know, Kirby, there are few old-timers like Dan McLain around anymore," said Monte, as they watched the two women. "I've known him a long time. He was working as a rancher and living with his wife and daughters in a cave on the Coconino. In those days, we pioneers did not feel we were sacrificing our dignity by taking advantage of such rudimentary shelters."

"I worked for that cantankerous old-timer on a few occasions," said Kirby. Monte seemed surprised but let Kirby continue, knowing he may have instigated a long spiel. "He used to regale me with canyon facts. Dan took on a younger partner; I can't remember his name right now, but together they added an automobile campground to their

Tusayan complex, with cabins renting for one dollar a day. The partners had a gasoline filling station, a general store, a coffee shop, and even a dance hall. Located three miles from the Village, they promoted their private establishment by claiming it rested on solid footing, a safe distance back from the dangerous rim of the Grand Canyon."

Monte added, "A forest ranger station sits there now." His own statement reminded him of his last outburst with Ranger Weinstein and past struggles with the Forest Service.

As Heidi headed back to the Village, Sabrina rejoined the conversation. "Heidi has quite an endearing personality. What are you men talking about?"

"You first, what were you women talking about?" countered Kirby.

"We were discussing how the government seems committed to resolving cases of private settlement within Grand Canyon National Park, even though the act creating the park reaffirmed the rights of resident landowners. For example, take Dan's roadwork; the government contends he never registered the roads with the county, so they were not official."

Kirby interjected, "Sounds like an excuse to close his roads."

"Yes, and now the government is threatening further use by Dan McLain, casting him as a trespasser on government property!" Sabrina shook her long braids in disgust. "It's just not right."

"That's what we were discussing—how the government ran Dan out of business and forced him to take up residence just outside the park, but as we know, he's at least still keeping his hand in roadbuilding," commented Kirby.

Monte, peering at Kirby over the rim of his coffee mug, said, "I remember Dan talking about the purchase of a seven-passenger Studebaker automobile for fifteen hundred dollars. I think the high cost deterred him, but his plan would have worked, especially with his auto experience."

Sabrina perked up. "Now see Uncle Monte, that's what you need to do—get that Flagstaff-Summit automobile line going and you can have a profitable enterprise. I hope it is not too late." Sabrina added, "As you know, Kirby and I are ready to help."

"Yes, ma'am, I'll get to it!" replied Monte, then squirming in his rocker, he added, "Before we turn in, I'd like you two to hear something from me." Kirby and Sabrina had that worried but quizzical look on their faces, wondering what Uncle Monte had on his mind.

"Despite all the government harassment, despite the loss of most of what we worked so hard for, despite the fighting and bickering that has taken place over the years, one great thing has happened through it all." Monte had their undivided attention.

"This is one of the most spectacular places in America, and while I do not agree with how it was done or how we pioneers were treated, we now have Grand Canyon National Park. This Canyon was the most magnificent place when I came here, and it will be the most magnificent place when I leave here. We need to cherish this wondrous treasure, its natural resources, its rich history and its romance as a sacred American heritage. More to the point, we cannot allow greedy men or corporate interests to steal our canyon country. Under this vaulted Arizona sky, we have a spiritual land with spiritual power—magical powers that can draw folks into its dizzying depths—and it will be here for many generations to come. It's been an honor and a privilege to live on the edge of such spell-binding geography."

During an awkward pause, Monte seemed to swallow his pride. "I think my rough edges have eroded with age; I sound like the late Teddy Roosevelt, but this Canyon, with its magnificent congregation of buttes and towers, is sacred—a great American treasure."

Sabrina added, "Uncle Monte, it's a land made for legends like you. You helped forge a frontier and in doing so you shaped the destiny of the Grand Canyon. I believe national park status was inevitable."

"Yeah, inevitability has an insidious way of sneaking up from behind, but I agree, the Canyon becoming a national park is a great thing," concluded the aging pioneer.

Monte became silent, appearing as though he had drifted off into another world. Kirby and Sabrina sat still, not knowing whether to stay or go. Another fifteen minutes passed; Monte broke the silence.

"In a way," he said dryly, "I'll be sorry to see the frontier pass into history. I've spent so much of my life here at the Canyon I feel very much at home here. In fact, there is no place I would rather be. But I have mixed feelings. On one hand, I welcome visitors and want to share my knowledge with them. On the other hand, it makes me sad to think once developers line the rim with hotels, livery stables and saloons, all to attract hordes of tourists, the quiet solitude of this grand place may vanish forever."

"That's the story of America's westward expansion and settlement," chimed Sabrina. "I've seen it happen twice in my lifetime, first in Texas and then in Arizona. And they're both better for it."

"Sabrina, you are right to a point. But here, in this very special place, there are those who want rim-to-river cable-car rides, and others who want to dam the Colorado and flood the Canyon up to the brink of Granite Gorge to form a giant lake for recreation; not as high as the Coconino bathtub ring, mind you, but a flood that would ruin many a side canyon."

Kirby, feeling left out of the conversation, broke in. "I know what you mean, Monte. I see continuing conflicts arising between the National Park Service and burgeoning industries calling for more rails to the rim to support ranching, timber-cutting and mining, and yes, tourism."

"Well, you two will have to deal with that. As for me, I'm just going to sit here on the rim and stare at this wondrous place—its golden haze and memories of my canyon days. The Park Service may soon force me out of this old burned-out hotel and shoo me away from Summit Point. But whenever you can get away from your Circle K ranch, come visit me and Anna, either here or at our Coconino Basin Ranch. You are the only real friends we have left." In a matter of minutes, Monte dozed off. Kirby and Sabrina tip-toed down from the hotel veranda, trying to keep the weathered boards from creaking. They walked around to their horses. Then the raucous caw of a raven, followed by a series of garbled chuckles, jolted Monte out of his light slumber. He watched the O'Briens, remembering the good old days—young at heart and full of energy.

Heeding Sabrina's reminder to pursue his auto transportation idea, Monte started to lay out a plan. He thought it better to have a challenging project than to spend his days moping around his Summit place. Besides, the timing seemed right, with rutted wagon trails turning into well-traveled roadways. Before long, Grand Canyon National Park featured a dirt road approach and an entry station where park rangers lived in tent-houses and charged one-dollar entrance fees.

Long aware of the surrounding corruption and scandal, Monte still presented his plan to develop an auto transportation line between Flagstaff and the South Rim. Even though he designated his South Rim terminal as Grand Canyon Village, instead of Summit, the government quashed his auto fleet plan and his application to operate as a transportation concessionaire. It based its blunt denial on the fact that the Trails West Company had the exclusive concession to offer lodging, camping and, to Monte's dismay, transportation services.

This was the proverbial last straw. Even though Grand Canyon tourism first took hold at Summit and Clancy's old ranch, it became obvious the Santa Fe Railway and Trails West coalition had won out. Monte had hung on as long as he could, but the time had come to move to his late son's ranch. He thought to himself, "*I'm nothing but a caretaker for the properties I built and owned. I sold my mines to Canyon Copper Company, my Summit homestead to Hearst and my beloved Grand Canyon Hotel is in shambles. It's time to move on.*"

***

The Santa Fe purchased many canyon pioneer properties, including camps, mines, mill-sites and trails, and transferred them to the government under a move to rid the park of pockets of privately held land, despite the park bill stipulating protection of existing owners' rights. The Santa Fe relished seeing its pesky competition demolished.

Riding on a Republican landslide, Arizona elected Clint McCarty for a six-year term as U.S. Senator. As the first Republican to represent Arizona in the Senate, he served on Senate committees overseeing irrigation and reclamation matters. His most noteworthy accomplishments involved reclamation of desert land. However, he opposed damming the lower Colorado River on the premise that California would rob precious water destined for Arizona, but he supported an act providing funds for study and test borings on the upper Colorado River. He objected to the government's planned entry in the power generation business, because he still hoped to develop such a massive undertaking himself.

McCarty promoted measures that benefited Arizona stockmen, including reducing forest grazing fees. He sponsored an act providing for the location and purchase of lands containing concentrated minerals and lobbied for import tariffs on foreign copper. He fought a bill for construction of a new approach road to the canyon because it involved Coconino County trading the Pioneer Trail to the government for one hundred thousand dollars in road funds.

The indomitable senator used his public office as an agent to restore his own eroding footholds at the Canyon and to wreak havoc on the National Park Service. Following a personal vendetta, he tried to oust the director. He actually succeeded in deleting from the Interior Department bill all appropriations for Grand Canyon National Park, which he had opposed from the beginning. Some of his constituents in Flagstaff charged Clint with using Coconino County as a political pawn in his continuing fight with the Santa Fe Railway, Trails West Company, Forest Service, and National Park Service.

Voters viewed McCarty as an obstructionist rather than a progressive legislator with the best interests of Arizona at heart. Negative press and seething legal battles cast doubt for his reelection. Having alienated many of his colleagues and constituents, Clint lost his bid for re-election. With this political defeat, he also lost all hope of continuing his control of the canyon's development. Separating himself from unhappy memories in his Grand Canyon State, he moved back to the East Coast.

**

One moonlit summer evening at the Circle K, Kirby and Sabrina sat on their porch watching faint moving shadows—a small herd of pronghorn antelope—in the distance.

"Sabrina, this sure is beautiful country, and the Circle K sure is a fine ranch." A lone coyote started his mournful cry. It soon evolved into a full-throated chilling serenade as other coyotes joined in.

"There go the prairie tenors again."

Sabrina looked at him, "What? Oh, you mean those coyotes. I swear, Kirby, sometimes you have quite a way with words." The howling pack created a staccato chorus and then it cut off abruptly. Without the coyote commotion, the two could hear the wind sigh through the pinyon pines.

"I'm going to fetch our coffee; it should be ready."

As Sabrina returned with two steaming cups, Kirby said, "I miss the Canyon."

"Now you see why I made so many trips over the years. I was not there just for treasure-hunting. I was there for the Canyon's mind-boggling expanse, depth and beauty. There's nothing else like it." Sabrina became pensive for a minute or two. "About your way with words, I have an idea. We should write a book about Uncle Monte and his life and times at the Canyon."

Kirby had to put a stop to that thinking. "I'm not a writer, Sabrina. I have trouble crafting a short letter."

"Well, I'm not a writer either but Ryan Perkins is!"

Sabrina's mind buzzed with ideas. "We could all go up to Summit where incredulous views and indelible memories abound, and interview Monte, have him tell his story in his own words. We could use some of Heidi's photographs in the book and I'll hire a publisher. I worry about Monte and Anna being so isolated. They must be very lonely. A book project would keep Monte's mind active and it would be a good excuse for some long visits." Sabrina, breathless, "Let's run up there tomorrow."

Kirby, with a broad smile, whispered, "I was about to suggest such a trip when I became distracted by the prairie tenors."

***

In replacing its old ramshackle hotel, Trails West reduced McCarty's old hotel building to its original single-story cabin. Once a historic cabin on the old stage road, it became an integral part of the new Starlight Lodge. A suspension bridge replaced the old cableway across the Colorado, resulting in a safer canyon crossroad and easy access to a new park development—the Dancing Ghost Ranch, on the east bank of Skeleton Creek. In mid-June the following year, Trails West opened its lodge with a large family-style dining room and kitchen. Three rustic cabins were constructed with colorful native stone and grey-green roof shingles to blend with the surrounding greenery.

Monte and Anna remained aloof of other canyon residents and tourists; few passed their way and they only drove to the Village for supplies. Monte hunted wolf and trapped fox and sold the furs. He operated a small trading post on his ranch which happened to straddle Dan McLain's Gray Mountain Road used by Trails West excursions to Navajo Country.

Sometimes Park Service patrols stopped at the ranch for lunch and information. Every few days Monte checked the Grand Canyon Hotel to make sure it remained secure—and not on fire.

Sabrina had broached the book-writing project with Monte, but it got off to a very slow start. Ryan Perkins agreed to collaborate on telling Monte's story. Sabrina, reasoning the book would appeal to many Americans interested in the Grand Canyon, planned to get it published in New York City at her expense. But Monte seemed slow to come around to the book idea.

"Uncle Monte, if you tell me your story—the story of the canyon pioneers' claims to the Grand Canyon, I will present that story in your own words in our book." Sabrina spoke with a depth of sincerity Monte could not deny. "Tell me your side, how you felt, and I promise every word you speak will appear in our book and in the spirit you intended."

Kirby often accompanied Sabrina to the South Rim, but not as a major contributor to the project. They borrowed Monte's Hudson autocar for the runs back and forth on the old stage road.

Many meetings at the abandoned Grand Canyon Hotel followed, with Monte, Ryan and Sabrina in detailed discussions about the pioneer days at the Canyon. The meetings went on for months. Ryan, having retired from his job as a reporter for the *Frontier Times*, had the time to devote to the book project.

Two weeks before the stock market crashed, Dan McLain passed away. His estate included three patented mining claims, six hundred acres of grazing land, thirty range horses, and various farm and road implements, all designated for his two daughters. He also left forty-five cans of Prince Albert tobacco, six cartons of Camel cigarettes, and three pounds of Hills coffee in his cabin.

In the early days of Grand Canyon living, a rudimentary, single-wire telephone line connected the Canyon Queen Hotel with fire patrols at an old pioneer's cabin, which had been confiscated and used as a Forest Ranger station. Monte had a key to the telephone box for emergency fire use, but the newfangled device became a major aggravation for him as he often could not make it work. He became partially crippled by a fall while restringing the line after a ponderosa fell on it. He blamed the fall on his lame right foot. It was never the same after his plunge in the river decades ago.

When both Monte and Anna suffered from poor health, the Park Service provided a phone tap to Monte's ranch from its line to Navajo Point. Each morning, park rangers expected Monte to report in; if they did not receive a call, a ranger would come to investigate.

Monte became petrified of using the telephone. On one frigid January day, Anna became deathly ill and Monte, after much hesitation, determined he had to use the wretched thing. He cranked and cranked, but neglected to flip the switch, and so did not make a connection. And the tragedy of it all—Anna Bridgestone died of blood poisoning. Remembered as one of the best loved canyon citizens, they buried her in Pioneer Cemetery, next to Monte's son.

Throughout the year, Kirby, Sabrina and Ryan made frequent trips to Monte's ranch. While lonely and in failing health, he always seemed happy to see his trusted friends, but less enthusiastic about working on the book. Ryan often complained about running out of time.

As the Hudson neared the turnoff to the ranch, Kirby spoke about the project's slow progress. "Sabrina, Monte may not be in the mood to continue telling his canyon story today. During our last time here, I sensed his interest dwindling."

"Fellas, we may not make much progress today. Ever since Anna died, Monte has been in the doldrums, like he's hit rock bottom. He is lonely without Anna at his side. Now winter is coming." Sabrina had a thought. "I wonder if we should take Uncle Monte back to the Circle K with us."

Ryan, who still called Flagstaff home, observed, "Traveling to Little Springs instead of the South Rim would be easier for me. Why do you call your ranch the Circle K?"

Sabrina answered, "The K is for the Klostermeyers who developed the ranch long before it became a stage stop. Kirby, what about Monte staying with us?"

"No, he would never stand for it. He loves his Canyon too much," said Kirby. "Let's keep trudging on with the book as best we can."

When Monte became snowbound at the ranch, Kirby and Sabrina checked on him by telephone. The book meetings continued through the winter months, weather permitting. Ryan saw increased progress in the spring and estimated they had reached the halfway mark in capturing Monte's story on paper.

But that summer, Monte became very sick; Kirby took him to Flagstaff where he spent several weeks in the hospital. When he grew homesick in mid-August, Kirby brought him back to his ranch. He and Sabrina cared for the seventy-four-year-old canyon pioneer as best they could. They spent most of their time at his ranch to be near their dear friend and to help in any way they could.

"Sabrina, I always thought growing old would take longer."

"Uncle Monte don't talk like that, you'll be fine. I believe life needs to develop on its own terms, in its own time, in its own way. You never quite know what will happen next in life, or when your allotted time span will end. What I'm saying is—"

Sabrina stopped short as Monte got up on one elbow. "Why do you call me Uncle Monte? We are not relatives."

"Because you are like family to Kirby and I. Why are you trying to get up?"

Kirby steadied Monte as he propped himself against the headboard. Then Monte surprised them both.

"You know I've never been much of a drinking man, even in my tavern-keeping days, but I sure could use a shot of brandy."

Monte suffered excruciating stomach pains, and they took their toll on his strength and disposition. Sabrina obliged. Monte watched her long straight hair sway as she reached for a bottle on a high shelf. She poured him a shot, fearing it might do more harm than good. He took a swig.

"Sabrina, I have traveled my—" Monte sputtered and coughed, unable to finish. He switched to water and repeated his statement. "I have traveled my last trail. I'm not long for this world now. Kirby, take me over to Summit Point so I can take in some last views of my Canyon." Monte had determined not to die until he had a last look—nor did he want to die alone.

Chapter Fourteen

ONLY THE ROCKS LIVE FOREVER

God bless America and her magnificent Grand Canyon, my home, my life.

The shuffling between the ranch and the rim became a routine for Kirby in late August and early September. Sabrina often accompanied the men on the rim visits.

"Uncle Monte, don't give in to this sickness. I've seen improvement in your strength and stamina over the last three days. You'll pull through."

"Sabrina, I've always admired your positive attitude and cheerful disposition but there's no doubt my time has almost expired. I'm not improving; I've come to know life and death at close quarters; I'm dying. I've had a long productive life and with you—the daughter I never had—the best part of it; these last ten years have been a joy beyond measure. You, with your heart of gold, believed in me when I no longer believed in myself. Unfortunately, all did not go according to plan. My mines did not pay. My lodges could not compete with those in the Village. My auto service plan never got past Park Service approval. But I've lived many years here in the Grand Canyon—surely the most spectacular place in the world."

Sabrina's eyes flooded with tears. It took several minutes to regain her composure. She and Kirby continued to encourage Monte to think positive.

"Uncle Monte, you are like the rocks that make up this Canyon," said Sabrina, in a sweeping move of her arms across the sun-painted landscape. "You still have some good years left," expressing an air of guarded optimism.

"Sabrina, only the rocks live forever. We have no say in our arrival, and we are never consulted about our departure, no matter how many more years we go on breathing," and with that Monte stopped breathing.

Kirby kept him from slumping forward while trying to console his sobbing wife. "He's gone. We have lost a dear friend, Sabrina."

"The Grand Canyon has also lost a great man." Sabrina could not stop the tears and Kirby could not pry her away from Monte.

"Kirby, I hear shallow breathing, like faint wheezing! Monte is still with us!"

Monte's breathing seemed strained. He opened his eyes, and mumbled something neither could understand. "Say again, Monte, what are you trying to tell us?"

"I think I . . . I dozed off. Have I been out long? Several hours?"

Sabrina, her voice trembling, "Only minutes, Monte, only minutes, but you sure scared us! We thought we lost you."

Kirby and Sabrina insisted on driving Monte to town in his autocar. Reluctant to make the trip, he finally conceded. At the Flagstaff hospital, doctors examined the aging pioneer and gave him a supply of medicine to relieve his stomach pain.

"Doc, will these pills help my ankle? I don't think the bones ever healed right as I've had a hitch in my get-along ever since ol' Levi Jackson rescued me from the river." Monte did not expect a cure, just some relief, but the doctor doubted they would help fifty-year-old bone injuries.

Monte continued. "Then, what about my back? Ever since I fell while working on that dad-blamed telephone line at my ranch, intermittent back pains have plagued me. I've been hobbling around with cracked bones ever since then." This time the doctor thought he might get some relief and prescribed two pills every evening.

Sabrina then interrupted. "Kirby, let's get our hobbling friend back to the Canyon. Please get the Hudson running while I help him out of the hospital."

On the long drive back to the South Rim, Monte slept most of the way. The first two pills made him drowsy. Sabrina and Kirby whispered occasionally but stayed quiet most of the trip. Both entertained the same thought. They needed to take turns staying with Monte.

***

The pills seemed to relieve most of Monte's discomfort and allowed him to sleep well during short naps and at night. With Ryan's help, they made great progress on the book, tentatively titled *The Life and Times of Monte Bridgestone*. Monte's interest in telling his story exploded. In fact, it seemed to give him a purpose, a reason to keep going. He also seemed buoyed by frequent visits to Summit Point. Kirby enjoyed hauling his old friend to the brink of the Canyon. The two stared into the abyss for hours, reminiscing about the old days.

Monte often instigated the conversation. "Kirby, look down there at Windsong Mesa. It sure conjures up old memories, doesn't it?" Without waiting for a response, he continued. "I remember when the explosion sent us running down to the mine, and another time when we hauled that big block of copper up the trail, and a couple times when I spotted you and Sabrina down there at Arrowhead Spring." He grinned.

Monte had never seen such a look of surprise when Kirby craned his neck toward him. He blurted, "You saw us? You said nothing! And here I thought Sabrina and I remained out of sight."

"Well, I regard some places below the rim as intimately mine and Arrowhead Spring is one of them. I liked scanning around with my field glasses, not spying mind you, just enjoying the views when I happened upon the two of you, quite by accident, but I must confess I discovered you on three separate occasions. I suspected you two would have a future together. So, when you came out to the hotel that day and shared your secret, I feigned my surprise."

"Well, you did a good job, Monte. You sure fooled me. I felt bad about not telling you earlier but I wanted to wait until Sabrina was ready for me to divulge her secret." Kirby shook his head; still shocked Monte already had a strong inkling about their blossoming romance.

Days like that on the rim with Monte drew the two together and when Sabrina joined them, the three had a joyful time. Kirby and Sabrina both felt the pride in giving their ailing friend pleasant times in his favorite place on the planet.

During one of those times, Sabrina broke some great news. "Monte, I received a letter from our publisher in New York City. Your book is being printed. Sixteen boxes should arrive by train in about three weeks!"

"Imagine that" said Monte, "a book about me!" Kirby caught him wincing when he spoke.

"Monte, we need to get you back to your ranch. Time for those pain pills and Sabrina has some more good news for you." Kirby helped him to his feet. "Sabrina, do you want to tell him now or wait till we get back?"

"Monte, also in the mail today I received the preliminary plans for your Grand Canyon Pioneer Museum from the architect. I'd like to show his design drawings to you when we get you settled in." She grinned with pride as she had already studied the plans.

"I see you two have been busy; first the book, now the museum," said Monte. "No one could have better . . . friends than you." He winced halfway through his sentence as a shooting pain pierced his stomach.

As Sabrina spread the drawings out on an oak table, Kirby helped Monte to a chair. The pain pills had not yet taken effect.

"I cannot do this tonight," said Monte, looking at Sabrina. "I did not realize you were this far along in the project. In the morning you can show me what the designer has in mind." He turned in for the night. Kirby and Sabrina had already planned to stay overnight.

After a short while, the two talked in the kitchen. Sabrina spoke first. "Kirby, I'm worried about him. His pain is worsening. He may not hold out long enough to see the museum completed. The architect says it's a three-month construction job." She handed a cup of coffee to Kirby.

"Sabrina, we'll have his book in our hands soon and you already have Park Service approval pending final review of the design drawings. Let's schedule a joint book-signing and ground-breaking event as soon as we receive the book shipment." Kirby watched her eyes light up with approval. She almost spilled her coffee.

"That's a great idea. And from now on, at least one of us needs to be here with Monte. His health is deteriorating. We may not get him to Summit Point as often as he wants," concluded Sabrina, concerned about the clock running out for their old friend.

***

Kirby and Sabrina had been planning the joint book-signing and ground-breaking ceremony for two weeks. They sent out invitations; Park Rangers made themselves available to help and Monte, although weak, grinned with pride as he hobbled from his Hudson autocar to the construction site. Teresa Cordova had delivered four boxes of books just two days earlier. Heidi Sherman stood by, ready to capture the historic event with her camera. On that beautiful October day at the South Rim, one man became noticeably absent—Clint McCarty.

The selected site for the museum occupied an outstanding promontory known as Inspiration Point, just a few miles east of the Village. At one time, it was the site of the Road-to-Ruin Saloon. At another time, the Forest Service planned to construct a rest house there. The Park Service already constructed a Geology Museum nearby. Being so close to the Village, the combined facilities assured frequent tours and visits for the traveling public.

After some opening remarks by the Park Superintendent, Kirby took the podium and addressed the crowd of sixty or seventy of Monte's fans.

"Ladies and gentlemen, we are here today to honor a great man, a man you all know and love, one of the last canyon pioneers, Monte Bridgestone. In a few moments, I will ask him to say a few words. Monte came to this magnificent place about fifty years ago and became infatuated with the Grand Canyon's majesty and overpowering immensity, became consumed by its many changing colors and moods, and he never left. He pioneered in building trails, tourist enterprises and copper mines. But that is only part of the story you will read in his book. He fought for fairness and compromise with respect to government control and commercial development. He is the last of the hard rock pick-and-shovel miners. Now we will ask him to take that shovel over there and one more time dig into the Canyon, thus initiating the excavation for the Grand Canyon Pioneer Museum."

Sabrina helped Monte to the ceremonial shovel leaning against a juniper. With a firm grip on the handle, Monte ambled over to a survey marker designating the northwest cornerstone.

"Kirby, I recognize this shovel. It's from our Shooting Star Mine, right?"

"Yes sir, it was always your favorite." Kirby stepped back as a piece of caprock gave way to Monte's thrust into the rim. The crowd clapped and cheered. Monte, wincing, suppressed a series of pains, and took the podium. With Kirby on one side and Sabrina on the other, he addressed the crowd, while using his coveted shovel for support.

"I am honored today to represent all the canyon pioneers. It is important to name them: Levi Jackson, Clancy Jennings, Francois LaRue, Buckey O'Neill, Stuart Casey, Cole Campbell, Slim Broadway, and yes, Clint McCarty. They are no longer with us. If they were here, they too would express their sincere appreciation for recognizing their time, their contributions, and their love affair with the Grand Canyon. Now with this shovel as a crutch, and with Sabrina O'Brien's help, I'll make my way to that pile of books on the table. There, I will sign personalized copies for everyone present. God bless America and her magnificent Grand Canyon, my home, my life."

***

Kirby received permission from the Hearst Corporation, owners of the abandoned Grand Canyon Hotel at Summit Point, to retrieve about twenty lightly scorched logs for the Grand Canyon Pioneer Museum. The architect's drawings showed a flat-roof, pueblo-style building using ponderosa vigas and native stone similar to the rock walls of Anasazi cliff dwellings. In a way, it paid homage to the first inhabitants of this hallowed place on the planet.

The design called for four distinct sections in the building. It was finally time to review the design drawings with Monte. He already knew what he wanted in the mining section. Sabrina took copious notes.

"Kirby, take Jeremy with you and head down to the Shooting Star Mine and start retrieving some of the heavy equipment before it disappears. In this section of the museum, I would like to include an ore cart on a section of track; mining tools including pickaxe, shovels and wheelbarrow; our winch with some hoisting cable; our gasoline-powered blower and a section of ductwork; and some ore sacks filled to the brim with colorful copper ore. Although we never used one, see if you can find an old canvas boat. We want to represent all prospectors and miners who spent a good portion of their lives on both sides of the river."

Kirby added a few more items to the list. "Monte, let's include kerosene lanterns, empty giant powder crates, a reconstructed rock monument with a mining claim visible inside, and some wall exhibits showing assay reports, mining claims, and underground plan and profile maps with descriptions from the most encouraging mining report we received back in aught seven."

"Excellent ideas, Kirby. Only a mining man would think of these details. Sabrina, please pass this information to the interior designers."

"I have it all down on paper, Monte. This is very exciting." Sabrina and Kirby were overwhelmed by Monte's enthusiasm, much stronger than when they collaborated on the book. Their brainstorming session seemed to give Monte a real boost in fighting his nagging stomach pains.

"Monte, as you can see from these drawings, there is another section dedicated to trail-building. I'm sure you have ideas about this area too."

"Let's see. Yes, this is where we can feature trail-building tools like rod-and-feathers for splitting rock, drills and jacks for inserting dynamite sticks in holes, miners' spoons for ladling blasting powder, and even a few empty powder kegs." Monte was on a roll. "And let us not forget some juniper logs, iron rods, some with heads for pounding, some with eyes for threading cables."

Kirby added, "Monte, we'll have plenty of wall space for trail signs and survey maps."

"Good point. Got that Mrs. Notetaker?" Monte was in an exceptionally good mood. "What's next?"

Sabrina rolled open another drawing in the set of plans. "Monte, this section is devoted to tourism in the Canyon. Without treading into the mission of the neighboring geology museum, this is the perfect place for stalac—stalactites and stalag—stalagmites from the Windsong caves. I always seem to trip on those two words."

"Don't feel bad, Sabrina. I have the same problem," added Kirby.

"Me too," Monte jumped back into the discussion, bubbling with ideas. "Let's display some canteens, knapsacks, walking sticks, field glasses—I think they are called binoculars now. That takes care of the hikers. Oh, and we should post stagecoach schedules and rates, after all, that's how early tourists got here. And hotel signs with room rates. And livery signs for saddle horses and carriage rides."

Kirby had several more suggestions. "Let's add some water barrels that we used for hauling drinking water from the spring to the hotel. I'm very familiar with those ol' barrels."

"Good idea, Kirby, and I have another suggestion," said Monte. "Let's set aside a corner for story relics. This canyon is just brimming with stories. Clancy always used so-called physical evidence, like battered pans or rusty rifle parts, even bullet holes in trees, to demonstrate authenticity to his wild stories. And add some Twin Oaks whiskey bottles. Maybe dress up the walls with bighorn sheep horns and deer antlers, and Navajo rugs from Moonflower Yazzie's clan."

"Monte, there is one more section of the museum building that caters to visitor pocketbooks. Sabrina, do you want to walk us through the gift shop and photograph gallery?"

Monte hovered over the fourth section drawing. "Here is the counter with its mechanical register, a kind of cash box," explained Sabrina, pointing to an area near the main entrance. And here are the sales tables with stacks of your *Monte Bridgestone – Pioneer of the Grand Canyon* book, plus picture postcards by professional photographers, and folded trail guides and road maps. And along this wall is a collection of historic photographs showing the mining operations, different views of various trails, all the pioneers who opened the Canyon for others to see and experience, plus distinguished visitors. In fact, we have a rare photograph of President Teddy Roosevelt having lunch in the Grand Canyon Hotel dining room."

Sabrina directed the men's attention back to the set of architect's drawings. "We skipped over the title sheet on these plans, which is a site plan for the museum building and its immediate surroundings. We plan to park a stagecoach, with harnesses and tack, a Studebaker wagon, and a scattering of heavy oak benches in front of the building. Below the Grand Canyon Pioneer Museum sign there will be a copper plaque dedicating the museum to Levi, Clancy, Francois, Casey, Buckey, Clint, Cole, Slim and, of course, you Monte. And on the canyon side, there will be a stone patio with more viewing benches."

"Sabrina and Kirby, I could not be more impressed." With a broad smile, Monte tried to express his deep appreciation. "This project is truly remarkable and will be a worthy addition to Grand Canyon National Park. Thank you for your thoughtfulness, dedication, and support toward making this dream become a reality."

***

On a cold gray winter day, Ben Saxton drifted north to Williams. Forty years had passed since he left Flagstaff for the gritty railroad and mining town of Benson, north of Tombstone. Ben had aged significantly; the lines on his forehead ran in such dense profusion that to call them wrinkles seemed inadequate; instead more like crevices hovering over bushy eyebrows. He needed suspenders to contain his pudgy middle. Haggard, homeless and moody, and still carrying a grudge about the rough treatment rendered by his former business partners, he avoided Flagstaff.

The crotchety old man spent the frigid night wrapped in a grungy blanket on a bench at the Williams train station. He awoke to the stationmaster's violent shaking.

"Hey, mister, can't you read the sign about no loitering? Now, be on your way or I'll call the sheriff."

"Leave me alone. I'm waiting for the train to the Canyon," countered Ben, in a gravelly voice.

"Then step inside. I trust you have money for a ticket," replied the stationmaster, a fair question since the nation still had not dug itself out of the Great Depression.

Ben had no real plan except to look over his old stomping grounds at the Canyon, but then demonizing old enemies came to mind. He pulled some dirty, crumpled bills from his back pocket and bought a one-way ticket. Just after sunrise, he took a window seat in the back of a car and started his long, slow train ride to Grand Canyon Village. With the station at the foot of the Canyon Queen Hotel, he had no problem locating the nearest bar, even though the village looked nothing like it did when he worked there.

After two shots of Old Crow Whiskey, he hung over the bar with his elbows holding himself steady, and asked the bartender if he knew Monte Bridgestone. Ben did not know why he asked that question.

Perhaps deep down, with the spring-loaded poise of a coiled rattlesnake, he still had a score to settle.

"Why are you asking? A stranger here are ya?" The bartender seemed wary and waited for an explanation.

Ben scowled. "He used to work for me when I ran the Shooting Star mining operation below Summit Point. He also helped me build the Pioneer Trail over yonder." With that he ordered a double.

"Well, I don't know about that. I never met the man yer asking about. After this drink, mister, you should call it quits and go out on the veranda and get some air." The bartender had known Monte for years but refused to divulge that information to this unsavory character.

A gentleman near the end of the bar, having overheard Ben's inquiry, walked over to introduce himself.

"Howdy, mister, my ears perked up when you mentioned Monte Bridgestone. I guess you have not heard."

Ben downed his glass of redeye and asked, "Who are you?" His blurry eyes narrowed into slits.

"I'm Jesse Parks, and you are?" Ben ordered another drink.

"I'm Ben Saxton and what is it I ain't heard?" asked Ben, his speech slurred and his voice almost inaudible. Jesse felt the tension bristling about this grousing old-timer.

"Hm-m, I remember you," said Jesse. "Many years have passed. A real troublemaker as I recall. And you have your facts a mite twisted. You worked for Monte, not the other way around. I'm using the term 'worked' rather loosely. Monte never had anything good to say about you or your work habits. Anyway, for your information, he is terminally ill and not long for this world." With that, Jesse left the bar.

Ben snatched his fourth, perhaps his fifth, drink off the bar and stumbled out onto the veranda to take in the canyon's splendors—and pitfalls. Already mid-afternoon, ominous dark clouds piled up on the

North Rim. He slumped down into a rocking chair and grumbled to himself about how life had beaten him up. He sunk into a mood of delusion and self-pity, and, despite the cold, soon passed out.

When he awoke in the dark, he found his drink still sitting on a side table. Clutching his glass, Ben staggered off the veranda and over to the rim. Raising his drink high, he shouted, "Here's to you, Monte Bridgestone—and good riddance!" He swallowed and leaned forward, then teetered on the edge, lost his balance, and toppled over the side. The old man's scream of terror diminished as he plunged to his death seven hundred feet below where he downed his last drink of redeye. Ben Saxton had lived on the ragged edge of the law and died on the ragged edge of the Canyon. Somewhere on an inaccessible ledge, he rests, albeit splattered, but in peace—a peace that eluded him in life.

***

On the other side of the Canyon, Kurt Ritter's waning years continued—but not for long. As the Texas Republic celebrated its centennial, the eighty-seven-year-old former Texan's heart gave out at his nephew's home in Afton, New Mexico. The nephew buried Uncle Kurt twenty miles northeast of Afton, in the Masonic Cemetery in Las Cruces, about six hundred miles from the North Rim of the Grand Canyon.

The canyon pioneers were a dying breed. Uncle Kurt would be remembered for his efforts to save the beleaguered buffalo, his own dying breed. He witnessed vast herds roaming the plains and later bemoaned their diminishing numbers. At least Kurt saved a few. He cherished his days among his small herd on the North Rim's Walhalla Plateau, surrounded by cliffs and side canyons.

About the time of Kurt Ritter's passing, a contractor hired to dismantle Clancy's rim cabin at the head of his old trail discovered a map tucked away in an old book. When asked about how he found it, he explained he had just pried a soot-covered shelf off the cabin wall behind the woodstove and a Mark Twain book tumbled onto the plank floor. Clancy had placed the hand-drawn map in Huckleberry Finn's protective custody, perhaps for future use in conjuring up a buried treasure story. The contractor made tracings for his fellow workers, last seen heading down the Jackson Trail.

It is unfortunate the Canyon Copper Company did not fully develop the famous Shooting Star Mine. Throughout America's industrial revolution, the insatiable demand for copper in markets associated with electrical wiring, piping and even brass shells for the military would have fetched higher prices, making canyon copper worth mining. But such outlandish operations would have been contrary to preserving the pristine nature and supreme majesty of Grand Canyon. Monte Bridgestone himself always seemed torn between the two opposing tenets.

***

Frustration prevailed over Monte's declining health. Kirby and Sabrina refused to accept the conclusion that nothing could be done for their ailing friend. When Monte slept, they talked for hours. To pass the time, Kirby disclosed little tidbits he had learned over the years about Monte's farming days, his Colorado mining days, his failed marriage to Marcy, and how he and Monte met.

"Monte was once a farmer?"

"Yes Sabrina, he told me he had over one hundred acres of rich farmland in southwestern Missouri, but he really never took to farming. Neither did his older brother John who also had about one hundred acres. They sold their land and joined a small silver boom in Colorado's San Juan mountains. While their quartz mines contained high-grade silver, they found living at such a high mountain elevation very rough, especially during long, brutally frigid winter months."

"Monte told me his brother quit their pick-and-shovel mining operations first and headed south to Arizona Territory, settling in the railroad town we know as Flagstaff. John entered the saloon business by establishing the Ponderosa Tavern. You've no doubt seen it during your rare trips to the town center."

Sabrina asked, "So I assume Monte followed in his brother's footsteps and partnered with him?"

"Exactly, and all went well until John was shot during a scuffle. Monte, who was prospecting in the Canyon, always thought the shooting was an accident. John had married an Albuquerque woman named Marcy Parker. Monte described her as a hot-tempered Irish lass who insisted the killing was murder, not an accident."

Sabrina knew Monte and Marcy married but had always been perplexed about the strange relationship—Monte marrying his brother's widow. "I assume it was not love, at least not at the beginning."

Kirby made the same assumption. "I think Monte felt obliged to come to Marcy's rescue. He never talked about their marriage except to say those were rough times, eventually ending in divorce and Monte relocating to Summit Point. That's where he devoted the rest of his life to mining, trail-building and tourism. And I joined him in those enterprises."

"Before you and I met, Monte and I would sit on the rim watching shadows glide across red-tinted buttes standing in mute testimony of massive erosion, and muse over unknowable stories of the planet's trouble past. He used to ask, 'How can a giant swath in the planet's surface be so deep, so wide, so quiet, so breathtaking? From this spot on the rim, I can view places I always thought I wanted to visit but they seemed inaccessible to exploration by foot or mule.' Then he'd add,

'Kirby, what made us think we could prosper here? After all, the mineral was copper, not gold.' Then we'd just sit there, staring, with nothing else to say."

"How sad," said Sabrina, "Monte has seen his share of melancholy days." Even Kirby seemed to sink into Monte's doldrums. She decided to inject a bit of dry humor. "Think of our Grand Canyon as a very slow-paced play; so slow you feel like giving up your sitting rock—your center-stage seat—before the final act; that is, unless you have been glued to your seat by pinyon pine pitch."

Kirby often missed the hidden messages his sassy wife conveyed in her clever prose. Rather than ask for clarification, he changed the subject. "I propose we take a few days and celebrate our twenty-fifth anniversary at the Canyon Queen Hotel. I've asked Jeremy Livingston to care for Monte while we're away."

***

One day in Albuquerque, an elderly lady, probably in her late eighties, walked into a bookstore on the downtown plaza. After spending a half-hour browsing in the store's southwest section, her hand gravitated toward an inch-thick book on the shelf. It had a copper foil cover, unique for a hardbound book, engraved with the title *Monte Bridgestone—Pioneer of the Grand Canyon*. Startled, she dropped her cane and the book on the floor. A clerk picked them up for her. "Ma'am, are you interested in this book? We received a new supply last week. It's one of our most popular sellers, just can't keep it on the shelf. You may have noticed the pile on the table near the front door."

"Yes sir, I am interested in the book. I have never been to the Grand Canyon, but this might help satisfy my curiosity. Will you take a check?"

"Of course, just make it out to Treasure House Bookstore. Shall I wrap it for you?" The clerk guided her to the counter with a clear place for writing.

"No need. It's not a gift. I'm just buying it for myself," explained the lady.

She handed the clerk a check for two dollars, picked up her book and started out the door. "Thank you for your help. Good day to you, sir." And with that the lady disappeared around the corner.

The clerk glanced down at the check. He read the signature—Marcy Bridgestone.

***

Kirby had booked the presidential luxury suite, the uppermost suite at the Canyon Queen. When they checked in, the clerk mentioned Teddy Roosevelt once stayed in that same north-facing room. It connected to an open deck with sweeping views of the Canyon.

Sitting back in their rocking chairs, they watched the canyon glow as the last rays of sunshine colored the landscape in deep reds and oranges—a riot of shifting shapes and dazzling colors. Glorious sunsets and sunrises always started Kirby and Sabrina reminiscing about the early days of the canyon pioneers. Now in their early sixties, they had lived most of those days themselves and cherished their memories.

Sabrina giggled.

"What are you finding so amusing, Mrs. O'Brien?"

"Well, Mr. O'Brien, I'm sure you have heard that a contractor working for the Park Service on the demolition of Clancy's old cabin found a crumpled map showing the whereabouts of lost gold on the old Jackson Trail. Several workmen have already taken time off, a break of sorts, ostensibly for a leisurely stroll down the old trail. Do you think they'll find the gold?" Sabrina, cocking her head, and contriving to look wide-eyed and innocent, reached for her coffee mug.

Kirby, reaching for his own mug, stated flatly, "Not a chance." Then he raised his mug, "Here's to this moment and the next moment to come."

Suddenly they heard a rowdy disturbance on the lawn between the hotel and the rim. Peering over the railing, Kirby and Sabrina found a small crowd gathered around a hunched-back old-timer. "Yah! ol' Lucas Randall found the gold! Lee's lost gold!"

"What?!" exclaimed Kirby as he turned to Sabrina. He shouted down to the crowd, "Hey down there; what's all the commotion about?"

One of the men looked up to the luxury suite and shouted, "Ol' Lucas here found a whole passel of gold nuggets along the old Jackson Trail!"

About the Author

Dick Brown has always been fascinated by western history—mountain men, wagon trains, gold rushes, cattle drives, notorious outlaws, ghost towns, and transcontinental railroads; however, he has concentrated much of his recent writing on one region of the American West in particular—the Grand Canyon. He has spent decades researching the early pioneers and the Canyon's bumpy road from unbridled backcountry to a national park. It is the venerable pioneers of the late nineteenth century, with their struggles to survive and thrive on the ragged edge of this tremendous abyss, that inspired Dick to write this historical novel.

During his writing career, Dick has authored and co-authored six award-winning books and has been published in numerous periodicals. He is a retired systems engineer and past president of the Grand Canyon Historical Society. As a former Navy submariner, he is a regular contributor to the journal *The Submarine Review* for which he has won three literary awards. He is also past editor of the magazine *Ballooning*. Dick lives in the forested mountains of central New Mexico, enjoying retirement with his wife and two feral cats.

Upcoming New Release!

DICK BROWN'S

GUARDING THE TREASURE
UNDER THE CANYON SKY
BOOK THREE

Guarding the Treasure is the final historical novel in this trilogy about the early Grand Canyon pioneers. By day, the Canyon, the main character in this story, flaunts wild colors and teasing shadows; by night, it sleeps under a canopy of shimmering stars. Sadly, the Federal government contemplates destruction of parts of Grand Canyon—that it worked so hard to protect—by damming the Colorado River and obliterating precious natural and cultural resources.

Witness a suspension bridge collapse, river drownings, a train wreck, demolition of early historic hotels, a uranium scare, and the beginning of commercial river-running. Cross the troubled waters of the Colorado on a riveted steel replacement bridge leading to both an Army camp and a creek-fed swimming pool in the inner gorge. Wince at outlandish river dam proposals, high-strung cableways, intrusive canyon overflights, corporate greed, clashing government missions, and other incredible assaults on the Grand Canyon.

For more information
visit: www.SpeakingVolumes.us

Now Available!

MICAH S. HACKLER'S
SHERIFF LANSING MYSTERIES
BOOKS 1 – 11

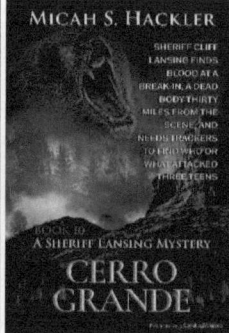

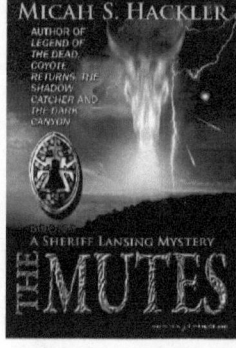

**For more information
visit:** www.SpeakingVolumes.us

Now Available!
ROBERT WESTBROOK'S
HOWARD MOON DEER MYSTERIES
BOOKS 1 – 9

 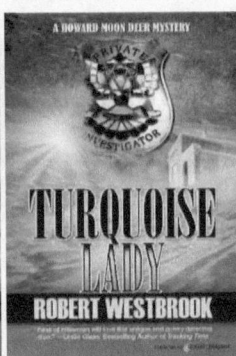 

**For more information
visit: www.SpeakingVolumes.us**

www.ingramcontent.com/pod-product-compliance
Lightning Source LLC
LaVergne TN
LVHW091631070526
838199LV00044B/1016